|||||||| ||| | ||||||||| ||||| |||| ||||| |||
W9-AVL-821

Praise for *New York Times* bestselling author

# DEBBIE MACOMBER

"Macomber has a gift for evoking the emotions
that are at the heart of the genre's popularity."
—*Publishers Weekly*

"Debbie Macomber shows why
she is one of the most powerful, highly regarded
authors on the stage today."
—*Midwest Book Review*

"Romance readers everywhere will
cherish the books of Debbie Macomber."
—Susan Elizabeth Phillips

"Macomber...is no stranger to the
*New York Times* bestseller list. She knows
how to please her audience."
—*Oregon Statesman Journal*

"Sometimes the best things come in small packages.
Such is the case here...."
—*Publishers Weekly* on *Return to Promise*

"Debbie Macomber is one of the most reliable,
versatile romance authors around. Whether she's
writing light-hearted romps or more serious
relationship books, her novels are always engaging
stories that accurately capture the foibles of real-life
men and women with warmth and humor."
—*Milwaukee Journal Sentinel*

Dear Readers,

*My Hero* and *My Funny Valentine* are two of my favorite stories.

*My Funny Valentine* was first published in 1991. My heroine, Dianne Williams, needs a date for a Valentine's dinner and very cleverly goes about finding one. Of course, he turns out to be the hero of her story.

Speaking of heroes… Every woman needs one, don't you think? Bailey York, a struggling romance writer, is working hard to get her book published. According to her critique partner, she has a fantastic plot, but unfortunately Bailey can't seem to get the hero right. Then…she sees *him* on the subway. Her plan to study him is perfect until… Okay, it probably isn't a good idea to give away the whole plot of *My Hero*.

If you've ever been in the position of having to convince someone to take you out on a date or if you've struggled with finding the perfect hero, then this book's for you. As for finding a hero of your own, they *are* out there. I know, because I found one. The real hero in my own life is my husband, Wayne.

P.S. I love to hear from readers. You can reach me at www.debbiemacomber.com or on Facebook, or write me at P.O. Box 1458, Port Orchard, WA 98366.

Happy Valentine's Day!

*Debbie Macomber*

PS I love to hear from readers. You can reach me at www.debbiemacomber.com or P.O. Box 1458, Port Orchard, WA 98366.

# DEBBIE MACOMBER

## *Be My Valentine*

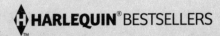
HARLEQUIN® BESTSELLERS

If you purchased this book without a cover you should be aware that this book is stolen property. It was reported as "unsold and destroyed" to the publisher, and neither the author nor the publisher has received any payment for this "stripped book."

ISBN-13: 978-0-373-60591-0

BE MY VALENTINE

Copyright © 2007 by MIRA Books.

The publisher acknowledges the copyright holder of the individual works as follows:

MY FUNNY VALENTINE
Copyright © 1991 by Debbie Macomber.

MY HERO
Copyright © 1992 by Debbie Macomber.

Recycling programs
for this product may
not exist in your area.

All rights reserved. Except for use in any review, the reproduction or utilization of this work in whole or in part in any form by any electronic, mechanical or other means, now known or hereafter invented, including xerography, photocopying and recording, or in any information storage or retrieval system, is forbidden without the written permission of the publisher, Harlequin Enterprises Limited, 225 Duncan Mill Road, Don Mills, Ontario M3B 3K9, Canada.

This is a work of fiction. Names, characters, places and incidents are either the product of the author's imagination or are used fictitiously, and any resemblance to actual persons, living or dead, business establishments, events or locales is entirely coincidental.

This edition published by arrangement with Harlequin Books S.A.

For questions and comments about the quality of this book, please contact us at CustomerService@Harlequin.com.

® and TM are trademarks of Harlequin Enterprises Limited or its corporate affiliates. Trademarks indicated with ® are registered in the United States Patent and Trademark Office, the Canadian Trade Marks Office and in other countries.

**Printed in U.S.A.**

HARLEQUIN®
www.Harlequin.com

# CONTENTS

# MY FUNNY VALENTINE

# One

Dianne Williams had the scenario all worked out. She'd be pushing her grocery cart down the aisle of the local grocery store and gazing over the frozen-food section when a tall, dark, handsome man would casually stroll up to her and with a brilliant smile say, "Those low-cal dinners couldn't possibly be for you."

She'd turn to him and suddenly the air would fill with the sounds of a Rimsky-Korsakov symphony, or bells would chime gently in the distance—Dianne didn't have that part completely figured out yet—and in that instant she would know deep in her heart that this was the man she was meant to spend the rest of her life with.

All right, Dianne was willing to admit, the scenario was childish and silly, the kind of fantasy only a teenage girl should dream up. But reentering the dating scene after umpteen years of married life created problems Dianne didn't even want to consider.

Three years earlier, Dianne's husband had left her and the children to find himself. Instead he found a SYT (sweet young thing), promptly divorced Dianne and moved across the country. It hurt; in fact, it hurt more than anything Dianne had ever known, but she was a survivor, and always had been. Perhaps that was the reason Jack didn't seem to suffer a single pang of guilt about abandoning her to raise Jason and Jill on her own.

Her children, Dianne had discovered, were incredibly resilient. Within a year of their father's departure, they were urging her to date. Their father did, they reminded Dianne with annoying frequency. And if it wasn't her children pushing her toward establishing a new relationship, it was her own dear mother.

When it came to locating Mr. Right for her divorced daughter, Martha Janes knew no equal. For several months, Dianne had been subjected to a long parade of single men. Their unmarried status, however, seemed their sole attribute.

After dinner with the man who lost his toupee on a low-hanging chandelier, Dianne had insisted enough was enough and she would find her own dates.

This proved to be easier said than done. Dianne hadn't gone out once in six months. Now, within the next week, she needed a man. Not just any man, either. One who was tall, dark and handsome. It would be a nice bonus if he was exceptionally wealthy, too, but she didn't have time to be choosy. The Valentine's dinner at the Port Blossom Community Center was Saturday night. *This* Saturday night.

From the moment the notice was posted six weeks earlier, Jason and Jill had insisted she attend. Surely their mother could find a date given that much time! And someone handsome to boot. It seemed a matter of family honor.

Only now the dinner was only days away and Dianne was no closer to achieving her goal.

"I'm home," Jason yelled as he walked into the house. The front door slammed in his wake, hard enough to shake the kitchen windows. He threw his books on the counter, moved directly to the refrigerator, opened the door and stuck the upper half of his fourteen-year-old body inside.

"Help yourself to a snack," Dianne said, smiling and shaking her head.

Jason reappeared with a chicken leg clenched between his teeth like a pirate's cutlass. One hand was filled with a piece of leftover cherry pie while the other held a platter of cold fried chicken.

"How was school?"

He shrugged, set down the pie and removed the chicken leg from his mouth. "Okay, I guess."

Dianne knew what was coming next. It was the same question he'd asked her every afternoon since the notice about the dinner had been posted.

"Do you have a date yet?" He leaned against the counter as his steady gaze pierced her. Her son's eyes could break through the firmest resolve, and cut through layers of deception.

"No date," she answered cheerfully. At least as cheerfully as she could under the circumstances.

"The dinner's this Saturday night."

As if she needed reminding. "I know. Stop worrying, I'll find someone."

"Not just anyone," Jason said emphatically, as though he were speaking to someone with impaired hearing. "He's got to make an impression. Someone decent."

"I know, I know."

"Grandma said she could line you up with—"

"No," Dianne interrupted. "I categorically refuse to go on any more of Grandma's blind dates."

"But you don't have the time to find your own now. It's—"

"I'm working on it," she insisted, although she knew she wasn't working very hard. She *was* trying to find someone to accompany her to the dinner, only she'd never dreamed it would be this difficult.

Until the necessity of attending this affair had been forced upon her, Dianne hadn't been aware of how limited her choices were. In the past couple of years, she'd met few single men, apart from the ones her mother had thrown at her. There were a couple of unmarried men at the office where she was employed part-time as a bookkeeper. Neither, however, was anyone she'd seriously consider dating. They were both too suave, too urbane—too much like Jack. Besides, problems might arise if she were to mingle her social life with her business one.

The front door opened and closed again, a little less noisily this time.

"I'm home!" ten-year-old Jill announced from the entryway. She dropped her books on the floor and marched toward the kitchen. Then she paused on the threshold and planted both hands on her hips as her eyes sought out her brother. "You better not have eaten all the leftover pie. I want some too, you know."

"Don't grow warts worrying about it," Jason said sarcastically. "There's plenty."

Jill's gaze swiveled from her brother to her mother. The level of severity didn't diminish one bit. Dianne met her daughter's eye and mouthed the words along with her.

"Do you have a date yet?"

Jason answered for Dianne. "No, she doesn't. And she's got five days to come up with a decent guy and all she says is that she's working on it."

"Mom…" Jill's brown eyes filled with concern.

"Children, please."

"Everyone in town's going," Jill claimed as if Dianne wasn't already aware of that. "You've *got* to be there, you've just got to. I told all my friends you're going."

More pressure! That was the last thing Dianne needed. Nevertheless, she smiled serenely at her two children and assured them they didn't have a thing to worry about.

An hour or so later, while she was making dinner, she could hear Jason and Jill's voices in the living room. They were huddled together in front of the television, their heads close together. Plotting, it looked like, charting her barren love life. Doubtless deciding who their mother should take to the dinner. Probably the guy with the toupee.

"Is something wrong?" Dianne asked, standing in the doorway. It was unusual for them to watch television this time of day, but more unusual for them to be so chummy. The fact that they'd turned on the TV to drown out their conversation hadn't escaped her.

They broke guiltily apart.

"Wrong?" Jason asked, recovering first. "I was just talking to Jill, is all. Do you need me to do something?"

That offer alone was enough evidence to convict them both. "Jill, would you set the table for me?" she asked, her gaze lingering on her two children for another moment before she returned to the kitchen.

Jason and Jill were up to something. Dianne could only guess what. No doubt the plot they were concocting included their grandmother.

Sure enough, while Jill was setting the silverware on the kitchen table, Jason used the phone, stretching the cord as far as it would go and mumbling into the mouthpiece so there was no chance Dianne could overhear his conversation.

Dianne's suspicions were confirmed when her mother arrived shortly after dinner. And within minutes, Jason and Jill had deserted the kitchen, saying they had to get to their homework. Also highly suspicious behavior.

"Do you want some tea, Mom?" Dianne felt obliged to ask, dreading the coming conversation. It didn't take Sherlock Holmes to deduce that her children had called their grandmother hoping she'd find a last-minute date for Dianne.

"Don't go to any trouble."

This was her mother's standard reply. "It's no trouble," Dianne said.

"Then make the tea."

Because of her evening aerobics class—W.A.R. it was called, for Women After Results—Dianne had changed and was prepared to make a hasty exit.

While the water was heating, she took a white ceramic teapot from the cupboard. "Before you ask, and I know you will," she said with strained patience, "I haven't got a date for the Valentine's dinner yet."

Her mother nodded slowly as if Dianne had just announced something of profound importance. Martha was from the old school, and she took her time getting around to whatever was on her mind, usually preceding it with a long list of questions that hinted at the subject. Dianne loved her mother, but there wasn't anyone on this earth who could drive her crazier.

"You've still got your figure," Martha said, her expression serious. "That helps." She stroked her chin a couple of times and nodded. "You've got your father's brown eyes, may he rest in peace, and your hair is nice and thick. You can thank your grandfather for that. He had hair so thick—"

"Ma, did I mention I have an aerobics class tonight?"

Her mother's posture stiffened. "I don't want to bother you."

"It's just that I might have to leave before you say what you're obviously planning to say, and I didn't want to miss the reason for your unexpected visit."

Her mother relaxed, but just a little. "Don't worry. I'll say what must be said and then you can leave. Your mother's words are not as important as your exercise class."

An argument bubbled up like fizz from a can of soda, but Dianne successfully managed to swallow it. Showing any sign of weakness in front of her mother was a major tactical error. Dianne made the tea, then carried the pot over to the table and sat across from Martha.

"Your skin's still as creamy as—"

"Mom," Dianne said, "there's no need to tell me all this. I know my coloring is good. I also know I've still got my figure and that my hair is thick and that you approve of my keeping it long. You don't need to sell me on myself."

"Ah," Martha told her softly, "that's where you're wrong."

Dianne couldn't help it—she rolled her eyes. When Dianne was fifteen her mother would have slapped her hand, but now that she was thirty-three, Martha used more subtle tactics.

Guilt.

"I don't have many years left."

"Mom—"

"No, listen. I'm an old woman now and I have the right to say what I want, especially since the good Lord may choose to call me home at any minute."

Stirring a teaspoon of sugar into her tea offered Dianne a moment to compose herself. Bracing her elbows on the table, she raised the cup to her lips. "Just say it."

Her mother nodded, apparently appeased. "You've lost confidence in yourself."

"That's not true."

Martha Janes's smile was meager at best. "Jack left you, and now you think there must be something wrong with you. But, Dianne, what you don't understand is that he would've gone if you were as beautiful as Marilyn Monroe. Jack's leaving had nothing to do with you and everything to do with Jack."

This conversation was taking a turn Dianne wanted

to avoid. Jack was a subject she preferred not to discuss. As far as she could see, there wasn't any reason to peel back the scars and examine the wound at this late date. Jack was gone. She'd accepted it, dealt with it, and gone on with her life. The fact that her mother was even mentioning her ex-husband had taken Dianne by surprise.

"My goodness," Dianne said, checking her watch. "Look at the time—"

"Before you go," her mother said quickly, grabbing her wrist, "I met a nice young man this afternoon in the butcher's shop. Marie Zimmerman told me about him and I went to talk to him myself."

"Mom—"

"Hush and listen. He's divorced, but from what he said it was all his wife's fault. He makes blood sausage and insisted I try some. It was so good it practically melted in my mouth. I never tasted sausage so good. A man who makes sausage like that would be an asset to any family."

Oh, sweet heaven. Her mother already had her married to the guy!

"I told him all about you and he generously offered to take you out."

"Mother, *please*. I've already said I won't go out on any more blind dates."

"Jerome's a nice man. He's—"

"I don't mean to be rude, but I really have to leave now, or I'll be late." Hurriedly, Dianne stood, collected her coat, and called out to her children that she'd be back in an hour.

The kids didn't say a word.

It wasn't until she was in her car that Dianne realized they'd been expecting her to announce that she finally had a date.

# Two

"Damn," Dianne muttered, scrambling through her purse for the tenth time. She knew it wasn't going to do the least bit of good, but she felt compelled to continue the search.

"Double damn," she said as she set the bulky leather handbag on the hood of her car. Rain drops spattered all around her.

Expelling her breath, she stalked back into the Port Blossom Community Center and stood in front of the desk. "I seem to have locked my keys in my car," she told the receptionist. "Along with my cell."

"Oh, dear. Is there someone you can get in touch with?"

"I'm a member of the auto club so I can call them for help. I also want to call home and say I'll be late. So if you'll let me use the phone?"

"Oh, sure." The young woman smiled pleasantly,

and lifted the phone onto the counter. "We close in fifteen minutes, you know."

A half hour later, Dianne was leaning impatiently against her car in the community center parking lot when a red tow truck pulled in. It circled the area, then eased into the space next to hers.

The driver, whom Dianne couldn't see in the dark, rolled down his window and stuck out his elbow. "Are you the lady who phoned about locking her keys in the car?"

"No. I'm standing out in the rain wearing a leotard for the fun of it," she muttered.

He chuckled, turned off the engine and hopped out of the driver's seat. "Sounds like this has been one of those days."

She nodded, suddenly feeling a stab of guilt at her churlishness. He seemed so friendly.

"Why don't you climb in my truck where it's nice and warm while I take care of this?" He opened the passenger-side door and gestured for her to enter.

She smiled weakly, and as she climbed in, said, "I didn't mean to snap at you just now."

He flashed her a grin. "No problem." She found herself taking a second look at him. He was wearing gray-striped coveralls and the front was covered with grease stains. His name, Steve, was embroidered in red across the top of his vest pocket. His hair, which was neatly styled, appeared to have been recently cut. His eyes were a warm shade of brown and—she searched for the right word—gentle, she decided.

After ensuring that she was comfortable in his truck, Steve walked around to the driver's side of her compact car and used his flashlight to determine the type of lock.

Dianne lowered the window. "I don't usually do things like this. I've never locked the keys in my car before—I don't know why I did tonight. Stupid."

He returned to the tow truck and opened the passenger door. "No one can be smart all the time," he said cheerfully. "Don't be so hard on yourself." He moved the seat forward a little and reached for a toolbox in the space behind her.

"I've had a lot on my mind lately," she said.

Straightening, he looked at her and nodded sympathetically. He had a nice face too, she noted, easy on the eyes. In fact, he was downright attractive. The coveralls didn't detract from his appeal, but actually suggested a certain ruggedness. He was thoughtful and friendly just when Dianne was beginning to think there wasn't anyone in the world who was. But then, standing in the dark and the rain might make anyone feel friendless, even though Port Blossom was a rural community with a warm, small-town atmosphere.

Steve went back to her car and began to fiddle with the lock. Unable to sit still, Dianne opened the truck door and climbed out. "It's the dinner that's got me so upset."

"The dinner?" Steve glanced up from his work.

"The Valentine's dinner the community center's sponsoring this Saturday night. My children are forcing me to go. I don't know for sure, but I think they've got money riding on it, because they're making it sound like a matter of national importance."

"I see. Why doesn't your husband take you?"

"I'm divorced," she said bluntly. "I suppose no one expects it to happen to them. I assumed after twelve years my marriage was solid, but it wasn't. Jack's remarried now, living in Boston." Dianne had no idea why she was rambling on like this, but once she'd opened her mouth, she couldn't seem to stop. She didn't usually relate the intimate details of her life to a perfect stranger.

"Aren't you cold?"

"I'm fine, thanks." That wasn't entirely true—she was a little chilled—but she was more worried about not having a date for the stupid Valentine's dinner than freezing to death. Briefly she wondered if Jason, Jill and her mother would accept pneumonia as a reasonable excuse for not attending.

"You're sure? You look like you're shivering."

She rubbed her palms together and ignored his question. "That's when my mother suggested Jerome."

"Jerome?"

"She seems to think I need help getting my feet wet."

Steve glanced up at her again, clearly puzzled.

"In the dating world," Dianne explained. "But I've had it with the dates she's arranged."

"Disasters?"

"Encounters of the worst kind. On one of them, the guy set his napkin on fire."

Steve laughed outright at that.

"Hey, it wasn't funny, trust me. I was mortified. He panicked and started waving it around in the air until the maitre d' arrived with a fire extinguisher and chaos broke loose."

Dianne found herself smiling at the memory of the unhappy episode. "Now that I look back on it, it was rather amusing."

Steve's gaze held hers. "I take it there were other disasters?"

"None I'd care to repeat."

"So your mother's up to her tricks again?"

Dianne nodded. "Only this time my kids are involved. Mom stumbled across this butcher who specializes in…well, never mind, that's not important. What is important is if I don't come up with a date in the next day or two, I'm going to be stuck going to this stupid dinner with Jerome."

"It shouldn't be so bad," he said. Dianne could hear the grin in his voice.

"How generous of you to say so." She crossed her arms over her chest. She'd orbited her vehicle twice before she spoke again.

"My kids are even instructing me on the kind of man they want me to date."

"Oh?"

Dianne wasn't sure he'd heard her. Her lock snapped free and he opened the door and retrieved her keys, which were in the ignition. He handed them to her, and with a thank-you, Dianne made a move to climb into her car.

"Jason and Jill—they're my kids—want me to go out with a tall, dark, handsome—" She stopped abruptly, thrusting out her arm as if to keep her balance.

Steve looked at her oddly. "Are you all right?"

Dianne brought her fingertips to her temple and nodded. "I think so…." She inhaled sharply and motioned toward the streetlight. "Would you mind stepping over there for a minute?"

"Me?" He pointed to himself as though he wasn't sure she meant him.

"Please."

He shrugged and did as she requested.

The idea was fast gaining momentum in her mind. He was certainly tall—at least six foot three, which was a nice complement to her own slender five ten. And he was dark—his hair appeared to be a rich shade of mahogany. As for the handsome part, she'd noticed that right off.

"Is something wrong?" he probed.

"No," Dianne said, grinning shyly—although what

she was about to propose was anything but shy. "By the way, how old are you? Thirty? Thirty-one?"

"Thirty-five."

"That's good. Perfect." A couple of years older than she was. Yes, the kids would approve of that.

"Good? Perfect?" He seemed to be questioning her sanity.

"Married?" she asked.

"Nope. I never got around to it, but I came close once." His eyes narrowed suspiciously.

"That's even better. I don't suppose you've got a jealous girlfriend—or a mad lover hanging around looking for an excuse to murder someone?"

"Not lately."

Dianne sighed with relief. "Great."

"Your car door's open," he said, gesturing toward it. He seemed eager to be on his way. "All I need to do is write down your auto club number."

"Yes, I know." She stood there, arms folded, studying him in the light. He was even better-looking than she'd first thought. "Do you own a decent suit?"

He chuckled as if the question amused him. "Yes."

"I mean something really nice, not the one you wore to your high-school graduation."

"It's a really nice suit."

Dianne didn't mean to be insulting, but she had to have all her bases covered. "That's good," she said. "How would you like to earn an extra hundred bucks Saturday night?"

"I beg your pardon?"

"I'm offering you a hundred dollars to escort me to the Valentine's dinner here at the center."

Steve stared at her as though he suspected she'd escaped from a mental institution.

"Listen, I know this is a bit unusual," Dianne rushed on, "but you're perfect. Well, not perfect, but you're exactly the kind of man the kids expect me to date, and frankly I haven't got time to do a whole lot of recruiting. Mr. Right hasn't showed up, if you know what I mean."

"I think I do."

"I need a date for one night. You fit the bill and you could probably use the extra cash. I realize it's not much, but a hundred dollars sounds fair to me. The dinner starts at seven and should be over by nine. I suspect fifty dollars an hour is more than you're earning now."

"Ah…"

"I know what you're thinking, but I promise you I'm not crazy. I've got a gold credit card, and they don't issue those to just anyone."

"What about a library card?"

"That, too, but I do have a book overdue. I was planning to take it back tomorrow." She started searching through her purse to prove she had both cards before she saw that he was teasing her.

"Ms.…"

"Dianne Williams," she said stepping forward to offer him her hand. His long, strong fingers wrapped around hers and he smiled, studying her for perhaps the first time. His eyes softened as he shook her hand. The gesture, though small, reassured Dianne that he was the man she wanted to take her to this silly dinner. Once more she found herself rushing to explain.

"I'm sure this all sounds crazy. I don't blame you for thinking I'm a nut case. But I'm not, really I'm not. I attend church every Sunday, do volunteer work at the grade school, and help coach a girls' soccer team in the fall."

"Why'd you pick me?"

"Well, that's a bit complicated, but you have nice eyes, and when you suggested I sit in your truck and get out of the rain—actually it was only drizzling—" she paused and inhaled a deep breath "—I realized you were a generous person, and you just might consider something this…"

"…weird," he finished for her.

Dianne nodded, then looked him directly in the eye. Her defenses were down, and there was nothing left to do but admit the truth.

"I'm desperate. No one but a desperate woman would make this kind of offer."

"Saturday night, you say?"

The way her luck was running, he'd suddenly remember he had urgent plans for the evening. Something important like dusting his bowling trophies.

"From seven to nine. No later, I promise. If you don't think a hundred is enough…"

"A hundred's more than generous."

She sagged with relief. "Does this mean you'll do it?"

Steve shook his head slowly, as though to suggest he ought to have it examined for even contemplating her proposal.

"All right," he said after a moment. "I never could resist a damsel in distress."

# Three

"Hello, everyone!" Dianne sang out as she breezed in the front door. She paused just inside the living room and watched as her mother and her two children stared openly. A sense of quiet astonishment pervaded the room. "Is something wrong?"

"What happened to you?" Jason cried. "You look awful!"

"You look like Little Orphan Annie, dear," her mother said, her hand working a crochet hook so fast the yarn zipped through her fingers.

"I phoned to tell you I'd be late," Dianne reminded them.

"But you didn't say anything about nearly drowning. What happened?"

"I locked my keys in the car—I already explained that."

Jill walked over to her mother, took her hand and

led her to the hallway mirror. The image that greeted Dianne was only a little short of shocking. Her long thick hair hung in limp sodden curls over her shoulders. Her mascara, supposedly no-run, had dissolved into black tracks down her cheeks. She was drenched to the skin and looked like a prize the cat had dragged onto the porch.

"Oh, dear," she whispered. Her stomach muscles tightened as she recalled the odd glances Steve had given her, and his comment that it must be "one of those days." No wonder!

"Why don't you go upstairs and take a nice hot shower?" her mother said. "You'll feel worlds better."

Humbled, for more reasons than she cared to admit, Dianne agreed.

As was generally the rule, her mother was right. By the time Dianne reappeared a half hour later, dressed in her terry-cloth robe and fuzzy pink slippers, she felt considerably better.

Making herself a cup of tea, she reviewed the events of the evening. Even if Steve had agreed to attend the Valentine's dinner out of pity, it didn't matter. What did matter was the fact that she had a date. As soon as she told her family, they'd stop hounding her.

"By the way," she said as she carried her tea into the living room, "I have a date for Saturday night."

The room went still. Even the television sound seemed to fade into nothingness. Her two children and her mother did a slow turn, their faces revealing their surprise.

"Don't look so shocked," Dianne said with a light, casual laugh. "I told you before that I was working on it. No one seemed to believe I was capable of finding a date on my own. Well, that isn't the case."

"Who?" Martha demanded, her eyes disbelieving.

"Oh, ye of little faith," Dianne said, feeling only a small twinge of guilt. "His name is Steve Creighton."

"When did you meet him?"

"Ah…"Dianne realized she wasn't prepared for an inquisition. "A few weeks ago. We happened to bump into each other tonight, and he asked if I had a date for the dinner. Naturally I told him I didn't and he suggested we go together."

"Steve Creighton." Her mother repeated the name slowly, rolling the syllables over her tongue, as if trying to remember where she'd last heard it. Then she shook her head and resumed crocheting.

"You never said anything about this guy before." Jason's gaze was slightly accusing. He sat on the carpet, knees tucked under his chin.

"Of course I didn't. If I had, all three of you would be bugging me about him, just the way you are now."

Martha gave her ball of yarn a hard jerk. "How'd you two meet?"

Dianne wasn't ready for this line of questioning. She'd assumed letting her family know she had the necessary escort would've been enough to appease them. Silly of her.

They wanted details. Lots of details, and the only thing Dianne could do was make them up as she went along. She couldn't very well admit she'd only met Steve that night and was so desperate for a date that she'd offered to pay him to escort her to the dinner.

"We met, ah, a few weeks ago in the grocery store," she explained haltingly, averting her gaze. She prayed that would satisfy their curiosity. But when she paused to sip her tea, the three faces were riveted on her.

"Go on," her mother urged.

"I…I was standing in the frozen-food section and…Steve was there, too, and…he smiled at me and introduced himself."

"What did he say after that?" Jill wanted to know, eager for the particulars. Martha shared her grand-daughter's interest. She set her yarn and crochet hook aside, focusing all her attention on Dianne.

"After he introduced himself, he said surely those low-cal dinners couldn't be for me—that I looked perfect just the way I was." The words fell stiffly from her lips. She had to be desperate to divulge her own fantasy to her family like this.

All right, she *was* desperate.

Jill's shoulders rose with an expressive sigh. "How romantic!"

Jason, however, was frowning. "The guy sounds

like a flake to me. A real man doesn't walk up to a woman and say something stupid like that."

"Steve's very nice."

"Maybe, but he doesn't sound like he's got all his oars in the water."

"I think he sounds sweet," Jill countered, immediately defending her mother by championing Steve. "If Mom likes him, then he's good enough for me."

"There are a lot of fruitcakes out there." Apparently her mother felt obliged to tell her that.

It was all Dianne could do not to remind her dear, sweet mother that she'd arranged several dates for her with men who fell easily into that category.

"I think we should meet him," Jason said, his eyes darkening with concern. "He might turn out to be a serial murderer or something."

"Jason—" Dianne forced another light laugh "—you're being silly. Besides, you're going to meet him Saturday night."

"By then it'll be too late."

"Jason's got a point, dear," Martha Janes said. "I don't think it would do any harm to introduce your young man to the family before Saturday night."

"I…he's probably busy…. He's working all sorts of weird hours and…"

"What does he do?"

"Ah…" She couldn't think fast enough to come up with a lie and had to admit the truth. "He drives a truck."

Her words were followed by a tense silence as her children and mother exchanged meaningful looks. "I've heard stories about truck drivers," Martha said, pinching her lips tightly together. "None I'd care to repeat in front of the children, mind you, but...stories."

"Mother, you're being—"

"Jason's absolutely right. I insist we meet this Steve. Truck drivers and cowboys simply aren't to be trusted."

Dianne rolled her eyes.

Her mother forgave her by saying, "I don't expect you to know this, Dianne, since you married so young."

"You married Dad when you were eighteen—younger than I was when I got married," Dianne said, not really wanting to argue, but finding herself trapped.

"Yes, but I've lived longer." She waved her crochet hook at Dianne. "A mother knows these things."

"Grandma's right," Jason said, sounding very adult. "We need to meet this Steve before you go out with him."

Dianne threw her hands in the air in frustration. "Hey, I thought you kids were the ones so eager for me to be at this dinner!"

"Yes, but we still have standards," Jill said, now siding with the others.

"I'll see what I can do," Dianne mumbled.

"Invite him over for dinner on Thursday night," her mother said. "I'll make my beef stroganoff and bring over a fresh apple pie."

"Ah…he might be busy."

"Then tell him Wednesday night," Jason advised in a voice that was hauntingly familiar. It was the same tone Dianne used when she meant business.

With nothing left to do but agree, Dianne said, "Okay. I'll try for Thursday." Oh, Lord, she thought, what had she got herself into?

She waited until the following afternoon to contact Steve. He'd given her his business card, which she'd tucked into the edging at the bottom of the bulletin board in her kitchen. She wasn't pleased about having to call him. She'd need to offer him more money if he agreed to this dinner. She couldn't very well expect him to come out of the generosity of his heart.

"Port Blossom Towing," a crisp female voice answered.

"Ah…this is Dianne Williams. I'd like to leave a message for Steve Creighton."

"Steve's here." Her words were followed by a click and a ringing sound.

"Steve," he answered distractedly.

"Hello." Dianne found herself at a loss for words. She'd hoped to just leave a message and ask him to return the call at his convenience. Having him there, on the other end of the line, when she wasn't expecting it left her at a disadvantage.

"Is this Dianne?"

"Yes. How'd you know?"

He chuckled softly, and the sound was pleasant and warm. "It's probably best if I don't answer that. Are you checking up to make sure I don't back out of Saturday night? Don't worry, I won't. In fact, I stopped off at the community center this morning and picked up tickets for the dinner."

"Oh, you didn't have to do that, but thanks. I'll reimburse you later."

"Just add it to my tab," he said lightly.

Dianne cringed, then took a breath and said, "Actually, I called to talk to you about my children."

"Your children?"

"Yes," she said. "Jason and Jill, and my mother, too, seem to think it would be a good idea if they met you. I assured them they would on Saturday night, but apparently that isn't good enough."

"I see."

"According to Jason, by then it'll be too late, and you might turn out to be a serial murderer or something. And my mother found the fact that you drive a truck worrisome."

"Do you want me to change jobs, too? I might have a bit of a problem managing all that before Saturday night."

"Of course not. Now, about Thursday—that's

when they want you to come for dinner. My mother's offered to fix her stroganoff and bake a pie. She uses Granny Smith apples," Dianne added, as though that bit of information would convince him to accept.

"Thursday night?"

"I'll give you an additional twenty dollars."

"Twenty dollars?" He sounded insulted, so Dianne raised her offer.

"All right, twenty-five, but that's as high as I can go. I'm living on a budget, you know." This fiasco was quickly running into a big chunk of cash. The dinner tickets were thirty each, and she'd need to reimburse Steve for those. Plus, she owed him a hundred for escorting her to the silly affair, and now an additional twenty-five if he came to dinner with her family.

"For twenty-five you've got yourself a deal," he said at last. "Anything else?"

Dianne closed her eyes. This was the worst part. "Yes," she said, swallowing tightly. The lump in her throat had grown to painful proportions. "There's one other thing. I…I want you to know I don't normally look that bad."

"Hey, I told you before—don't be so hard on yourself. You'd had a rough day."

"It's just that I don't want you to think I'm going to embarrass you at this Valentine's dinner. There may be people there you know, and after I made such a big deal over whether you had a suit and everything, well, I thought you might be more comfortable knowing…" She paused, closed her eyes and then blurted, "I've decided to switch brands of mascara."

His hesitation was only slight. "Thank you for sharing that. I'm sure I'll sleep better now."

Dianne decided to ignore his comment since she'd practically invited it. She didn't understand why she should find herself so tongue-tied with this man, but then again, perhaps she did. She'd made a complete idiot of herself. Paying a man to escort her to a dinner wasn't exactly the type of thing she wanted to list on a résumé.

"Oh, and before I forget," Dianne said, determined to put this unpleasantness behind her, "my mother and the kids asked me several questions about…us. How we met and the like. It might be a good idea if we went over my answers so our stories match."

"You want to meet for coffee later?"

"Ah…when?"

"Say seven, at the Pancake Haven. Don't worry, I'll buy."

Dianne had to bite back her sarcastic response. Instead she murmured, "Okay, but I won't have a lot of time."

"I promise not to keep you any longer than necessary."

# *Four*

"All right," Steve said dubiously, once the waitress had poured them each a cup of coffee. "How'd we meet?"

Dianne told him, lowering her voice when she came to the part about the low-cal frozen dinners. She found it rather humiliating to have to repeat her private fantasy a second time, especially to Steve.

He looked incredulous when she'd finished. "You've got to be kidding."

Dianne took offense at his tone. This was *her* romantic invention he was ridiculing, and she hadn't even mentioned the part about the Rimsky-Korsakov symphony or the chiming bells.

"I didn't have time to think of anything better," Dianne explained irritably. "Jason hit me with the question first thing and I wasn't prepared."

"What did Jason say when you told him that story?"

"He said you sounded like a flake."

"I don't blame him."

Dianne's shoulders sagged with defeat.

"Don't worry about it," Steve assured her, still frowning. "I'll clear everything up when I meet him Thursday night." He said it in a way that suggested the task would be difficult.

"Good—only don't make me look like any more of a fool than I already do."

"I'll try my best," he said with the same dubious inflection he'd used when they'd first sat down.

Dianne sympathized. This entire affair was quickly going from bad to worse, and there was no one to fault but her. Who would've dreamed finding a date for the Valentine's dinner would cause so many problems?

As they sipped their coffee, Dianne studied the man sitting across from her. She was somewhat surprised to discover that Steve Creighton looked even better the second time around. He was dressed in slacks and an Irish cable-knit sweater the color of winter wheat. His smile was a ready one and his eyes, now that she had a chance to see them in the light, were a deep, rich shade of brown like his hair. The impression he'd given her of a considerate, generous man persisted. He must be. No one else would have agreed to this scheme, at least not without a more substantial inducement.

"I'm afraid I might've painted my kids a picture of

you that's not quite accurate," Dianne admitted. Both her children had been filled with questions about Steve when they'd returned from school that afternoon. Jason had remained skeptical, but Jill, always a romantic—Dianne couldn't imagine where she'd inherited that!—had bombarded her for details.

"I'll do my best to live up to my image," Steve was quick to assure her.

Placing her elbows on the table, Dianne brushed a thick swatch of hair away from her face and tucked it behind her ear. "Listen, I'm sorry I ever got you involved in this."

"No backing out now—I've laid out cold hard cash for the dinner tickets."

Which was a not-so-subtle reminder that she owed him for those. She dug through her bag and brought out her checkbook. "I'll write you a check for the tickets right now."

"I'm not worried." He dismissed her offer with a wave of his hand.

Nevertheless, Dianne insisted. If she paid him in increments, she wouldn't have to think about how much this fiasco would end up costing her. She had the distinct feeling that by the time the Valentine's dinner was over, she would've spent as much as if she'd taken a Hawaiian vacation. Or gone to Seattle for the weekend, anyway.

After adding her signature, with a flair, to the bottom of the check, she kept her eyes lowered and said,

"If I upped the ante ten dollars do you think you could manage to look...besotted?"

"Besotted?" Steve repeated the word as though he'd never heard it before.

"You know, smitten."

"Smitten?"

Again he made it sound as though she were speaking a foreign language. "Attracted," she tried for the third time, loud enough to catch the waitress's attention. The woman appeared and splashed more coffee into their nearly full cups.

"I'm not purposely being dense," he said. "I'm just not sure what you mean."

"Try to look as though you find me attractive," she said, leaning halfway across the table and speaking in a heated whisper.

"I see. So that's what 'besotted' means." He took another sip of his coffee, and Dianne had the feeling he did so in an effort to hide a smile.

"You aren't supposed to find that amusing." She took a gulp of her own drink and nearly scalded her mouth. Under different circumstances she would've grimaced with pain, or at least reached for the water glass. She did none of those things. A woman has her pride.

"Let me see if I understand you correctly," Steve said matter-of-factly. "For an extra ten bucks you want me to look 'smitten.'"

"Yes," Dianne answered with as much dignity as she could muster, which at the moment wasn't a lot.

"I'll do it, of course," Steve said, grinning and making her feel all the more foolish, "only I'm not sure I know how." He straightened, squared his shoulders and momentarily closed his eyes.

"Steve?" Dianne whispered, glancing around, hoping no one was watching them. He seemed to be attempting some form of Eastern meditation. She half expected him to start chanting. "What are you doing?"

"Thinking about how to look smitten."

"Are you making fun of me?"

"Not at all. If you're willing to offer me an extra ten bucks, it must be important to you. I want to do it right."

Dianne thought she'd better tell him. "This isn't for me," she said. "It's for my ten-year-old daughter, who happens to have a romantic nature. Jill was so impressed with the story of how we supposedly met, that I…I was kind of hoping you'd be willing to…you know." Now that she was forced to spell it out, Dianne wasn't certain of anything. But she knew one thing—suggesting he look smitten with her had been a mistake.

"I'll try."

"I'd appreciate it," she said.

"How's this?" Steve cocked his head at a slight angle, then slowly lowered his eyelids until they were half closed. His mouth curved upward in an off-center smile while his shoulders heaved in what Dianne suspected was meant to be a deep sigh of longing. As though in afterthought, he pressed his open hands over his heart while making soft panting sounds.

"Are you doing an imitation of a Saint Bernard?" Dianne snapped, still not sure whether he was laughing at her. "You look like a…a dog. Maybe Jason's right and you really are a flake."

"I was trying to look besotted," Steve said. "I thought that was what you wanted." As if it would improve the image, he cocked his head the other way and repeated the performance.

"You're making fun of me, and I don't appreciate it one bit." Dianne tossed her napkin on the table and stood. "Thursday night, six o'clock, and please don't be late." With that she slipped her purse strap over her shoulder and stalked out of the restaurant.

Steve followed her to her car. "All right, I apologize. I got carried away in there."

Dianne nodded. She'd gone a little overboard herself, but not nearly as much as Steve. Although she claimed she wanted him to give the impression of being attracted to her for Jill's sake, that wasn't entirely true. Steve was handsome and kind, and to have him looking at her with his heart in his eyes was a fantasy that was strictly her own.

Admitting that, even to herself, was a shock. The walls around her battered heart had been reinforced by three years of loneliness. For reasons she couldn't really explain, this tow-truck driver made her feel vulnerable.

"I'm willing to try again if you want," he said. "Only…"

"Yes?" Her car was parked in the rear lot where the lighting wasn't nearly as good. Steve's face was hidden in the shadows, and she couldn't tell if he was being sincere or not.

"The problem," he replied slowly, "comes from the fact that we haven't kissed. I don't mean to be forward, you understand. You want me to wear a certain look, but it's a little difficult to manufacture without having had any, er, physical closeness."

"I see." Dianne's heart was pounding hard enough to damage her rib cage.

"Are you willing to let me kiss you?"

It was a last resort and she didn't have much choice. But she didn't have anything to lose, either. "If you insist."

With a deep breath, she tilted her head to the right, shut her eyes and puckered up. After waiting what seemed an inordinate amount of time, she opened her eyes. "Is something wrong?"

"I can't do it."

Embarrassed in the extreme, Dianne set her hands on her hips. "What do you mean?"

"You look like you're about to be sacrificed to appease the gods."

"I beg your pardon!" Dianne couldn't believe she was hearing him correctly. Talk about humiliation— she was only doing what he'd suggested.

"I can't kiss a woman who acts like she's about to undergo the most revolting experience of her life."

"You're saying I'm...oh...oh!" Too furious to speak, Dianne gripped Steve by the elbow and jerked him over to where his tow truck was parked, a couple of spaces down from her own car. Hopping onto the running board, she glared down at him. Her higher vantage point made her feel less vulnerable. Her eyes flashed with anger; his were filled with mild curiosity.

"Dianne, what are you doing now?"

"I'll have you know I was quite a kisser in my time."

"I don't doubt it."

"You just did. Now listen and listen well, because I'm only going to say this once." Waving her index finger under his nose, she paused and lowered her hand abruptly. He was right, she hadn't been all that thrilled to fall into this little experiment. A kiss was an innocent-enough exchange, she supposed, but kissing Steve put her on the defensive. And that troubled her.

"Say it."

Self-conscious now, she shifted her gaze and stepped off the running board, feeling ridiculous.

"What was so important that you were waving your finger under my nose?" Steve pressed.

Since she'd made such a fuss, she didn't have any alternative but to finish what she'd begun. "When I was in high school...the boys used to like to kiss me."

"They still would," Steve said softly, "if you'd give them a little encouragement."

She looked up at him and had to blink back unexpected tears. A woman doesn't have her husband walk out on her and not find herself awash in pain and self-doubt. Once she'd been confident; now she was dubious and insecure.

"Here," Steve said, holding her by the shoulders. "Let's try this." Then he gently, sweetly slanted his mouth over hers. Dianne was about to protest when their lips met and the option to refuse was taken from her.

Mindlessly she responded. Her arms slid around his middle and her hands splayed across the hard muscles of his back. And suddenly, emotions that had been simmering just below the surface rose like a tempest within her, and her heart went on a rampage.

Steve buried his hands in her hair, his fingers twisting and tangling in its thickness, bunching it at the back of her head. His mouth was soft, yet possessive. She gave a small, shocked moan when his tongue breached the barrier of her lips, but she adjusted quickly to the deepening quality of his kiss.

Reluctantly, Steve eased his mouth from hers. For a long moment, Dianne didn't open her eyes. When she finally did, she found Steve staring down at her.

He blinked.

She blinked.

Then, in the space of a heartbeat, he lowered his mouth back to hers.

Unable to stop, Dianne sighed deeply and leaned into his strength. Her legs felt like mush and her head was spinning with confusion. Her hands crept up and closed around the folds of his collar.

This kiss was long and thorough. It was the sweetest kiss Dianne had ever known—and the most passionate.

When he lifted his mouth from hers, he smiled tenderly. "I don't believe I'll have any problem looking besotted," he whispered.

# Five

"Steve's here!" Jason called, releasing the living-room curtain. "He just pulled into the driveway."

Jill's high-pitched voice echoed her brother's. "He brought his truck. It's red and—"

"—wicked," Jason said, paying Steve's choice of vehicles the highest form of teenage compliment.

"What did I tell you," Dianne's mother said, as she briskly stirred the stroganoff sauce. "He's driving a truck that's red and wicked." Her voice rose hysterically. "The man's probably a spawn of the devil!"

"Mother, 'wicked' means 'wonderful' to Jason."

"I've never heard anything so absurd in my life."

The doorbell chimed just then. Unfastening the apron from around her waist and tossing it aside, Dianne straightened and walked into the wide entryway. Jason, Jill and her mother followed closely, crowding her.

"Mom, please," Dianne pleaded, "give me some room here. Jason. Jill. Back up a little would you?"

All three moved several paces back, allowing Dianne some space. But the moment her hand went for the doorknob, they crowded forward again.

"Children, Ma, please!" she whispered frantically. The three were so close to her she could barely breathe.

Reluctantly Jason and Jill shuffled into the living room and slumped onto the sofa near the television set. Martha, however, refused to budge.

The bell chimed a second time, and after glaring at her mother and receiving no response, Dianne opened the door. On the other side of the screen door stood Steve, a huge bouquet of red roses in one hand and a large stuffed bear tucked under his other arm.

Dianne stared as she calculated the cost of long-stemmed roses, and a stuffed animal. She couldn't even afford carnations. And if he felt it necessary to bring along a stuffed bear, why hadn't he chosen a smaller, less costly one?

"May I come in?" he asked after a lengthy pause.

Her mother elbowed Dianne in the ribs and smiled serenely as she unlatched the lock on the screen door.

"You must be Steve. How lovely to meet you," Martha said as graciously as if she'd always thought the world of truck drivers.

Holding the outer door for him, Dianne managed to produce a weak smile as Steve entered her home.

Jason and Jill had come back into the hallway to stand next to their grandmother, eyeing Dianne's newfound date with open curiosity. For all her son's concern that Steve might turn out to be an ax-murderer, one look at the bright red tow truck and he'd been won over.

"Steve, I'd like you to meet my family," Dianne said, gesturing toward the three.

"So, you're Jason," Steve said, holding out his hand. The two exchanged a hearty handshake. "I'm pleased to meet you. Your mother speaks highly of you."

Jason beamed.

Turning his attention to Jill, Steve held out the oversize teddy bear. "This is for you," he said, giving her the stuffed animal. "I wanted something extra-special for Dianne's daughter, but this was all I could think of. I hope you aren't disappointed."

"I *love* teddy bears!" Jill cried, hugging it tight. "Did Mom tell you that?"

"Nope," Steve said, centering his high-voltage smile on the ten-year-old. "I just guessed."

"Oh, thank you, thank you." Cuddling the bear, Jill raced up the stairs, giddy with delight. "I'm going to put him on my bed right now."

Steve's gaze followed her daughter, and then his eyes briefly linked with Dianne's. In that split second, she let him know she wasn't entirely pleased. He frowned slightly, but recovered before presenting the roses to Dianne's mother.

"For me?" Martha brought her fingertips to her

mouth as though shocked by the gesture. "Oh, you shouldn't have! Oh, my heavens, I can't remember the last time a man gave me roses." Reaching for the corner of her apron, she discreetly dabbed her eyes. "This is such a treat."

"Mother, don't you want to put those in water?" Dianne said pointedly.

"Oh, dear, I suppose I should. It was a thoughtful gesture, Steve. Very thoughtful."

"Jason, go help your grandmother."

Her son looked as though he intended to object, but changed his mind and obediently followed Martha into the kitchen.

As soon as they were alone, Dianne turned on Steve. "Don't you think you're laying it on a little thick?" she whispered. She was so furious she was having trouble speaking clearly. "I can't afford all this!"

"Don't worry about it."

"I am worried. In fact I'm experiencing a good deal of distress. At the rate you're spending my money, I'm going to have to go on an installment plan."

"Hush, now, before you attract everyone's attention."

Dianne scowled at him. "I—"

Steve placed his fingers over her lips. "I've learned a very effective way of keeping you quiet—don't force me to use it. Kissing you so soon after my arrival might create the wrong impression."

"You wouldn't dare!"

The way his mouth slanted upward in a slow smile made her afraid he would. "I was only doing my best to act besotted," he said.

"You didn't have to spend this much money doing it. Opening my door, holding out my chair—that's all I wanted. First you roll your eyes like you're going into a coma and pant like a Saint Bernard, then you spend a fortune."

"Dinner's ready," Martha shouted from the kitchen.

With one last angry glare, Dianne led him into the big kitchen. Steve moved behind Dianne's chair and pulled it out for her. "Are you happy now?" he whispered close to her ear as she sat down.

She nodded, thinking it was too little, too late, but she didn't have much of an argument since she'd specifically asked for this.

Soon the five were seated around the wooden table. Dianne's mother said the blessing, and while she did, Dianne offered up a fervent prayer of her own. She wanted Steve to make a good impression—but not too good.

After the buttered noodles and the stroganoff had been passed around, along with a lettuce-and-cucumber salad and homemade rolls, Jason embarked on the topic that had apparently been troubling him from the first.

"Mom said you met at the grocery store."

Steve nodded. "She was blocking the aisle and I had to ask her to move her cart so I could get to the Hearty Eater Pot Pies."

Jason straightened in his chair, looking more than a little satisfied. "I thought it might be something like that."

"I beg your pardon?" Steve asked, playing innocent.

Her son cleared his throat, glanced carefully around before answering, then lowered his voice. "You should hear Mom's version of how you two met."

"More noodles?" Dianne said, shoving the bowl toward her son.

Jill looked confused. "But didn't you smile at Mom and say she's perfect just the way she is?"

Steve took a moment to compose his thoughts while he buttered his third dinner roll. Dianne recognized that he was doing a balancing act between her two children. If he said he'd commented on the low-cal frozen dinners and her figure, then he risked offending Jason, who seemed to think no man in his right mind would say something like that. On the other hand, if he claimed otherwise, he might wound Jill's romantic little heart.

"I'd be interested in knowing that myself," Martha added, looking pleased that Steve had taken a second helping of her stroganoff. "Dianne's terribly close-mouthed about these things. She didn't even mention you until the other night."

"To be honest," Steve said, sitting back in his chair, "I don't exactly recall what I said to Dianne. I remember being irritated with her for hogging the aisle, but when I asked her to move, she apologized and immediately pushed her cart out of the way."

Jason nodded, appeased.

"But when I got a good look at her, I couldn't help thinking she was the most beautiful woman I'd seen in a long while."

Jill sighed, mollified.

"I don't recall any of that," Dianne said, reaching for another roll. She tore it apart with a vengeance and smeared butter on both halves before she realized she had an untouched roll balanced on the edge of her plate.

"I was thinking that after dinner I'd take Jason out for a ride in the truck," Steve said when a few minutes had passed.

"You'd do that?" Jason nearly leapt from his chair in his eagerness.

"I was planning to all along," Steve explained. "I thought you'd be more interested in seeing how all the gears worked than in any gift I could bring you."

"I am." Jason was so excited he could barely sit still.

"When Jason and I come back, I'll take you out for a spin, Dianne."

She shook her head. "I'm not interested, thanks."

Three pairs of accusing eyes flashed in her direction. It was as if she'd committed an act of treason.

"I'm sure my daughter didn't mean that," Martha said, smiling sweetly at Steve. "She's been very tired lately and not quite herself."

Bewildered, Dianne stared at her mother.

"Can we go now?" Jason asked, already standing.

"If your mother says it's okay," Steve said, with a glance at Dianne. She nodded, and Steve finished the last of his roll and stood.

"I'll have apple pie ready for you when you get back," Martha promised, quickly ushering the two out the front door.

As soon as her mother returned to the kitchen, Dianne asked, "What was all that about?"

"What?" her mother demanded, feigning ignorance.

"That I've been very tired and not myself lately?"

"Oh, that," Martha said, clearing the table. "Steve wants to spend a few minutes alone with you. It's only natural. So I had to make some excuse for you."

"Yes, but—"

"Your behavior, my dear, was just short of rude. When a gentleman makes it clear he wants to spend some uninterrupted time in your company, you should welcome the opportunity."

"Mother, I seem to recall your saying Steve was a spawn of the devil, remember?"

"Now that I've met him, I've had a change of heart."

"What about Jerome, the butcher? I thought you were convinced he was the one for me."

"I like Steve better. I can tell he's a good man, and you'd be a fool to let him slip through your fingers by pretending to be indifferent."

"I am indifferent."

With a look of patent disbelief, Martha Janes shook her head. "I saw the way your eyes lit up when Steve walked into the house. You can fool some folks, but you can't pull the wool over your own mother's eyes. You're falling in love with this young man, and frankly, I'm pleased. I like him."

Dianne frowned. If her eyes had lit up when Steve arrived, it was because she was busy trying to figure out a way to repay him for the roses and the teddy bear. What she felt for him wasn't anything romantic. Or was it?

Dear Lord, she couldn't actually be falling for this guy, could she?

The question haunted Dianne as she loaded the dishwasher.

"Steve's real cute," Jill announced. Her daughter would find Attila the Hun cute, too, if he brought her a teddy bear, but Dianne resisted the impulse to say so.

"He looks a little bit like Hugh Jackman, don't you think?" Jill continued.

"I can't say I've noticed." A small lie. Dianne had noticed a lot more about Steve than she was willing to admit. Although she'd issued a fair number of complaints, he really was being a good sport about this. Of course, she was paying him, but he'd gone above and beyond the call of duty. Taking Jason out for a spin in the tow truck was one example, although why anyone would be thrilled to drive around in that contraption was something Dianne didn't understand.

"I do believe Steve Creighton will make you a decent husband," her mother stated thoughtfully as she removed the warm apple pie from the oven. "In fact, I was just thinking how nice it would be to have a summer wedding. It's so much easier to ask relatives to travel when the weather's good. June or July would be perfect."

"Mother, please! Steve and I barely know each other."

"On the contrary," Steve said, sauntering into the kitchen. He stepped behind Dianne's mother and sniffed appreciatively at the aroma wafting from her apple pie. "I happen to be partial to summer weddings myself."

# *Six*

"Don't you think you're overdoing it a bit?" Dianne demanded as Steve eased the big tow truck out of her driveway. She was belted into the seat next to him, feeling trapped—not to mention betrayed by her own family. They had insisted Steve take her out for a spin so the two of them could have some time alone. Steve didn't want to be alone with her, but her family didn't know that.

"Maybe I did come on a little strong," Steve agreed, dazzling her with his smile.

It was better for her equilibrium if she didn't glance his way, Dianne decided. Her eyes would innocently meet his and he'd give her one of those heart-stopping, lopsided smiles, and something inside her would melt. If this continued much longer, she'd be nothing more than a puddle by the end of the evening.

"The flowers and the stuffed animal I can understand," she said stiffly, willing to grant him that much. "You wanted to make a good impression, and that's fine, but the comment about being partial to summer weddings was going too far. It's just the kind of thing my mother was hoping to hear from you."

"You're right."

The fact that he was being so agreeable should have forewarned Dianne that something was amiss. She'd sensed it from the first moment she'd climbed into the truck. He'd closed the door and almost immediately something pulled wire-taut within her. The sensation was peculiar, even wistful—a melancholy pining she'd never felt before.

She squared her shoulders and stared straight ahead, determined not to fall under his spell the way her children and her mother so obviously had.

"As it is, I suspect Mom's been faithfully lighting votive candles every afternoon, asking God to send me a husband. She thinks God needs her help—that's why she goes around arranging dates for me."

"You're right, of course. I should never have made that comment about summer weddings," Steve said, "but I assumed that's just the sort of thing a *besotted* man would say."

Dianne sighed, realizing once again that she didn't have much of an argument. But he was doing everything in his power to make her regret that silly request.

"Hey, where are you taking me?" she asked when he turned off her street onto a main thoroughfare.

Steve turned his smile on her full force and twitched his thick eyebrows a couple of times for effect. "For a short drive. It wouldn't look good if we were to return five minutes after we left the house. Your family—"

"—will be waiting at the front door. They expect me back any minute."

"No, they don't."

"And why don't they?" she asked, growing uneasy. This wasn't supposed to be anything more than a ride around the block, and she'd had to be coerced into even that.

"Because I told your mother we'd be gone for an hour."

"An hour?" Dianne cried, as though he'd just announced he was kidnapping her. "But you can't do that! I mean, what about your time? Surely it's valuable."

"I assumed you'd want to pay me a few extra dollars—after all, I'm doing this to create the right impression. It's what—"

"I know, I know," she interrupted. "You're just acting smitten." The truth of the matter was that Dianne was making a fuss over something that was actually causing her heart to pound hard and fast. The whole idea of being alone with Steve appealed to her too much. *That* was the reason she fought it so hard. Without even trying, he'd managed to cast a spell on her family, and although she hated to admit it, he'd cast one on her, too. Steve Creighton was laughter and magic. Instinctively she knew he wasn't another Jack. Not the type of man who would walk away from his family.

Dianne frowned as the thought crossed her mind. It would be much easier to deal with the hand life had dealt her if she wasn't forced to associate with men as seemingly wonderful as Steve. It was easier to view all men as insensitive and inconsiderate.

Dianne didn't like that Steve was proving to be otherwise. He was apparently determined to crack the hard shell around her heart, no matter how hard she tried to reinforce it.

"Another thing," she said stiffly, crossing her arms with resolve, but refusing to glance in his direction. "You've got to stop being so free with my money."

"I never expected you to reimburse me for those gifts," he explained quietly.

"I insist on it."

"My, my, aren't we prickly. I bought the flowers and the toy for Jill of my own accord. I don't expect you to pick up the tab," he said again.

Dianne didn't know if she should argue with him or not. Although his tone was soft, a thread of steel ran through his words, just enough to let her know nothing she said was going to change his mind.

"That's not all," she said, deciding to drop that argument for a more urgent one. She probably did sound a bit shrewish, but if he wasn't going to be practical about this, *she'd* have to be.

"You mean there's more?" he cried, pretending to be distressed.

"Steve, please," she said, shocked at how feeble she sounded. She scarcely recognized the voice as her own. "You've got to stop being so…so wonderful," she finally said.

He came to a stop at a red light and turned to her, draping his arm over the back of the seat. "I don't think I heard you right. Would you mind repeating that?"

"You can't continue to be so—" she paused, searching for another word "—charming."

"Charming," he echoed. "Charming?"

"To my children and my mother," she elaborated. "The gifts were one thing. Giving Jason a ride in the tow truck was fine, too, but agreeing with my mother about summer weddings and then playing basketball with Jason—none of that was necessary."

"Personally, I would've thought your mother measuring my chest and arm length so she could knit me a sweater would bother you the most."

"That, too!"

"Could you explain why this is such a problem?"

"Isn't it obvious? If you keep doing that sort of thing, they'll expect me to continue dating you after the Valentine's dinner, and, frankly, I can't afford it."

He chuckled at that as if she was making some kind

of joke. Only it wasn't funny. "I happen to live on a budget—"

"I don't think we should concern ourselves with that," he broke in.

"Well, I *am* concerned." She expelled her breath sharply. "One date! That's all I can afford and that's all I'm interested in. If you continue to be so...so..."

"Wonderful?" he supplied.

"Charming," she corrected, "then I'll have a whole lot to answer for when I don't see you again after Saturday."

"So you want me to limit the charm?"

"Please."

"I'll do my best," he said, and his eyes sparked with laughter, which they seemed to do a good deal of the time. If she hadn't been so flustered, she might have been pleased that he found her so amusing.

"Thank you." She glanced pointedly at her watch. "Shouldn't we head back to the house?"

"No."

"No? I realize you told my mother we'd be gone an hour, but that really is too long and—"

"I'm taking you to Jackson Point."

Dianne's heart reacted instantly, zooming into her throat and then righting itself. Jackson Point overlooked a narrow water passage between the Kitsap Peninsula and Vashon Island. The view, either at night or during the day, was spectacular, but those who came to appreciate it at night were generally more interested in each other than the glittering lights of the island and Seattle farther beyond.

"I'll take the fact that you're not arguing with me as a positive sign," he said.

"I think we should go back to the house," she stated with as much resolve as she could muster. Unfortunately it didn't come out sounding very firm. The last time she'd been to Jackson Point had been a lifetime ago. She'd been a high-school junior and madly in love for the first time. The last time.

"We'll go back in a little while."

"Steve," she cried, fighting the urge to cry, "why are you doing this?"

"Isn't it obvious? I want to kiss you again."

Dianne pushed her hair away from her face with both hands. "I don't think that's such a good idea." Her voice wavered, just like her teenage son's.

Before she could come up with an argument, Steve pulled off the highway and down the narrow road that led to the popular lookout. She hadn't wanted to think about that kiss they'd shared. It had been a mistake. Dianne knew she'd disappointed Steve—not because of the kiss itself, but her reaction to it. He seemed to be waiting for her to admit how deeply it had affected her, but she hadn't given him the satisfaction.

Now, she told herself, he wanted revenge.

Her heart was still hammering when Steve stopped the truck and turned off the engine. The lights across the water sparkled in welcome. The closest lights were from Vashon Island, a sparsely populated place accessible only by ferry. The more distant ones came from West Seattle.

"It's really beautiful," she whispered. Some of the tension eased from her shoulders and she felt herself begin to relax.

"Yes," Steve agreed. He moved closer and placed his arm around her shoulder.

Dianne closed her eyes, knowing she didn't have the power to resist him. He'd been so wonderful with her children and her mother—more than wonderful. Now it seemed to be her turn, and try as she might to avoid it, she found herself a willing victim to his special brand of magic.

"You *are* going to let me kiss you, aren't you?" he whispered close to her ear.

She nodded.

His hands were in her hair as he directed his mouth to hers. The kiss was slow, as though he was afraid of frightening her. His mouth was warm and moist over her own, gentle and persuasive. Dianne could feel her bones start to dissolve and knew that if she was going to walk away from this experience unscathed, she needed to think fast. Unfortunately, her mind was already overloaded.

When at last they drew apart, he dragged in a deep breath. Dianne sank back against the seat and noted that his eyes were still closed. Taking this moment to gather her composure, she scooted as far away from him as she could, pressing the small of her back against the door handle.

"You're very good at this," she said, striving to sound unaffected, and knowing she hadn't succeeded.

He opened his eyes and frowned. "I'll assume that's a compliment."

"Yes. I think you should." Steve was the kind of man who'd attract attention from women no matter where he went. He wouldn't be interested in a divorcée and a ready-made family, and there was no use trying to convince herself otherwise. The only reason he'd agreed to take her to the Valentine's dinner was because she'd offered to pay him. This was strictly a business arrangement.

His finger lightly grazed the side of her face. His eyes were tender as he studied her, but he said nothing.

"It would probably be a good idea if we talked about Saturday night," she said, doing her best to keep her gaze trained away from him. "There's a lot to discuss and…there isn't much time left."

"All right." His wayward grin told her she hadn't fooled him. He knew exactly what she was up to.

"Since the dinner starts at seven, I suggest you arrive at my house at quarter to."

"Fine."

"We don't need to go to the trouble or the expense of a corsage."

"What are you wearing?"

Dianne hadn't given the matter a second's thought. "Since it's a Valentine's dinner, something red, I suppose. I have a red-and-white striped dress that will do." It was a couple of years old, but this dinner wasn't exactly the fashion event of the year, and she didn't have the money for a new outfit, anyway.

She looked at her watch, although she couldn't possibly read it in the darkness.

"Is that a hint you want to get back to the house?"

"Yes," she said.

Her honesty seemed to amuse him. "That's what I thought." Without argument, he started the engine and put the truck in reverse.

The minute they turned onto her street, Jason and Jill came vaulting out the front door. Dianne guessed they'd both been staring out the upstairs window, eagerly awaiting her return.

She was wrong. It was Steve they were eager to see.

"Hey, what took you so long?" Jason demanded as Steve climbed out of the truck.

"Grandma's got the apple pie all dished up. Are you ready?" Jill hugged Steve's arm, gazing anxiously up at him.

Dianne watched the unfolding scene with dismay. Steve walked into her house with one arm around Jason and Jill clinging to the other.

It was as if she were invisible. Neither of her children had said a single word to her!

To his credit, Jason paused at the front door. "Mom, you coming?"

"Just bringing up the rear," she muttered.

Jill shook her head, her shoulders lifting, then falling, in a deep sigh. "You'll have to forgive my mother," she told Steve confidingly. "She can be a real slowpoke sometimes."

# Seven

"Oh, Mom," Jill said softly. "You look so beautiful."

Dianne examined her reflection in the full-length mirror. At the last moment, she'd been gripped by another bout of insanity. She'd gone out and purchased a new dress.

She couldn't afford it. She couldn't rationalize that expense on top of everything else, but the instant she'd seen the flowered pink creation in the shop window, she'd decided to try it on. That was her first mistake. Correction: that was just one mistake in a long list of recent mistakes where Steve Creighton was concerned.

The dress was probably the most flattering thing she'd ever owned. The price tag had practically caused her to clutch her chest and stagger backward. She hadn't purchased it impulsively. No, she was too smart for that. The fact that she was nearly penniless and it was only the middle of the month didn't help matters. She'd sat down in the coffee shop next door and juggled figures for ten or fifteen minutes before crumpling up the paper and deciding to buy the dress, anyway. It was her birthday, Mother's Day and Christmas gifts to herself all rolled into one.

"I brought my pearls," Martha announced as she bolted breathlessly into Dianne's bedroom. She was late, which wasn't like Martha, but Dianne hadn't been worried. She knew her mother would be there before she had to leave for the dinner.

Martha stopped abruptly, folding her hands prayerfully and nodding with approval. "Oh, Dianne. You look…"

"Beautiful," Jill finished for her grandmother.

"Beautiful," Martha echoed. "I thought you were going to wear the red dress."

"I just happened to be at the mall and stumbled across this." She didn't mention that she'd made the trip into Tacoma for the express purpose of looking for something new to wear.

"Steve's here," Jason yelled from the bottom of the stairs.

"Here are my pearls," Martha said, reverently handing them to her daughter. The pearls were a family heirloom and worn only on the most special occasions.

"Mom, I don't know…"

"Your first official date with Steve," she said as though that event was on a level with God giving Moses the Ten Commandments. Without further ado, Martha draped the necklace around her daughter's neck. "I insist. Your father insists."

"Mom?" Dianne asked, turning around to search her mother's face. "Have you been talking to Dad again?" Dianne's father had been gone for more than ten years. However, for several years following his death, Martha Janes claimed they carried on regular conversations.

"Not exactly, but I know your father would have insisted, had he been here. Now off with you. It's rude to keep a date waiting."

Preparing to leave her bedroom, Dianne closed her eyes. She was nervous. Which was silly, she told herself. This wasn't a *real* date, since she was paying Steve for the honor of escorting her. She'd reminded herself of that the entire time she was dressing. The only reason they were even attending this Valentine's dinner was because she'd asked him. Not only asked, but offered to pay for everything.

Jill rushed out of the bedroom door and down the stairs. "She's coming and she looks beautiful."

"Your mother always looks beautiful," Dianne heard Steve say matter-of-factly as she descended the steps. Her eyes were on him, standing in the entryway dressed in a dark gray suit, looking tall and debonair.

He glanced up and his gaze found hers. She was gratified to see that his eyes widened briefly.

"I was wrong, she's extra-beautiful tonight," he whispered, but if he was speaking to her children, he wasn't looking at them. In fact, his eyes were riveted on her, which only served to make Dianne more uneasy.

They stood staring at each other like star-crossed lovers until Jill tugged at Steve's arm. "Aren't you going to give my mom the corsage?"

"Oh, yes, here," he said. Apparently he'd forgotten he was holding an octagon-shaped plastic box.

Dianne frowned. They'd agreed earlier that he wasn't going to do this. She was already over her budget, and flowers were a low-priority item, as far as Dianne was concerned.

"It's for the wrist," he explained, opening the box for her. "I thought you said the dress was red, so I'm afraid this might not go with it very well." The corsage was fashioned of three white rosebuds between a froth of red-and-white silk ribbons. Although her dress was several shades of pink, there was a smattering of red in the center of the flowers that matched the color in the ribbon perfectly. It was as if Steve had seen the dress and chosen the flowers to complement it. "It's…"

"Beautiful," Jill supplied once more, smugly pleased with herself.

"Are you ready?" Steve asked.

Jason stepped forward with her wool coat as though he couldn't wait to be rid of her. Steve took the coat from her son's hands and helped Dianne into it, while her son and daughter stood back looking as proud as if they'd arranged the entire affair themselves.

Before she left the house, Dianne gave her children their instructions and kissed them each on the cheek. Jason wasn't much in favor of letting his mother kiss him, but he tolerated it.

Martha continued to stand at the top of the stairs, dabbing her eyes with a tissue and looking down as if the four of them together were the most romantic sight she'd ever witnessed. Dianne sincerely prayed that Steve wouldn't notice.

"I won't be late," Dianne said as Steve opened the front door.

"Don't worry about it," Jason said pointedly. "There's no need to rush home."

"Have a wonderful time," Jill called after them.

The first thing Dianne realized once they were out the door was that Steve's tow truck was missing from her driveway. She looked around, half expecting to find the red monstrosity parked on the street.

With his hand cupping her elbow, he led her instead to a luxury car. "What's this?" she asked, thinking he might have rented it. If he had, she wanted it understood this minute that she had no intention of paying the fee.

"My car."

"Your car?" she asked. He opened the door for her and Dianne slid onto the supple white leather. Tow-truck operators obviously made better money than she'd assumed. If she'd known that, she would've offered him seventy-five dollars for this evening instead of a hundred.

Steve walked around the front of the sedan and got into the driver's seat. They chatted on the short ride to the community center, with Dianne making small talk in an effort to cover her nervousness.

The parking lot was nearly full, but Steve found a spot on the side lot next to the sprawling brick building.

"You want to go in?" he asked.

She nodded. Over the years, Dianne had attended a dozen of these affairs. There was no reason to feel nervous. Her friends and neighbors would be there. Naturally there'd be questions about her and Steve, but this time she was prepared.

Steve came around the car, opened her door and helped her out. She saw that he was frowning.

"Is something wrong?" she asked anxiously.

"You look pale."

She was about to reply that it was probably nerves when he said, "Not to worry, I have a cure for that." Before she'd guessed his intention, he leaned forward and brushed his mouth over hers.

He was right. The instant his lips touched hers, hot

color exploded in her cheeks. She felt herself swaying toward him, and Steve caught her gently by the shoulders.

"That was a mistake," he whispered once they'd moved apart. "Now the only thing I'm hungry for is you. Forget the dinner."

"I…think we should go inside now," she said, glancing around the parking lot, praying no one had witnessed the kiss.

Light and laughter spilled out from the wide double doors of the Port Blossom Community Center. The soft strains of a romantic ballad beckoned them in.

Steve took her coat and hung it on the rack in the entry. She waited for him, feeling more jittery than ever. When he'd finished, Steve slipped his arm about her waist and led her into the main room.

"Steve Creighton!" They had scarcely stepped into the room when Steve was greeted by a robust man with a salt-and-pepper beard. Glancing curiously at Dianne, the stranger slapped Steve on the back and said, "It's about time you attended one of our functions."

Steve introduced Dianne to the man, whose name was Sam Horton. The name was vaguely familiar to her, but she couldn't quite place it.

Apparently reading her mind, Steve said, "Sam's the president of the Chamber of Commerce."

"Ah, yes," Dianne said, impressed to meet one of the community's more distinguished members.

"My wife, Renée," Sam said, absently glancing around, "is somewhere in this mass of humanity." Then he turned back to Steve. "Have you two found a table yet? We'd consider it a pleasure to have you join us."

"Dianne?" Steve looked at her.

"That would be very nice, thank you." Wait until her mother heard this. She and Steve dining with the Chamber of Commerce president! Dianne couldn't help smiling. No doubt her mother would attribute this piece of good luck to the pearls. Sam left to find his wife, in order to introduce her to Dianne.

"Dianne Williams! It's so good to see you." The voice belonged to Beth Martin, who had crossed the room, dragging her husband, Ralph, along with her. Dianne knew Beth from the PTA. They'd worked together on the spring carnival the year before. Actually, Dianne had done most of the work while Beth had done the delegating. The experience had been enough to convince Dianne not to volunteer for this year's event.

Dianne introduced Steve to Beth and Ralph. Dianne felt a small sense of triumph as she noted the way Beth eyed Steve. This man was worth every single penny of the money he was costing her!

The two couples chatted for a few moments, then Steve excused himself. Dianne watched him as he walked through the room, observing how the eyes of several women followed him. He did make a compelling sight, especially in his well-cut suit.

"How long have you known Steve Creighton?" Beth asked the instant Steve was out of earshot. She moved closer to Dianne, as though she was about to hear some well-seasoned gossip.

"A few weeks now." It was clear that Beth was hoping Dianne would elaborate, but Dianne had no intention of doing so.

"Dianne." Shirley Simpson, another PTA friend, moved to her side. "Is that Steve Creighton you're with?"

"Yes." She'd had no idea Steve was so well known.

"I swear he's the cutest man in town. One look at him and my toes start to curl."

When she'd approached Steve with this proposal, Dianne hadn't a clue she would become the envy of her friends. She really *had* got a bargain.

"Are you sitting with anyone yet?" Shirley asked. Beth bristled as though offended she hadn't thought to ask first.

"Ah, yes. Sam Horton's already invited us, but thanks."

"Sam Horton," Beth repeated and she and Shirley shared a significant look. "My, my, you are traveling in elevated circles these days. Well, more power to you. And good luck with Steve Creighton. I've been saying for ages that it's time someone bagged him. I hope it's you."

"Thanks," Dianne said, feeling more than a little confused by this unexpected turn of events. Everyone knew Steve, right down to her PTA friends. It didn't make a lot of sense.

Steve returned a moment later, carrying two slender flutes of champagne. "I'd like you to meet some friends of mine," he said, leading her across the room to where several couples were standing. The circle immediately opened to include them. Dianne recognized the mayor and a couple of others.

Dianne threw Steve a puzzled look. He certainly was a social animal, but the people he knew… Still, why should she be surprised? A tow-truck operator would have plenty of opportunity to meet community leaders. And Steve was such a likable man, who obviously made friends easily.

A four-piece band began playing forties' swing, and after the introductions, Dianne found her toe tapping to the music.

"Next year we should make this a dinner-dance," Steve suggested, smiling down on Dianne. He casually put his hand on her shoulder as if he'd been doing that for months.

"Great idea," Port Blossom's mayor said, nodding. "You might bring it up at the March committee meeting."

Dianne frowned, not certain she understood. It was several minutes before she had a chance to ask Steve about the comment.

"I'm on the board of directors for the community center," he explained briefly.

"You are?" Dianne took another sip of her champagne. Some of the details were beginning to get muddled in her mind, and she wasn't sure if it had anything to do with the champagne.

"Does that surprise you?"

"Yes. I thought you had to be, you know, a business owner to be on the board of directors."

Now it was Steve's turn to frown. "I am."

"You are?" Dianne asked. Her hand tightened around the long stem of her glass. "What business?"

"Port Blossom Towing."

That did it. Dianne drank what remained of her champagne in a single gulp. "You mean to say you *own* the company?"

"Yes. Don't tell me you didn't know."

She glared up at him, her eyes narrowed and distrusting. "I didn't."

# Eight

Steve Creighton had made a fool of her.

Dianne was so infuriated she couldn't wait to be alone with him so she could give him a piece of her mind. Loudly.

"What's that got to do with anything?" Steve asked.

Dianne continued to glare at him, unable to form any words yet. It wasn't just that he owned the towing company or even that he was a member of the board of directors for the community center. It was the fact that he'd deceived her.

"You should've told me you owned the company!" she hissed.

"I gave you my business card," he said, shrugging.

"You gave me your business card," she mimicked in a furious whisper. "The least you could've done was mention it. I feel like an idiot."

Steve was wearing a perplexed frown, as if he found

her response completely unreasonable. "To be honest, I assumed you knew. I wasn't purposely keeping it from you."

That wasn't the only thing disturbing her, but the second concern was even more troubling than the first. "While I'm on the subject, what are you? Some sort of…love god?"

*"What?"*

"From the moment we arrived all the women I know, and even some I don't, have been crowding around me asking all sorts of leading questions. One friend claims you make her toes curl and another…never mind."

Steve looked exceptionally pleased. "I make her toes curl?"

How like a man to fall for flattery! "That's not the point."

"Then what is?"

"Everyone thinks you and I are an item."

"So? I thought that's what you wanted."

Dianne felt like screaming. "Kindly look at this from my point of view. I'm in one hell of a mess because of you!" He frowned as she went on. "What am I supposed to tell everyone, including my mother and children, once tonight is over?" Why, oh why hadn't she thought of this sooner?

"About what?"

"About you and me," she said slowly, using short words so he'd understand. "I didn't even *want* to attend this dinner. I've lied to my own family and, worse, I'm actually paying a man to escort me. This is probably the lowest point of my life, and all you can do is stand there with a silly grin."

Steve chuckled and his mouth twitched. "This silly grin you find so offensive is my besotted look. I've been practicing it in front of a mirror all week."

Dianne covered her face with her hands. "Now… now I discover that I'm even more of a fool than I realized. You're this upstanding businessman and, worse, a…a playboy."

"I'm not a playboy," he corrected. "And that's a pretty dated term, anyway."

"Maybe—but that's the reputation you seem to have. There isn't a woman at this dinner who doesn't envy me."

All she'd wanted was someone presentable to escort her to this dinner so she could satisfy her children. She lived a quiet, uncomplicated life, and suddenly she was the most gossip-worthy member of tonight's affair.

Sam Horton stepped to the microphone in front of the hall and announced that dinner was about to be served, so would everyone please go to their tables.

"Don't look so discontented," Steve whispered in her ear. He was standing behind her, and his hands rested gently on her shoulders. "The woman who's supposed to be the envy of every other one here shouldn't be frowning. Try smiling."

"I don't think I can," she muttered, fearing she might break down and cry. Being casually held by Steve wasn't helping. She found his touch reassuring and comforting when she didn't want either, at least not from him. She was confused enough. Her head was telling her one thing and her heart another.

"Trust me, Dianne, you're blowing this out of proportion. I didn't mean to deceive you. Let's just enjoy the evening."

"I feel like such a fool," she muttered again. Several people walked past them on their way to the tables, pausing to smile and nod. Dianne did her best to respond appropriately.

"You're not a fool." He slipped his arm around her waist and led her toward the table where Sam and his wife, as well as two other couples Dianne didn't know, were waiting.

Dianne smiled at the others while Steve held out her chair. A gentleman to the very end, she observed wryly. He opened doors and held out chairs for her, and the whole time she was making an idiot of herself in front of the entire community.

As soon as everyone was seated, he introduced Dianne to the two remaining couples—Larry and Louise Lester, who owned a local restaurant, and Dale and Maryanne Atwater. Dale was head of the town's most prominent accounting firm.

The salads were delivered by young men in crisp white jackets. The Lesters and the Atwaters were discussing the weather and other bland subjects. Caught in her own churning thoughts, Dianne ate her salad and tuned them out. When she was least expecting it, she heard her name. She glanced up to find six pairs of eyes studying her. She had no idea why.

She lowered the fork to her salad plate and glanced at Steve, praying he'd know what was going on.

"The two of you make such a handsome couple," Renée Horton said. Her words were casual, but her expression wasn't. Everything about her said she was intensely curious about Steve and Dianne.

"Thank you." Steve answered, then turned to Dianne and gave her what she'd referred to earlier as a silly grin and what he'd said was his besotted look.

"How did you two meet?" Maryanne Atwater asked nonchalantly.

"Ah…" Dianne's mind spun, lost in a haze of half-truths and misconceptions. She didn't know if she dared repeat the story about meeting in the local grocery, but she couldn't think fast enough to come up with anything else. She thought she was prepared, but the moment she was in the spotlight, all her self-confidence deserted her.

"We both happened to be in the grocery store at the same time," Steve explained smoothly. The story had been repeated so often it was beginning to sound like the truth.

"I was blocking Steve's way in the frozen-food section," she said, picking up his version of the story. She felt embarrassed seeing the three other couples listening so intently to their fabrication.

"I asked Dianne to kindly move her cart, and she stopped to apologize for being so thoughtless. Before I knew it, we'd struck up a conversation."

"I was there!" Louise Lester threw her hands wildly in the air, her blue eyes shining. "That was the two of you? I saw the whole thing!" She dabbed the corners of her mouth with her napkin and checked to be sure she had everyone's attention before continuing. "I swear it was the most romantic thing I've ever seen."

"It certainly was," Steve added, smiling over at Dianne, who restrained herself from kicking him in the shin, although it was exactly what he deserved.

"Steve's cart inadvertently bumped into Dianne's," Louise went on, grinning broadly at Steve.

"Inadvertently, Steve?" Sam Horton teased, chuckling loudly enough to attract attention. Crazy though it was, it seemed that everyone in the entire community center had stopped eating in order to hear Louise tell her story.

"At any rate," Louise said, "the two of them stopped to chat, and I swear it was like watching a romantic comedy. Naturally Dianne apologized—she hadn't realized she was blocking the aisle. Then Steve started sorting through the stuff in her cart, teasing her. We all know how Steve enjoys kidding around."

The others shook their heads, their affection for their friend obvious.

"She was buying all these diet dinners," Steve said, ignoring Dianne's glare. "I told her she couldn't possibly be buying them for herself."

The three women at the table sighed audibly. It was all Dianne could do not to slide off her chair and disappear under the table.

"That's not the best part," Louise said, beaming with pride at the attention she was garnering. A dreamy look stole over her features. "They must've stood and talked for ages. I'd finished my shopping and just happened to stroll past them several minutes later, and they were still there. It was when I was standing in the checkout line that I noticed them coming down the aisle side by side, each pushing a grocery cart. It was so cute, I half expected someone to start playing a violin."

"How sweet," Renée Horton whispered.

"I thought so myself and I mentioned it to Larry once I got home. Remember, honey?"

Larry nodded obligingly. "Louise must've told me that story two or three times that night," her husband reported.

"I just didn't know it was you, Steve. Imagine, out of all the people to run into at the grocery store, I happened to stumble upon you and Dianne the first time you met. Life is so ironic, isn't it?"

"Oh, yes, life is very ironic," Dianne said. Steve sent her a subtle smile, and she couldn't hold back an answering grin.

"It was one of the most beautiful things I've ever seen," Louise finished.

"Can you believe that Louise Lester?" Steve said later. They were sitting in his luxury sedan waiting for their turn to pull out of the crowded parking lot.

"No," Dianne said simply. She'd managed to make it through the rest of the dinner, but it had demanded every ounce of poise and self-control she possessed. From the moment they'd walked in the front door until the time Steve helped her put on her coat at the end of the evening, they'd been the center of attention. And the main topic of conversation.

Like a bumblebee visiting a flower garden, Louise Lester had breezed from one dinner table to the next, spreading the story of how Dianne and Steve had met and how she'd been there to witness every detail.

"I've never been so…" Dianne couldn't think of a word that quite described how she'd felt. "This may have been the worst evening of my life." She slumped against the back of the seat and covered her eyes.

"I thought you had a good time."

"How could I?" she cried, dropping her hand long enough to glare at him. "The first thing I get hit with is that you're some rich playboy."

"Come on, Dianne. Just because I happen to own a business doesn't mean I'm rolling in money."

"Port Blossom Towing is one of the fastest-growing enterprises in Kitsap County," she said, repeating what Sam Horton had been happy to tell her. "What I don't understand is why my mother hasn't heard of you. She's been on the lookout for eligible men for months. It's a miracle she didn't—" Dianne stopped abruptly.

"What?"

"My mother was looking all right, but she was realistic enough to stay in my own social realm. You're a major-league player. The only men my mother knows are in the minors—butchers, teachers, every-day sort of guys."

Now that she thought about it, however, her mother had seemed to recognize Steve's name when Dianne first mentioned it. She probably *had* heard of him, but couldn't remember where.

"Major-league player? That's a ridiculous analogy."

"It isn't. And to think I approached you, offering you money to take me to this dinner." Humiliation washed over her again, then gradually receded. "I have one question—why didn't you already have a date?" The dinner had been only five days away, so surely the most eligible bachelor in town, a man who could have his choice of women, would've had a date!

He shrugged. "I'm not seeing anyone."

"I bet you got a good laugh when I offered to pay you." Not to mention the fact that she'd made such a fuss over his owning a proper suit.

"As a matter of fact, I was flattered."

"No doubt."

"Are you still upset?"

"You could say that, yes." *Upset* was putting it mildly.

Since Dianne's house was only a couple of miles from the community center, she reached for her purse and checkbook. She waited until he pulled into the driveway before writing a check and handing it to him.

"What's this?" Steve asked.

"What I owe you. Since I didn't know the exact cost of Jill's stuffed animal, I made an educated guess. The cost of the roses varies from shop to shop, so I took an average price."

"I don't think you should pay me until the evening's over," he said, opening his car door.

As far as Dianne was concerned, it had been over the minute she'd learned who he was. When he came around to her side of the car and opened her door, she said, "Just what are you planning now?" He led her by the hand to the front of the garage, which was illuminated by a floodlight. They stood facing each other, his hands on her shoulders.

She frowned, gazing up at him. "I fully intend to give you your money's worth," he replied.

"I beg your pardon?"

"Jason, Jill and your mother."

"What about them?"

"They're peering out the front window waiting for me to kiss you, and I'm not going to disappoint them."

"Oh, no, you don't," she objected. But the moment his eyes held hers, all her anger drained away. Then, slowly, as though he recognized the change in her, he lowered his head. Dianne knew he was going to kiss her, and in the same instant she knew she wouldn't do anything to stop him....

# *Nine*

"You have the check?" Dianne asked once her head was clear enough for her to think again. It was a struggle to pull herself free from the magic Steve wove so easily around her.

Steve pulled the check she'd written from his suit pocket. Then, without ceremony, he tore it in two. "I never intended to accept a penny."

"You have to! We agreed—"

"I want to see you again," he said, clasping her shoulders firmly and looking intently at her.

Dianne was struck dumb. If he'd announced he was an alien, visiting from the planet Mars, he couldn't have surprised her more. Not knowing what to say, she eyed him speculatively. "You're kidding, aren't you?"

A smile flitted across his lips as though he'd anticipated her reaction. The left side of his mouth rose slightly higher in that lazy, off-center grin of his. "I've never been more serious in my life."

Now that the shock had worn off, it took Dianne all of one second to decide. "Naturally, I'm flattered—but no."

"No?" Steve was clearly taken aback, and he needed a second or two to compose himself. "Why not?"

"After tonight you need to ask?"

"Apparently so," he said, stepping away from her a little. He paused and shoved his fingers through his hair with enough force to make Dianne flinch. "I can't believe you," he muttered. "The first time we kissed I realized we had something special. I thought you felt it, too."

Dianne couldn't deny it, but she wasn't about to admit it, either. She lowered her gaze, refusing to meet the hungry intensity of his eyes.

When she didn't respond, Steve continued, "I have no intention of letting you out of my life. In case you haven't figured it out yet—and obviously you haven't—I'm crazy about you, Dianne."

Unexpected tears clouded her vision as she gazed up at him. She rubbed her hands against her eyes and sniffled. This wasn't supposed to be happening. She wanted the break to be clean and final. No discussion. No tears.

Steve was handsome and ambitious, intelligent and charming. If anyone deserved an SYT, it was this oh-so-eligible bachelor. She'd been married, and her life was complicated by two children and a manipulative mother.

"Say something," he demanded. "Don't just stand there looking at me with tears in your eyes."

"Th-these aren't tears. They're…" Dianne couldn't finish as fresh tears scalded her eyes.

"Tomorrow afternoon," he said, his voice gentle, "I'll stop by the house, and you and the kids and I can all go to a movie. You can bring your mother, too, if you want."

Dianne managed to swallow a sob. "That's the lowest, meanest thing you've ever suggested."

He frowned. "Taking you and the kids to a movie?"

"Y-yes. You're using my own children against me and that's—"

"Low and mean," he finished, scowling more fiercely. "All right, if you don't want to involve Jason and Jill, then just the two of us will go."

"I already said no."

"Why?"

Her shoulders trembled slightly as she smeared the moisture across her cheek. "I'm divorced." She said it as if it had been a well-kept secret and no one but her mother and children were aware of it.

"So?" He was still scowling.

"I have children."

"I know that, too. You're not making a lot of sense, Dianne."

"It's not that—exactly. You can date any woman you want."

"I want to date *you*."

"No!" She was trembling from the inside out. She tried to compose herself, but it was hopeless with Steve standing so close, looking as though he was going to reach for her and kiss her again.

When she was reasonably sure she wouldn't crumble under the force of her fascination with him, she looked him in the eye. "I'm flattered, really I am, but it wouldn't work."

"You don't know that."

"But I do, I do. We're not even in the same league, you and I, and this whole thing has got completely out of hand." She stood a little straighter, as though the extra inch in height would help. "The deal was I pay you to escort me to the Valentine's dinner—but then I had to go and complicate matters by suggesting you look smitten with me and you did such a good job of it that you've convinced yourself you're attracted to me and you aren't. You couldn't be."

"Because you're divorced and have two children," he repeated incredulously.

"You're forgetting my manipulative mother."

Steve clenched his fists at his sides. "I haven't forgotten her. In fact, I'm grateful to her."

Dianne narrowed her eyes. "Now I *know* you can't be serious."

"Your mother's a real kick, and your kids are great,

and in case you're completely blind, I think you're pretty wonderful yourself."

Dianne fumbled with the pearls at her neck, twisting the strand between her fingers. The man who stood before her was every woman's dream, but she didn't know what was right anymore. She knew only one thing. After the way he'd humiliated her this evening, after the way he'd let her actually pay him to take her to the Valentine's dinner, make a total fool of herself, there was no chance she could see him again.

"I don't think so," she said stiffly. "Goodbye, Steve."

"You really mean it, don't you?"

She was already halfway to the front door. "Yes."

"All right. Fine," he said, slicing the air with his hands. "If this is the way you want it, then fine, just fine." With that he stormed off to his car.

Dianne knew her family would give her all kinds of flack. The minute she walked in the door, Jason and Jill barraged her with questions about the dinner. Dianne was as vague as possible and walked upstairs to her room, pleading exhaustion. There must have been something in her eyes that convinced her mother and children to leave her alone, because no one disturbed her again that night.

She awoke early the next morning, feeling more than a little out of sorts. Jason was already up, eating a huge bowl of cornflakes at the kitchen table.

"Well," he said, when Dianne walked into the kitchen, "when are you going to see Steve again?"

"Uh, I don't know." She put on a pot of coffee, doing her best to shove every thought of her dinner companion from her mind. And not succeeding.

"He wants to go out on another date with you, doesn't he?"

"Uh, I'm not sure."

"You're not sure?" Jason asked. "How come? I saw you two get mushy last night. I like Steve. He's fun."

"Yes, I know," she said, standing in front of the machine while the coffee dripped into the glass pot. Her back was to her son. "Let's give it some time. See how things work out," she mumbled.

To Dianne's relief, he seemed to accept that and didn't question her further. That, however, wasn't the case with her mother.

"So talk to me," Martha insisted later that day, working her crochet hook as she sat in the living room with Dianne. "You've been very quiet."

"No, I haven't." Dianne didn't know why she denied it. Her mother was right, she had been introspective.

"The phone isn't ringing. The phone should be ringing."

"Why's that?"

"Steve. He met your mother, he met your children, he took you out to dinner…"

"You make it sound like we should be discussing

wedding plans." Dianne had intended to be flippant, but the look her mother gave her said she shouldn't joke about something so sacred.

"When are you seeing him again?" Her mother tugged on her ball of yarn when Dianne didn't immediately answer, as if that might bring forth a response.

"We're both going to be busy for the next few days."

"Busy? You're going to let busy interfere with love?"

Dianne ignored the question. It was easier that way. Her mother plied her with questions on and off for the rest of the day, but after repeated attempts to get something more out of her daughter and not succeeding, Martha reluctantly let the matter drop.

Three days after the Valentine's dinner, Dianne was shopping after work at a grocery store on the other side of town—she avoided going anywhere near the one around which she and Steve had fabricated their story—when she ran into Beth Martin.

"Dianne," Beth called, racing down the aisle after her. Darn, Dianne thought. The last person she wanted to chitchat with was Beth, who would, no doubt, be filled with questions about her and Steve.

She was.

"I've been meaning to phone you all week," Beth said, her smile so sweet Dianne felt as if she'd fallen into a vat of honey.

"Hello, Beth." She made a pretense of scanning the grocery shelf until she realized she was standing in front of the disposable-diaper section. She jerked away as though she'd been burned.

Beth's gaze followed Dianne's. "You know, you're not too old to have more children," she said. "What are you? Thirty-three, thirty-four?"

"Around that."

"If Steve wanted children, you could—"

"I have no intention of marrying Steve Creighton," Dianne answered testily. "We're nothing more than friends."

Beth arched her eyebrows. "My dear girl, that's not what I've heard. All of Port Blossom is buzzing with talk about the two of you. Steve's been such an elusive bachelor. He dates a lot of women, or so I've heard, but from what everyone's saying, and I do mean *everyone,* you've got him hooked. Why, the way he was looking at you on Saturday night was enough to bring tears to my eyes. I don't know what you did to that man, but he's yours for the asking."

"I'm sure you're mistaken." Dianne couldn't very well announce that she'd paid Steve to look besotted. He'd done such a good job of it, he'd convinced himself and everyone else that he was head over heels in love with her.

Beth grinned. "I don't think so."

As quickly as she could, Dianne made her excuses, paid for her groceries and hurried home. Home, she soon discovered, wasn't exactly a haven. Jason and Jill were waiting for her, and it wasn't because they were eager to carry in the grocery sacks.

"It's been three days," Jill said. "Shouldn't you have heard from Steve by now?"

"If he doesn't phone you, then you should call him," Jason insisted. "Girls do that sort of thing all the time now, no matter what Grandma says."

"I…" Dianne looked for an escape. Of course there wasn't one.

"Here's his card," Jason said, taking it from the corner of the bulletin board. "Call him."

Dianne stared at the raised red lettering. Port Blossom Towing, it said, with the phone number in large numbers below. In the corner, in smaller, less-pronounced lettering, was Steve's name, followed by one simple word: *owner.*

Dianne's heart plummeted and she closed her eyes. He'd really meant it when he said he had never intentionally misled her. He assumed she knew, and with good reason. The business card he'd given her spelled it out. Only she hadn't noticed…

"Mom." Jason's voice fragmented her introspection.

She opened her eyes to see her son and daughter staring up at her, their eyes, so like her own, intent and worried.

"What are you going to do?" Jill wanted to know.

"W.A.R."

"Aerobics?" Jason said. "What for?"

"I need it," Dianne answered. And she did. She'd learned long ago that when something was weighing on her, heavy-duty exercise helped considerably. It cleared her mind. She didn't enjoy it, exactly; pain rarely thrilled her. But the aerobics classes at the community center had seen her through more than one emotional trauma. If she hurried, she could be there for the last session of the afternoon.

"Kids, put those groceries away for me, will you?" she said, heading for the stairs, yanking the sweater over her head as she raced. The buttons on her blouse were too time-consuming, so she peeled that over her head the moment she entered the bedroom, closing the door with her foot.

In five minutes flat, she'd changed into her leotard, kissed the kids and was out the door. She had a small attack of guilt when she pulled out of the driveway and glanced back to see both her children standing on the porch looking dejected.

The warm-up exercises had already begun when Dianne joined the class. For the next hour she leapt, kicked, bent and stretched, doing her best to keep up with everyone else. By the end of the session, she was exhausted—and no closer to deciding whether or not to phone Steve.

With a towel draped around her neck, she walked out to her car. Her cardiovascular system might've been fine, but nothing else about her was. She searched through her purse for her keys and then checked her coat pocket.

Nothing.

Dread filled her. Framing the sides of her face with her hands, she peered inside the car. There, innocently poking out of the ignition, were her keys.

# Ten

"Jason," Dianne said, closing her eyes in thanks that it was her son who'd answered the phone and not Jill. Her daughter would have plied her with questions and more advice than "Dear Abby."

"Hi, Mom. I thought you were at aerobics."

"I am, and I may be here a whole lot longer if you can't help me out." Without a pause, she continued, "I need you to go upstairs, look in my underwear drawer and bring me the extra set of car keys."

"They're in your underwear drawer?"

"Yes." It was the desperate plan of a desperate woman. She didn't dare contact the auto club this time for fear they'd send Port Blossom Towing to the rescue in the form of one Steve Creighton.

"You don't expect me to paw through your, uh, stuff, do you?"

"Jason, listen to me, I've locked my keys in the car, and I don't have any other choice."

"You locked your keys in the car? *Again?* What's with you lately, Mom?"

"Do we need to go through this now?" she demanded. Jason wasn't saying anything she hadn't already said to herself a hundred times over the past few minutes. She was so agitated it was a struggle not to break down and weep.

"I'll have Jill get the keys for me," Jason agreed, with a sigh that told her it demanded a good deal of effort, not to mention fortitude, for him to comply with this request.

"Great. Thanks." Dianne breathed out in relief. "Okay. Now, the next thing you need to do is get your bicycle out of the garage and ride it down to the community center."

"You mean you want me to *bring* you the keys?"

"Yes."

"But it's raining!"

"It's only drizzling." True, but as a general rule Dianne didn't like her son riding his bike in the winter.

"But it's getting dark," Jason protested next.

That did concern Dianne. "Okay, you're right. Call Grandma and ask her to come over and get the keys from you and then have her bring them to me."

"You want me to call Grandma?"

"Jason, are you hard of hearing? Yes, I want you to call Grandma, and if you can't reach her, call me back here at the community center." Needless to say, her cell phone was locked in the car. *Again.* "I'll be waiting." She read off the number for him. "And listen, if my car keys aren't in my underwear drawer, have Grandma bring me a wire clothes hanger, okay?"

He hesitated. "All right," he said after another burdened sigh. "Are you sure you're all right, Mom?"

"Of course I'm sure." But she was going to remember his attitude the next time he needed her to go on a Boy Scout camp-out with him.

Jason seemed to take hours to do as she'd asked. Since the front desk was now busy with the after-work crowd, Dianne didn't want to trouble the staff for the phone a second time to find out what was keeping her son.

Forty minutes after Dianne's aerobic class was over, she was still pacing the foyer of the community center, stopping every now and then to glance outside. Suddenly she saw a big red tow truck turn into the parking lot.

She didn't need to be psychic to know that the man driving the truck was Steve.

Mumbling a curse under her breath, Dianne walked out into the parking lot to confront him.

Steve was standing alongside her car when she approached. She noticed that he wasn't wearing the gray-striped coveralls he'd worn the first time they'd met. Now he was dressed in slacks and a sweater, as though he'd come from the office.

"What are you doing here?" The best defense was a good offense, or so her high-school basketball coach had advised her about a hundred years ago.

"Jason called me," he said, without looking at her.

"The traitor," Dianne muttered.

"He said something about refusing to search through your underwear and his grandmother couldn't be reached. And that all this has to do with you going off to war."

Although Steve was speaking in an even voice, it was clear he found the situation comical.

"W.A.R. is my aerobics class," Dianne explained stiffly. "It means Women After Results."

"I'm glad to hear it." He walked around to the passenger side of the tow truck and brought out the instrument he'd used to open her door the first time. "So," he said leaning against the side of her compact. "How have you been?"

"Fine."

"You don't look so good, but then I suppose that's because you're a divorced woman with two children and a manipulative mother."

Naturally he'd taunt her with that. "How kind of you to say so," she returned with an equal dose of sarcasm.

"How's Jerome?"

"Jerome?"

"The butcher your mother wanted to set you up with," he answered gruffly. "I figured by now the two of you would've gone out." His words had a biting edge.

"I'm not seeing Jerome." The thought of having to eat blood sausage was enough to turn her stomach.

"I'm surprised," he said. "I would've figured you'd leap at the opportunity to date someone other than me."

"If I wasn't interested in him before, what makes you think I'd go out with him now? And why aren't you opening my door? That's what you're here for, isn't it?"

He ignored her question. "Frankly, Dianne, we can't go on meeting like this."

"Funny, very funny." She crossed her arms defiantly.

"Actually I came here to talk some sense into you," he said after a moment.

"According to my mother, you won't have any chance of succeeding. I'm hopeless."

"I don't believe that. Otherwise I wouldn't be here." He walked over to her and gently placed his hands on her shoulders. "Maybe, Dianne, you've been fine these past few days, but frankly I've been a wreck."

"You have?" As Dianne looked at him she thought she'd drown in his eyes. And when he smiled, it was all she could do not to cry.

"I've never met a more stubborn woman in my life."

She blushed. "I'm awful, I know."

His gaze became more intent as he asked, "How about if we go someplace and talk?"

"I…think that would be all right." At the moment there was little she could refuse him. Until he'd arrived, she'd had no idea what to do about the situation between them. Now the answer was becoming clear….

"You might want to call Jason and Jill and tell them."

"Oh, right, I should." How could she have forgotten her own children?

Steve was grinning from ear to ear. "Don't worry, I already took care of that. While I was at it, I phoned your mother, too. She's on her way to your house now. She'll make the kids' dinner." He paused, then said, "I figured if I was fortunate enough, I might be able to talk you into having dinner with me. I understand Walker's has an excellent seafood salad."

If he was fortunate enough, he might be able to talk her into having dinner with him? Dianne felt like weeping. Steve Creighton was the sweetest, kindest, handsomest man she'd ever met, and *he* was looking at *her* as if he was the one who should be counting his blessings.

Steve promptly opened her car door. "I'm going to buy you a magnetic key attachment for keeping a spare key under your bumper so this doesn't happen again."

"You are?"

"Yes, otherwise I'll worry about you."

No one had ever worried about her, except her immediate family. Whatever situation arose, she handled. Broken water pipes, lost checks, a leaky roof—nothing had ever defeated her. Not even Jack had been able to break her spirit, but one kind smile from Steve Creighton and she was a jumble of emotions. She blinked back tears and made a mess of thanking him, rushing her words so that they tumbled over each other.

"Dianne?"

She stopped and bit her lower lip. "Yes?"

"Either we go to the restaurant now and talk, or I'm going to kiss you right here in this parking lot."

Despite everything, she managed to smile. "It wouldn't be the first time."

"No, but I doubt I'd be content with one kiss."

She lowered her lashes, thinking she probably wouldn't be, either. "I'll meet you at Walker's."

He followed her across town, which took less than five minutes, and pulled into the empty parking space next to hers. Once inside the restaurant, they were seated immediately by a window overlooking Sinclair Inlet.

Dianne had just picked up her menu when Steve said, "I'd like to tell you a story."

"Okay," she said, puzzled. She put the menu aside. Deciding what to eat took second place to listening to Steve.

"It's about a woman who first attracted the attention of a particular man at the community center about two months ago."

Dianne took a sip of water, her eyes meeting his above the glass, her heart thumping loudly in her ears. "Yes…"

"This lady was oblivious to certain facts."

"Such as?" Dianne prompted.

"First of all, she didn't seem to have a clue how attractive she was or how much this guy admired her. He did everything but stand on his head to get her attention, but nothing worked."

"What exactly did he try?"

"Working out at the same hours she did, pumping iron—and looking exceptionally good in his T-shirt and shorts."

"Why didn't this man say something to…this woman?"

Steve chuckled. "Well, you see, he was accustomed to women giving him plenty of attention. So this particular woman dented his pride by ignoring him, then she made him downright angry. Finally it occurred to him that she wasn't *purposely* ignoring him—she simply wasn't aware of him."

"It seems to me this man is rather arrogant."

"I couldn't agree with you more."

"You couldn't?" Dianne was surprised.

"That was when he decided there were plenty of fish in the sea and he didn't need a pretty divorcée with two children—he'd asked around about her, so he knew a few details like that."

Dianne smoothed the pink linen napkin across her lap. "What happened next?"

"He was sitting in his office one evening. The day had been busy and one of his men had phoned in sick, so he'd been out on the road all afternoon. He was ready to go home and take a hot shower, but just about then the phone rang. One of the night crew answered it and it was the auto club. Apparently some lady had locked her keys in her car at the community center and needed someone to come rescue her."

"So you, I mean this man, volunteered?"

"That he did, never dreaming she'd practically throw herself in his arms. And not because he'd unlocked her car, either, but because she was desperate for someone to take her to the Valentine's dinner."

"That part about her falling in your arms is a slight exaggeration," Dianne felt obliged to tell him.

"Maybe so, but it was the first time a woman had ever offered to pay him to take her out. Which was the most ironic part of this entire tale. For weeks he'd been trying to gain this woman's attention, practically killing himself to impress her with the amount of weight he was lifting. It seemed every woman in town was impressed except the one who mattered."

"Did you ever stop to think that was the very reason he found her so attractive? If she ignored him, then he must have considered her a challenge."

"Yes, he thought about that a lot. But after he met her and kissed her, he realized that his instincts had been right from the first. He was going to fall in love with this woman."

"He was?" Dianne's voice was little more than a hoarse whisper.

"That's the second part of the story."

"The second part?" Dianne was growing confused.

"The happily-ever-after part."

Dianne used her napkin to wipe away the tears, which had suddenly welled up in her eyes again. "He can't possibly know that."

Steve smiled then, that wonderful carefree, vagabond smile of his, the smile that never failed to lift her heart. "Wrong. He's known it for a long time. All he needs to do now is convince her."

Sniffing, Dianne said, "I have the strangest sensation that this woman has trouble recognizing a prince when she sees one. For a good part of her life, she was satisfied with keeping a frog happy."

"And now?"

"And now she's…now *I'm* ready to discover what happily-ever-after is all about."

# MY HERO

For Virginia Myers, my mentor—
thanks for your friendship and encouragement!

# *One*

The man was the source of all her problems, Bailey York decided. He just didn't cut it. The first time around he was too cold, too distant. Only a woman "who loved too much" could possibly fall for him.

The second time, the guy was a regular Milquetoast. A wimp. He didn't seem to have a single thought of his own. This man definitely needed to be whipped into shape, but Bailey wasn't sure she knew how to do it.

So she did the logical thing. She consulted a fellow romance writer. Jo Ann Davis and Bailey rode the subway together every day, and Jo Ann had far more experience in this. Three years of dealing with men like Michael.

"Well?" Bailey asked anxiously when they met on a gray, drizzly January morning before boarding San Francisco's Bay Area Rapid Transit system, or BART for short.

Jo Ann shook her head, her look as sympathetic as her words. "You're right—Michael's a wimp."

"But I've worked so hard." Bailey couldn't help feeling discouraged. She'd spent months on this, squeezing in every available moment. She'd sacrificed lunches, given up nighttime television and whole weekends. Even Christmas had seemed a mere distraction. Needless to say, her social life had come to a complete standstill.

"No one told me writing a romance novel would be so difficult," Bailey muttered, as the subway train finally shot into the station. It screeched to a halt and the doors slid open, disgorging a crowd of harried-looking passengers.

"What should I do next?" Bailey asked as she and Jo Ann made their way into one of the cars. She'd never been a quitter, and already she could feel her resolve stiffening.

"Go back to the beginning and start over again," Jo Ann advised.

"Again," Bailey groaned, casting her eyes about for a vacant seat and darting forward, Jo Ann close behind, when she located one. When they were settled, Jo Ann handed Bailey her battle-weary manuscript.

She thumbed through the top pages, glancing over the notes Jo Ann had made in the margins. Her first thought had been to throw the whole project in the garbage and put herself out of her misery, but she hated to admit defeat. She'd always been a determined person; once she set her mind to something, it took more than a little thing like characterization to put her off.

It was ironic, Bailey mused, that a woman who was such a failure at love was so interested in writing about it. Perhaps that was the reason she felt so strongly about selling her romance novel. True love had scurried past her twice, stepping on her toes both times. She'd learned her lesson the hard way. Men were wonderful to read about and to look at from afar, but when it came to involving herself in a serious relationship, Bailey simply wasn't interested. Not anymore.

"The plot is basically sound," Jo Ann assured her. "All you really need to do is rework Michael."

The poor man had been reworked so many times it was a wonder Janice, her heroine, even recognized him. And if *Bailey* wasn't in love with Michael, she couldn't very well expect Janice to be swept off her feet.

"The best advice I can give you is to re-read your favorite romances and look really carefully at how the author portrays her hero," Jo Ann went on.

Bailey heaved an expressive sigh. She shouldn't be complaining—not yet, anyway. After all, she'd only been at this a few months, unlike Jo Ann who'd been writing and submitting manuscripts for more than three years. Personally, Bailey didn't think it would take *her* that long to sell a book. For one thing, she had more time to write than her friend. Jo Ann was married, the mother of two school-age children, plus she worked full-time. Another reason Bailey felt assured of success was that she had a romantic heart. Nearly everyone in their writers' group had said so. Not that it had done her any good when it came to finding a man of her own, but in the romance-writing business, a sensitive nature was clearly an asset.

Bailey prayed that all her creative whimsy, all her romantic perceptions, would be brilliantly conveyed on the pages of *Forever Yours*. They were, too—except for Michael, who seemed bent on giving her problems.

Men had always been an enigma to her, Bailey mused, so it was unreasonable to expect that to be any different now.

"Something else that might help you…" Jo Ann began thoughtfully.

"Yes?"

"Writers' Input recently published a book on characterization. I read a review of it, and as I recall, the author claims the best way to learn is to observe. It sounded rather abstract at the time, but I've had a chance to think about it, and you know? It makes sense."

"In other words," Bailey mused aloud, "what I really need is a model." She frowned. "I sometimes think I wouldn't recognize a hero if one hit me over the head."

No sooner had the words left her mouth than a dull object smacked the side of her head.

Bailey let out a sharp cry and rubbed the tender spot, twisting around to glare at the villain who was strolling casually past. She wasn't hurt so much as surprised.

"Hey, watch it!" she cried.

"I beg your pardon," a man said crisply, continuing down the crowded aisle. He carried a briefcase in one hand, with his umbrella tucked under his arm. As far as Bailey could determine, the umbrella handle had been the culprit. She scowled after him. The least he could've done was inquire if she'd been hurt.

"You're coming to the meeting tonight, aren't you?" Jo Ann asked. The subway came to a stop, which lowered the noise level enough for them to continue their conversation without raising their voices. "Libby McDonald's going to be there." Libby had published several popular romances and was in the San Francisco area visiting relatives. Their romance writers' group was honored that she'd agreed to speak.

Bailey nodded eagerly. Meeting Jo Ann couldn't have come at a better time. They'd found each other on the subway when Bailey noticed they were both reading the same romance, and began a conversation. She soon learned that they shared several interests; they began to meet regularly and struck up a friendship.

A week or so after their first meeting, Bailey sheep-

ishly admitted how much she wanted to write a romance novel herself, not telling Jo Ann she'd already
finished and submitted a manuscript. It was then that
Jo Ann revealed that she'd written two complete
manuscripts and was working on her third historical
romance.

In the months since they'd met, Jo Ann's friendship had been invaluable to Bailey. Her mentor had
introduced her to the local writers' group, and Bailey had discovered others all striving toward the
same ultimate goal—publishing their stories. Since
joining the group, Bailey had come to realize she'd
made several mistakes, all typical of a novice writer,
and had started the rewriting project. But unfortunately that hadn't gone well, at least not according
to Jo Ann.

Bailey leafed through her manuscript, studying the
notes her friend had made. What Jo Ann said made a
lot of sense. "A romance hero is larger than life," Jo
Ann had written in bold red ink along one margin.
"Unfortunately, Michael isn't."

In the past few months, Bailey had been learning
about classic romance heroes. They were supposed to
be proud, passionate and impetuous. Strong, forceful
men who were capable of tenderness. Men of excellent taste and impeccable style. That these qualities
were too good to be true was something Bailey knew
for a fact. A hero was supposed to have a burning need
to find the one woman who would make his life

complete. That sounded just fine on paper, but Bailey knew darn well what men were *really* like.

She heaved an exasperated sigh and shook her head. "You'd think I'd know all this by now."

"Don't be so hard on yourself. You haven't been at this as long as I have. Don't make the mistake of thinking I have all the answers, either," Jo Ann warned. "You'll notice I haven't sold yet."

"But you will." Bailey was convinced of that. Jo Ann's historical romance was beautifully written. Twice her friend had been a finalist in a national writing competition, and everyone, including Bailey, strongly believed it was only a matter of time before a publishing company bought *Fire Dream*.

"I agree with everything you're saying," Bailey added. "I just don't know if I can do it. I put my heart and soul into this book. I can't do any better."

"Of course you can," Jo Ann insisted.

Bailey knew she'd feel differently in a few hours, when she'd had a chance to muster her resolve; by tonight she'd be revising her manuscript with renewed enthusiasm. But for now, she needed to sit back and recover her confidence. She was lucky, though, because she had Jo Ann, who'd taken the time to read *Forever Yours* and give much-needed suggestions.

Yet Bailey couldn't help thinking that if she had a model for Michael, her job would be much easier. Jo Ann used her husband, Dan. Half their writers' group was in love with him, and no one had even met the man.

Reading Jo Ann's words at the end of the first chapter, Bailey found herself agreeing once more. "Michael should be determined, cool and detached. A man of substance."

Her friend made it sound so easy. Again Bailey reflected on how disadvantaged she was. In all her life, she hadn't dated a single hero, only those who thought they were but then quickly proved otherwise.

Bailey was mulling over her dilemma when she noticed him. He was tall and impeccably dressed in a gray pin-striped suit. She wasn't an expert on men's clothing, but she knew quality when she saw it.

The stranger carried himself with an air of cool detachment. That was good. Excellent, in fact. Exactly what Jo Ann had written in the margin of *Forever Yours*.

Now that she was studying him, she realized he looked vaguely familiar, but she didn't know why. Then she got it. This was "a man of substance." The very person she was looking for…

Here she was, bemoaning her sorry fate, when lo and behold a handsome stranger strolled into her life. Not just any stranger. This man was Michael incarnate. The embodiment of everything she'd come to expect of a romantic hero. Only this version was living and breathing, and standing a few feet away.

For several minutes, Bailey couldn't keep her eyes off him. The subway cars were crowded to capacity in the early-morning rush, and while other people looked bored and uncomfortable, her hero couldn't have been more relaxed. He stood several spaces ahead of her, holding the overhead rail and reading the morning edition of the paper. His raincoat was folded over his arm and, unlike some of the passengers, he seemed undisturbed by the train's movement as it sped along.

The fact that he was engaged in reading gave Bailey the opportunity to analyze him without being detected. His age was difficult to judge, but she guessed him to be in his mid-thirties. Perfect! Michael was thirty-four.

The man in the pin-striped suit was handsome, too. But it wasn't his classic features—the sculpted cheekbones, straight nose or high forehead—that seized her attention.

It was his jaw.

Bailey had never seen a more determined jaw in her life. Exactly the type that illustrated a touch of arrogance and a hint of audacity, both attributes Jo Ann had mentioned in her critique.

His rich chestnut-colored hair was short and neatly trimmed, his skin lightly tanned. His eyes were dark. As dark as her own were blue.

His very presence seemed to fill the subway car. Bailey was convinced everyone else sensed it, too. She couldn't understand why the other women weren't all staring at him just as raptly. The more she studied him, the better he looked. He was, without a doubt, the most masculine male Bailey had ever seen—exactly the way she'd always pictured her hero. Unfortunately she hadn't succeeded in transferring him from her imagination to the page.

Bailey was so excited she could barely contain herself. After months of writing and rewriting *Forever Yours,* shaping and reshaping the characters, she'd finally stumbled upon a real-life Michael. She could hardly believe her luck. Hadn't Jo Ann just mentioned this great new book that suggested learning through observing?

"Do you see the man in the gray pin-striped suit?" Bailey whispered, elbowing Jo Ann. "You know who he is, don't you?"

Jo Ann's eyes narrowed as she identified Bailey's hero and studied him for several seconds. She shook her head. "Isn't he the guy who clobbered you on the head with his umbrella a few minutes ago?"

"He is?"

"Who did you think he was?"

"You mean you don't know?" Bailey had been confident Jo Ann would recognize him as quickly as she had.

"*Should* I know him?"

"Of course you should." Jo Ann had read *Forever Yours.* Surely she'd recognize Michael in the flesh.

"Who do *you* think he is?" Jo Ann asked, growing impatient.

"That's Michael—my Michael," she added when Jo Ann frowned.

"Michael?" Jo Ann echoed without conviction.

"The way he was meant to be. The way Janice, my heroine, and I want him to be." Bailey had been trying to create him in her mind for weeks, and now here he was! "Can't you feel the sexual magnetism radiating from him?" she asked out of the corner of her mouth.

"Frankly, no."

Bailey decided to ignore that. "He's absolutely perfect. Can't you sense his proud determination? That commanding presence that makes him larger than life?"

Jo Ann's eyes narrowed again, the way they usually did when she was doing some serious contemplating.

"Do you see it now?" Bailey pressed.

Jo Ann's shoulders lifted in a regretful shrug. "I'm honestly trying, but I just don't. Give me a couple of minutes to work on it."

Bailey ignored her fellow writer's lack of insight. It didn't matter if Jo Ann agreed with her or not. The man in the gray suit was Michael. Her Michael. Naturally she'd be willing to step aside and give him to Janice, who'd been waiting all these weeks for Michael to straighten himself out.

"It hit me all of a sudden—what you were saying about observing in order to learn. I need a model for Michael, someone who can help me gain perspective," Bailey explained, her gaze momentarily leaving her hero.

"Ah…" Jo Ann sounded uncertain.

"If I'm ever going to sell *Forever Yours* I've got to employ those kinds of techniques." Bailey's eyes automatically returned to the man. Hmm, a little over six feet tall, she estimated. He really was a perfect specimen. All this time she'd been feeling melancholy, wondering how she could ever create an authentic hero, then, almost by magic, this one appeared in living color….

"Go on," Jo Ann prodded, urging Bailey to finish her thought.

"The way I figure it, I may never get this characterization down right if I don't have someone to pattern Michael after."

Bailey half expected Jo Ann to argue with her. She was pleasantly surprised when her friend agreed with a quick nod. "I think you're right. It's an excellent idea."

Grinning sheepishly, Bailey gave herself a mental pat on the back. "I thought so myself."

"What are you planning to do? Study this guy—research his life history, learn what you can about his family and upbringing? That sort of thing? I hope you understand that this may not be as easy as it seems."

"Nothing worthwhile ever is," Bailey intoned solemnly. Actually, how she was going to do any of this research was a mystery to her, as well. Eventually she'd come up with some way of learning what she needed to know without being obvious about it. The sooner the better, of course. "I should probably start by finding out his name."

"That sounds like a good idea," Jo Ann said as though she wasn't entirely sure this plan was such a brilliant one, after all.

The train came to a vibrating halt, and a group of people moved toward the doors. Even while they disembarked, more were crowding onto the train. Bailey kept her gaze on the man in the pin-striped suit for fear he'd step off the subway without her realizing it. When she was certain he wasn't leaving, she relaxed.

"You know," Jo Ann said thoughtfully once the train had started again. "My Logan's modeled after Dan, but in this case, I'm beginning to have—"

"Did you see that?" Bailey interrupted, grabbing her friend's arm in her enthusiasm. The longer she studied the stranger, the more impressed she became.

"What?" Jo Ann demanded, glancing around her.

"The elegant way he turned the page." Bailey was thinking of her own miserable attempts to read while standing in a moving train. Any endeavor to turn the unwieldy newspaper page resulted in frustration to her and anyone unfortunate enough to be standing nearby. Yet he did it as gracefully and easily as if he were sitting at his own desk, in his own office.

"You're really hung up on this guy, aren't you?"

"You still don't see it, do you?" Bailey couldn't help being disappointed. She would've expected Jo Ann, of all her friends, to understand that this stranger was everything she'd ever wanted in Michael, from the top of his perfect hair to the tip of his (probably) size-eleven shoe.

"I'm still trying," Jo Ann said squinting as she stared at Bailey's hero, "but I don't quite see it."

"That's what I thought." But Bailey felt convinced she was right. This tall, handsome man was Michael, and it didn't matter if Jo Ann saw it or not. She did, and that was all that mattered.

The subway train slowed as it neared the next stop. Once again, passengers immediately crowded the doorway. Her hero slipped the newspaper into his briefcase, removed the umbrella hooked around his forearm and stood back, politely waiting his turn.

"Oh, my," Bailey said, panic in her voice. This could get complicated. Her heart was already thundering like a Midwest storm gone berserk. She reached for her purse and vaulted to her feet.

Jo Ann looked at her as though she suspected Bailey had lost her wits. She tugged the sleeve of Bailey's coat. "This isn't our stop."

"Yes, I know," Bailey said, pulling an unwilling Jo Ann to her feet.

"Then what are you doing getting off here?"

Bailey frowned. "We're following him, what else?"

"We? But what about our jobs?"

"You don't expect me to do this alone, do you?"

# *Two*

"You don't mean we're actually going to *follow* him?"

"Of course we are." They couldn't stand there arguing. "Are you coming or not?"

For the first time in recent history, Jo Ann seemed at a complete loss for words. Just when Bailey figured she'd have to do this on her own, Jo Ann nodded. The two dashed off the car just in time.

"I've never done anything so crazy in all my life," Jo Ann muttered.

Bailey ignored her. "He went that way," she said, pointing toward the escalator. Grabbing Jo Ann by the arm, she hurried after the man in the pin-striped suit, maintaining a safe distance.

"Listen, Bailey," Jo Ann said, jogging in order to keep up, but still two steps behind her. "I'm beginning to have second thoughts about this."

"Why? Not five minutes ago you agreed that modeling Michael on a real man was an excellent approach to characterization."

"I didn't know you planned to stalk the guy! Don't you think we should stay back a little farther?"

"No." Bailey was adamant. As it was, her hero's long, powerful strides were much faster than Bailey's normal walking pace. Jo Ann's short-legged stride was even slower.

By the time they reached the corner, Jo Ann was panting. She leaned against the street lamp and placed her hand over her heart, inhaling deeply. "Give me a minute, would you?"

"We might lose him." The look Jo Ann gave her suggested that might not be so bad. "Think of this as research," Bailey added, looping her arm through Jo Ann's again and dragging her forward.

Staying in the shadow of the buildings, the two trailed Bailey's hero for three more blocks. Fortunately he was walking in the direction of the area where Bailey and Jo Ann both worked.

When he paused for a red light, Bailey stayed several feet behind him, wandering aimlessly toward a widow display while glancing over her shoulder every few seconds. She didn't want to give him an opportunity to notice her.

"Do you think he's married?" Bailey demanded of her friend.

"How would I know?" Jo Ann snapped.

"Intuition."

The light changed and Bailey rushed forward. A reluctant Jo Ann followed on her heels. "I can't believe I'm doing this."

"You already said that."

"What am I going to tell my boss when I'm late?" Jo Ann groaned.

Bailey had to wait when Jo Ann came to a sudden halt, leaned against a display window and removed her high heel. She shook it out, then hurriedly put it back on.

"Jo Ann," Bailey said in a heated whisper, urging her friend to hurry.

"There was something in my shoe," she said from between clenched teeth. "I can't race down the streets of San Francisco with a stone in my shoe."

"I don't want to lose him," Bailey stopped abruptly, causing Jo Ann to collide with her. "Look, he went into the Cascade Building."

"Oh, good," Jo Ann muttered on the tail end of a sigh that proclaimed relief. "Does that mean we can go to work now?"

"Of course not." It was clear to Bailey that Jo Ann knew next to nothing about detective work. She probably didn't read mysteries. "I have to find out what his name is."

"What?" Jo Ann sounded as though Bailey had suggested they climb to the top of Coit Tower and leap off. "How do you plan to do that?"

"I don't know. I'll figure it out later." Clutching her friend's arm, Bailey urged her forward. "Come on, we can't give up now."

"Sure we can," Jo Ann muttered as they entered the Cascade Building.

"Hurry," Bailey whispered, releasing Jo Ann's elbow. "He's getting into the elevator." Bailey slipped past several people, mumbling. "Excuse me, excuse me" as she struggled to catch the same elevator, Jo Ann stumbling behind her.

They managed to make it a split second before the doors closed. There were four or five others on board, and Jo Ann cast Bailey a frown that doubted her intelligence.

Bailey had other concerns. She tried to remain as unobtrusive as possible, not wanting to call attention to herself or Jo Ann. Her hero seemed oblivious to them, which served her purposes nicely. All she intended to do was find out his name and what he did for a living, a task that shouldn't require the FBI.

Jo Ann jerked Bailey's sleeve and nodded toward the stranger's left hand. It took Bailey a moment to realize her friend was pointing out the fact that he wasn't wearing a wedding ring. The realization cheered Bailey and she made a circle with thumb and finger, grinning broadly.

As the elevator sped upward, Bailey saw Jo Ann anxiously check her watch. Then the elevator came to a smooth halt. A few seconds passed before the doors slid open and two passengers stepped out.

Her hero glanced over his shoulder, then moved to one side. For half a second, his gaze rested on Bailey and Jo Ann.

Half a second! Bailey straightened, offended at the casual way in which he'd dismissed her. She didn't want him to notice her, but at the same time, she felt cheated that he hadn't recognized the heroine in her— the same way she'd seen the hero in him. She was, after all, heroine material. She was attractive and... Well, attractive might be too strong a word. Cute and charming had a more comfortable feel. Her best feature was her thick dark hair that fell straight as a stick across her shoulders. The ends curved under just a little, giving it shape and bounce. She was taller than average, and slender, with clear blue eyes and a turned-up nose. As for her personality, she had spunk enough not to turn away from a good argument and spirit enough to follow a stranger around San Francisco.

Bailey noted that once again his presence seemed to fill the cramped quarters. His briefcase was tucked under his arm, while his hand gripped the curved handle of his umbrella. For all the notice he gave those around him, he might have been alone.

When Bailey turned to her friend, she saw that Jo Ann's eyes were focused straight ahead, her teeth gritted as though she couldn't wait to tell Bailey exactly what she thought of this crazy scheme. It *was* crazy, Bailey would be the first to admit, but these were desperate times in the life of a budding romance writer. She would stop at nothing to achieve her goal.

Bailey grinned. She had to agree that traipsing after her hero was a bit unconventional, but *he* didn't need to know about it. He didn't need to ever know how she intended to use him.

Her gaze moved from Jo Ann, then to the man with the umbrella. The amusement drained out of her as she found herself staring into the darkest pair of eyes she'd ever seen. Bailey was the first to look away, her pulse thundering in her ears.

The elevator stopped several times until, finally, only the three of them were left. Jo Ann had squeezed into the corner. Behind the stranger's back she mouthed several words that Bailey couldn't hope to decipher, then tapped one finger against the face of her watch.

Bailey nodded and raised her hand, fingers spread, to plead for five more minutes.

When the elevator stopped again, her hero stepped out, and Bailey followed, with Jo Ann trailing behind her. He walked briskly down the wide hallway, then entered a set of double doors marked with the name of a well-known architectural firm.

"Are you satisfied now?" Jo Ann burst out. "Honestly, Bailey, have you gone completely nuts?"

"You told me I need a hero who's proud and determined and I'm going to find one."

"That doesn't answer my question. Has it occurred to you yet that you've gone off the deep end?"

"Because I want to find out his name?"

"And how do you plan to do that?"

"I don't know yet," Bailey admitted. "Why don't I just ask?" Having said that, she straightened her shoulders and walked toward the same doors through which the man had disappeared.

The pleasant-looking middle-aged woman who sat at the reception desk greeted her with a warm smile. "Good morning."

"Good morning," Bailey returned, hoping her smile was as serene and trusting as the older woman's. "This may seem a bit unusual, but I...I was on the subway this morning and I thought I recognized an old family friend. Naturally I didn't want to make a fool of myself in case I was wrong. He arrived in your office a few minutes ago and I was wondering... I know it's unusual, but would you mind telling me his name?"

"That would be Mr. Davidson. He's been taking BART the last few months because of the freeway renovation project."

"Mr. Davidson," Bailey repeated slowly. "His first name wouldn't be Michael, would it?"

"No." The receptionist frowned slightly. "It's Parker."

"Parker," Bailey repeated softly. "Parker Davidson." She liked the way it sounded, and although it wasn't a name she would've chosen for a hero, she could see that it fit him perfectly.

"Is Mr. Davidson the man you thought?"

It took Bailey a second or two to realize the woman was speaking to her. "Yes," she answered with a bright smile. "I do believe he is."

"Why, that's wonderful." The woman was obviously delighted. "Would you like me to buzz him? I'm sure he'd want to talk to you himself. Mr. Davidson is such a nice man."

"Oh, no, please don't do that." Bailey hoped she was able to hide the panic she felt at the woman's suggestion. "I wouldn't want to disturb him and I really have to be getting to work. Thank you for your trouble."

"It was no trouble whatsoever." The receptionist glanced down at her appointment schedule and shook her head. "I was going to suggest you stop in at noon, but unfortunately Mr. Davidson's got a lunch engagement."

Bailey sighed as though with regret and turned away from the desk. "I'll guess I'll have to talk to him another time."

"That's really too bad. At least give me your name." The woman's soft brown eyes went from warm to sympathetic.

"Janice Hampton," Bailey said, mentioning the name of her heroine. "Thank you again for your help. You've been most kind."

Jo Ann was in the hallway pacing and muttering when Bailey stepped out of Parker's office. She stopped abruptly as Bailey appeared, her eyes filled with questions. "What happened?"

"Nothing. I asked the receptionist for his name and she told me. She even let it slip that he's got a lunch engagement…"

"Are you satisfied *now?*" Jo Ann sounded as though she'd passed from impatience to resignation. "In case you've forgotten, we're both working women."

Bailey glanced at her watch and groaned. "We won't be too late if we hurry." Jo Ann worked as an insurance specialist in a doctor's office and Bailey was a paralegal.

Luckily their office buildings were only a few blocks from the Cascade Building. They parted company on the next corner and Bailey half jogged the rest of the way.

No one commented when she slipped into the office ten minutes late. She hoped the same held true for Jo Ann, who'd probably never been late for work in her life.

Bailey settled down at her desk with her coffee and her files, then hesitated. Jo Ann was right. Discovering Parker's name was useless unless she could fill in the essential details about his life. She needed facts. Lots of facts. The kinds of people he associated with, his background, his likes and dislikes, everyday habits.

It wasn't until later in the morning that Bailey started wondering where someone like Parker Davidson would go for lunch. It might be important to learn that. The type of restaurant a man chose—casual? elegant? exotic?—said something about his personality. Details like that could make the difference between a sale and a rejection, and frankly, Bailey didn't know if Michael could tolerate another spurning.

At ten to twelve Bailey mumbled an excuse about having an appointment before she headed out the door. Her boss gave her a funny look, but Bailey made sure she escaped before anyone could ask any questions. It wasn't like Bailey to take her duties lightly.

Luck was with her. She'd only been standing at the street corner for five minutes when Parker Davidson came out of the building. He was deeply involved in conversation with another man, yet when he raised his hand to summon a taxi, one appeared instantly, as if by magic. If she hadn't seen it with her own eyes, Bailey wouldn't have believed it. Surely this was the confidence, the command, others said a hero should possess. Not wanting to miss a single detail, Bailey took a pen and pad out of her purse and started jotting them down.

As Parker's cab slowly pulled away, she ventured into the street and flagged down a second cab. In order to manage that, however, she'd had to wave her arms above her head and leap up and down.

She yanked open the door and leapt inside. "Follow that cab," she cried, pointing toward Parker's taxi.

The stocky driver twisted around. "Are you serious? You want me to follow that cab?"

"That's right," she said anxiously, afraid Parker's taxi would soon be out of sight.

Her driver laughed outright. "I've been waiting fifteen years for someone to tell me that. You got yourself a deal, lady." He stepped on the accelerator and barreled down the street, going well above the speed limit.

"Any particular reason, lady?"

"I beg your pardon?" The man was doing fifty in a thirty-mile-an-hour zone.

"I want to know why you're following that cab." The car turned a corner at record speed, the wheels screeching, and Bailey slid from one end of the seat to the other. If she'd hoped to avoid attention, it was a lost cause. Parker Davidson might not notice her, but nearly everyone else in San Francisco did.

"I'm doing some research for a romance novel," Bailey explained.

"You're doing *what?*"

"Research."

Apparently her answer didn't satisfy him, because he slowed to a sedate twenty miles an hour. "Research for a romance novel," he repeated, his voice flat. "I thought you were a private detective or something."

"I'm sorry to disappoint you. I write romance novels and— Oh, stop here, would you?" Parker's cab had pulled to the curb and the two men were climbing out.

"Sure, lady, don't get excited."

Bailey scrambled out of the cab and searched through her purse for her money. When she couldn't find it, she slapped the large bag onto the hood of the cab and sorted through its contents until she retrieved her wallet. "Here."

"Have a great day, lady," the cabbie said sardonically, setting his cap farther back on his head. Bailey offered him a vague smile.

She toyed with the idea of following the men into the restaurant and having lunch. She would have, too, if it weren't for the fact that she'd used all her cash to pay for the taxi.

But there was plenty to entertain her while she waited—although Bailey wasn't sure exactly what she was waiting for. The streets of Chinatown were crowded. She gazed about her at the colorful shops with their produce stands and souvenirs and rows of smoked ducks hanging in the windows. Street vendors displayed their wares and tried to coax her to come examine their goods.

Bailey bought a fresh orange with some change she scrounged from the bottom of her purse. Walking across the street, she wondered how long her hero would dawdle over his lunch. Most likely he'd walk back to the office. Michael would.

His lunch engagement didn't last nearly as long as Bailey had expected. When he emerged from the restaurant, he took her by surprise. Bailey was in the process of using her debit card to buy a sweatshirt she'd found at an incredibly low price and had to rush in an effort to keep up with him.

He hadn't gone more than a couple of blocks when she lost him. Stunned, she stood in the middle of the sidewalk, wondering how he could possibly have disappeared.

One minute he was there, and the next he was gone. Tailing a hero wasn't nearly as easy as she'd supposed.

Discouraged, Bailey clutched her bag with the sweatshirt and slung her purse over her shoulder, then started back toward her office. Heaven only knew what she was going to say to her boss once she arrived—half an hour late.

She hadn't gone more than a few steps when someone grabbed her arm and jerked her into the alley. She opened her mouth to scream, but the cry died a sudden death when she found herself staring up at Parker Davidson.

"I want to know why the hell you're following me."

# *Three*

"Ah... Ah..." For the life of her, Bailey couldn't string two words together.

"Janice Hampton, I presume?"

Bailey nodded, simply because it was easier than explaining herself.

Parker's eyes slowly raked her from head to foot. He obviously didn't see anything that pleased him. "You're not an old family friend, are you?"

Still silent, she answered him with a shake of her head.

"That's what I thought. What do you want?"

Bailey couldn't think of a single coherent remark.

"Well?" he demanded since she was clearly having a problem answering even the most basic questions. Bailey had no idea where to start or how much to say. The truth would never do, but she didn't know if she was capable of lying convincingly.

"Then you leave me no choice but to call the police," he said tightly.

"No…please." The thought of explaining everything to an officer of the law was too mortifying to consider.

"Then start talking." His eyes were narrow and as cold as the January wind off San Francisco Bay.

Bailey clasped her hands together, wishing she'd never given in to the whim to follow him on his lunch appointment. "It's a bit…complicated," she mumbled.

"Isn't it always?"

"Your attitude isn't helping any," she returned, straightening her shoulders. He might be a high-and-mighty architect—and her behavior might have been a little unusual—but that didn't give him the right to treat her as if she were some kind of criminal.

"*My* attitude?" he said incredulously.

"Listen, would you mind if we shorted this inquisition?" she asked, checking her watch. "I've got to be back at work in fifteen minutes."

"Not until you tell why you've been my constant shadow for the past hour. Not to mention this morning."

"You're exaggerating." Bailey half turned to leave when his hand flew out to grip her shoulder.

"You're not going anywhere until you've answered a few questions."

"If you must know," she said at the end of a protracted sigh, "I'm a novelist…"

"Published?"

"Not yet," she admitted reluctantly, "but I will be."

His mouth lifted at the corners and Bailey couldn't decide if the movement had a sardonic twist or he didn't believe a word she was saying. Neither alternative did anything to soothe her ego.

"It's true!" she said heatedly. "I am a novelist, only I've been having trouble capturing the true nature of a classic hero and, well, as I said earlier, it gets a bit involved."

"Start at the beginning."

"All right." Bailey was prepared now to do exactly that. He wanted details? She'd give him details. "It all began several months back when I was riding BART and I met Jo Ann—she's the woman I was with this morning. Over the course of the next few weeks I learned that she's a writer, too, and she's been kind enough to tutor me. I'd already mailed off my first manuscript when I met Jo Ann, but I quickly learned I'd made some basic mistakes. All beginning writers do. So I rewrote the story and—"

"Do you mind if we get to the part about this morning?" he asked, clearly impatient.

"All right, fine, I'll skip ahead, but it probably won't make much sense." She didn't understand why he was wearing that beleaguered look, since he was the one who'd insisted she start at the beginning. "Jo Ann and I were on the subway this morning and I was telling her I doubted I'd recognize a hero. You see,

Michael's the hero in my book and I'm having terrible problems with him. The first time around he was too harsh, then I turned him into a wimp. I just can't seem to get him to walk the middle of the road. He's got to be tough, but tender. Strong and authoritative, but not so stubborn or arrogant the reader wants to throttle him. I need to find a way to make Michael larger than life, but at the same time the kind of man any woman would fall in love with and—"

"Excuse me for interrupting you again," Parker said, folding his arms across his chest and irritably tapping his foot, "but could we finish this sometime before the end of the year?"

"Oh, yes. Sorry." His sarcasm didn't escape her, but she decided to be generous and overlook it. "I was telling Jo Ann I wouldn't recognize a hero if one hit me over the head, and no sooner had I said that than your umbrella whacked me." The instant the words were out, Bailey realized she should have passed over that part.

"I like the other version better," he said with undisguised contempt. He shook his head and stalked past her onto the busy sidewalk.

"What other version?" Bailey demanded, marching after him. She was only relaying the facts, the way *he'd* insisted!

"The one where you're an old family friend. This nonsense about being a novelist is—"

"The absolute truth," she finished with all the dignity she could muster. "You're the hero—well, not exactly the hero, don't get me wrong, but a lot like my hero, Michael. In fact, you could be his twin."

Parker stopped abruptly and just as abruptly turned around to face her. The contempt in his eyes was gone, replaced by some other emotion Bailey couldn't identify.

"Have you seen a doctor?" he asked gently.

"A doctor?"

"Have you discussed this problem with a professional?"

It took Bailey a moment to understand what he was saying. Once she did, she was so furious she couldn't formulate words fast enough to keep pace with her speeding mind.

"You think…mental patient…on the loose?"

He nodded solemnly.

"That's the most ridiculous thing I've ever heard in my life!" Bailey had never been more insulted. Parker Davidson thought she was a crazy person! She waved her arms haphazardly as she struggled to compose her thoughts. "I'm willing to admit that following you is a bit eccentric, but…but I did it in the name of research!"

"Then kindly research someone else."

"Gladly." She stormed ahead several paces, then whirled suddenly around, her fists clenched. "You'll have to excuse me, I'm new to the writing game. There's a lot I don't know yet, but obviously I have more to learn than I realized. I was right the first time—you're no hero."

Not giving him the opportunity to respond, she rushed back to her office, thoroughly disgusted with the man she'd assumed to be a living, breathing hero.

Max, Bailey's cat, was waiting anxiously for her when she arrived home that evening, almost an hour later than usual since she'd stayed to make up for her lengthy lunch. Not that Max would actually deign to let her think he was pleased to see her. Max had one thing on his mind and one thing only.

Dinner.

The sooner she fed him, the sooner he could go back to ignoring her.

"I'm crazy about you, too," Bailey teased, bending over to playfully scratch his ears. She talked to her cat the way she did her characters, although Michael had been suspiciously quiet of late—which was fine with Bailey, since a little time apart was sure to do them both good. She wasn't particularly happy with her hero after the Parker Davidson fiasco that afternoon. Once again Michael had led her astray. The best thing to do was lock him in the desk drawer for a while.

Max wove his fat fluffy body between Bailey's legs while she sorted through her mail. She paused, staring into space as she reviewed her confrontation with Parker Davidson. Every time she thought about the things he'd said, she felt a flush of embarrassment. It was all she could do not to cringe at the pitying look he'd given her as he asked if she was seeking professional help. Never in her life had Bailey felt so mortified.

"Meow." Max seemed determined to remind her that he was still waiting for his meal.

"All right, all right," she muttered, heading for the refrigerator. "I don't have time to argue with you tonight. I'm going out to hear Libby McDonald speak." She removed the can of cat food from the bottom shelf and dumped the contents on the dry kibble. Max had to have his meal moistened before he'd eat it.

With a single husky purr, Max sauntered over to his dish and left Bailey to change clothes for the writers' meeting.

Once she was in her most comfortable sweater and an old pair of faded jeans, she grabbed a quick bite to eat and was out the door.

Jo Ann had already arrived at Parklane College, the site of their meeting, and was rearranging the classroom desks to form a large circle. Bailey automatically helped, grateful her friend didn't question her about Parker Davidson. Within minutes, the room started to fill with members of the romance writers' group.

Bailey didn't know if she should tell Jo Ann about the meeting with Parker. No, she decided, the whole sorry episode was best forgotten. Buried under the heading of Mistakes Not to Be Repeated.

If Jo Ann did happen to ask, Bailey mused, it would be best to say nothing. She didn't make a habit of lying, but her encounter with that man had been too humiliating to describe, even to her friend.

The meeting went well, and although Bailey took copious notes, her thoughts persisted in drifting away from Libby's speech, straying to Parker. The man had his nerve suggesting she was a lunatic. Who did he think he was, anyway? Sigmund Freud? But then, to be fair, Parker had no way of knowing that Bailey didn't normally go around following strange men and claiming they were heroes straight out of her novel.

Again and again throughout the talk, Bailey had to stubbornly refocus her attention on Libby's speech. When Libby finished, the twenty or so writers who were gathered applauded enthusiastically. The sound startled Bailey, who'd been embroiled in yet another mental debate about the afternoon's encounter.

There was a series of questions, and then Libby had to leave in order to catch a plane. Bailey was disappointed that she couldn't stay for coffee. It had become tradition for a handful of the group's members to go across the street to the all-night diner after their monthly get-together.

As it turned out, everyone else had to rush home, too, except Jo Ann. Bailey was on the verge of making an excuse herself, but one glance told her Jo Ann was unlikely to believe it.

They walked across the street to the brightly lit and

almost empty restaurant. As they sat down in their usual booth, the waitress approached them with menus. Jo Ann ordered just coffee, but Bailey, who'd eaten an orange for lunch and had a meager dinner of five pretzels, a banana and two hard green jelly beans left over from Christmas, was hungry, so she asked for a turkey sandwich.

"All right, tell me what happened," Jo Ann said the moment the waitress left their booth.

"About what?" Bailey tried to appear innocent as she toyed with the edges of the paper napkin. She carefully avoided meeting Jo Ann's eyes.

"I phoned your office at lunchtime," her friend said in a stern voice. "Do I need to go into the details?" She studied Bailey, who raised her eyes to give Jo Ann a brief look of wide-eyed incomprehension. "Beth told me you'd left before noon for a doctor's appointment and weren't back yet." She paused for effect. "We both know you didn't have a doctor's appointment, don't we?"

"Uh…" Bailey felt like a cornered rat.

"You don't need to tell me where you were," Jo Ann went on, raising her eyebrows. "I can guess. You couldn't leave it alone, could you? My guess is that you followed Parker Davidson to his lunch engagement."

Bailey nodded miserably. So much for keeping one of her most humiliating moments a secret. She hadn't even told Max! Her cat generally heard everything, but today's encounter was best forgotten.

If only she could stop thinking about it. For most

of the afternoon she'd succeeded in pushing all thoughts of that man, that unreasonable insulting architect, out of her mind. Not so this evening.

"And?" Jo Ann prompted.

Bailey could see it was pointless to continue this charade with her friend. "And he confronted me, wanting to know why the hell I was following him."

Jo Ann closed her eyes, then slowly shook her head. After a moment, she reached for her coffee. "I can just imagine what you told him."

"At first I had no idea what to say."

"That part I can believe, but knowing you, I'd guess you insisted on telling him the truth and nothing but the truth."

"You're right again." Not that it had done Bailey any good.

"And?" Jo Ann prompted again.

Bailey's sandwich arrived and for a minute or so she was distracted by that. Unfortunately she wasn't able to put off Jo Ann's questions for long.

"Don't you dare take another bite of that sandwich until you tell me what he said!"

"He didn't believe me." Which was putting it mildly.

"He didn't believe you?"

"All right, if you have to know, he thought I was an escaped mental patient."

Anger flashed in Jo Ann's eyes, and Bailey was so grateful she could have hugged her.

"Good grief, why'd you do anything so stupid as

to tell him you're a writer?" Jo Ann demanded vehemently.

So much for having her friend champion her integrity, Bailey mused darkly.

"I can't understand why you'd do that," Jo Ann continued, raking her hand furiously through her hair. "You were making up stories all over the place when it came to discovering his name. You left me speechless with the way you walked into his office and spouted that nonsense about being an old family friend. Why in heaven's name didn't you make up something plausible when he confronted you?"

"I couldn't think." That, regrettably, was the truth.

Not that it would've made much difference even if she'd been able to invent a spur-of-the-moment excuse. She was convinced of that. The man would have known she was lying, and Bailey couldn't see the point of digging herself in any deeper than she already was. Of course she hadn't had time to reason that out until later. He'd hauled her into the alley and she'd simply followed her instincts, right or wrong.

"It wasn't like you didn't warn me," Bailey said, half her turkey sandwich poised in front of her mouth. "You tried to tell me from the moment we followed him off the subway how dumb the whole idea was. I should've listened to you then."

But she'd been so desperate to get a real hero down on paper. She'd been willing to do just about anything to straighten out this problem of Michael's. What she hadn't predicted was how foolish she'd end up feeling as a result. Well, no more—she'd learned her lesson. If any more handsome men hit her on the head, she'd hit them back!

"What are you going to do now?" Jo Ann asked.

"Absolutely nothing," Bailey answered without a second's hesitation.

"You mean you're going to let him go on thinking you're an escaped mental patient?"

"If that's what he wants to believe." Bailey tried to create the impression that it didn't matter to her one way or the other. She must have done a fairly good job because Jo Ann remained speechless, raising her coffee mug to her mouth three times without taking a single sip.

"What happens if you run into him on the subway again?" she finally asked.

"I don't think that'll be a problem," Bailey said blithely, trying hard to sound unconcerned. "What are the chances we'll be on the same car again at exactly the same time?"

"You're right," Jo Ann concurred. "Besides, after what happened today, he'll probably go back to driving, freeway renovation or not."

It would certainly be a blessing if he did, Bailey thought.

He didn't.

Jo Ann and Bailey were standing at the end of the crowded subway car, clutching the metal handrail when Jo Ann tugged hard at the sleeve of Bailey's bulky-knit cardigan.

"Don't turn around," Jo Ann murmured.

They were packed as tight as peas in a pod, and Bailey had no intention of moving in any direction.

"He's staring at you."

"Who?" Bailey whispered back.

She wasn't a complete fool. When she'd stepped onto the train earlier, she'd done a quick check and was thankful to note that Parker Davidson wasn't anywhere to be seen. She hadn't run into him in several days and there was no reason to think she would. He might have continued to take BART, but if that was the case their paths had yet to cross, which was fine with her. Their second encounter would likely prove as embarrassing as the first.

"He's here," Jo Ann hissed. "The architect you followed last week."

Bailey was convinced everyone in the subway car had turned to stare at her. "I'm sure you're mistaken," she muttered, furious with her friend for her lack of discretion.

"I'm not. Look." She motioned with her head.

Bailey did her best to be nonchalant about it. When she did slowly twist around, her heart sank all the way to her knees. Jo Ann was right. Parker stood no more than ten feet from her. Fortunately, they were separated by a number of people—which didn't disguise the fact that he was staring at Bailey as if he expected men in white coats to start descending on her.

She glared back at him.

"Do you see him?" Jo Ann asked.

"Of course. Thank you so much for pointing him out to me."

"He's staring at you. What else was I supposed to do?"

"Ignore him," Bailey suggested sarcastically. "I certainly intend to." Still, no matter how hard she tried to concentrate on the advertising posted above the seats, she found Parker Davidson dominating her thoughts.

A nervous shaky feeling slithered down her spine. Bailey could *feel* his look as profoundly as a caress. This was exactly the sort of look she struggled to describe in *Forever Yours.*

Casually, as if by accident, she slowly turned her head and peeked in his direction once more, wondering if she'd imagined the whole thing. For an instant the entire train seemed to go still. Her blue eyes met his brown ones, and an electric jolt rocked Bailey, like nothing she'd ever felt before. A breathless panic filled her and she longed to drag her eyes away, pretend she didn't recognize him, anything to escape this fluttery sensation in the pit of her stomach.

This was exactly how Janice had felt the first time she met Michael. Bailey had spent days writing that scene, studying each word, each phrase, until she'd achieved the right effect. That was the moment Janice had fallen in love with Michael. Oh, she'd fought it, done everything but stand on her head in an effort to control her feelings, but Janice had truly fallen for him.

Bailey, however, was much too wise to be taken in by a mere look. She'd already been in love. Twice. Both times were disasters and she wasn't willing to try it again soon. Her heart was still bleeding from the last go-round.

Of course she was leaping to conclusions. She was the one with the fluttery stomach. Not Parker. He obviously hadn't been affected by their exchange. In fact, he seemed to be amused, as if running into Bailey again was an unexpected opportunity for entertainment.

She braced herself, and with a resolve that would've impressed Janice, she dropped her gaze. She inhaled sharply, then twisted her mouth into a sneer. Unfortunately, Jo Ann was staring at her in complete—and knowing—fascination.

"What's with you—and him?"

"Nothing," Bailey denied quickly.

"That's not what I saw."

"You're mistaken," Bailey replied in a voice that said the subject was closed.

"Whatever you did worked," Jo Ann whispered a couple of minutes later.

"I don't know what you're talking about."

"Fine, but in case you're interested, he's coming this way."

"I beg your pardon?" Bailey's forehead broke out in a cold sweat at the mere prospect of being confronted by Parker Davidson again. Once in a lifetime was more than enough, but twice in the same week was well beyond her capabilities.

Sure enough, Parker Davidson boldly stepped forward and squeezed himself next to Bailey.

"Hello again," he said casually.

"Hello," she returned stiffly, refusing to look at him.

"You must be Jo Ann," he said, turning his attention to Bailey's friend.

Jo Anne's eyes narrowed. "You told him my name?" she asked Bailey in a loud distinct voice.

"I... Apparently so."

"Thank you very much," she muttered in a sarcastic voice. Then she turned toward Parker and her expression altered dramatically as she broke into a wide smile. "Yes, I'm Jo Ann."

"Have you been friends with Janice long?"

"Janice? Oh, you mean..." Bailey quickly nudged her friend in the ribs with her elbow. "Janice," Jo Ann repeated in a strained voice. "You mean *this* Janice?"

Parker frowned. "So that was a lie, as well?"

"As well," Bailey admitted coolly, deciding she had no alternative. "That was my problem in the first place. I told you the truth. Now, for the last time, I'm a writer and so is Jo Ann." She gestured toward her friend. "Tell him."

"We're both writers," Jo Ann confirmed with a sad lack of conviction. It wasn't something Jo Ann willingly broadcast, though Bailey had never really understood why. She supposed it was a kind of superstition, a fear of offending the fates by appearing too presumptuous—and thereby ruining her chances of selling a book.

Parker sighed, frowning more darkly. "That's what I thought."

The subway stopped at the next station, and he moved toward the door.

"Goodbye," Jo Ann said, raising her hand. "It was a pleasure to meet you."

"Me, too." He glanced from her to Bailey; she could have sworn his eyes hardened briefly before he stepped off the car.

"You told him your name was Janice?" Jo Ann cried the minute he was out of sight. "Why'd you do that?"

"I…I don't know. I panicked."

Jo Ann wiped her hand down her face. "Now he *really* thinks you're nuts."

"It might have helped if you hadn't acted like you'd never heard the word 'writer' before." Before Jo Ann could heap any more blame on her shoulders, Bailey had some guilt of her own to spread around.

"That isn't information I tell everyone, you know. I'd appreciate if you didn't pass it out to just anyone."

"Oh, dear," Bailey mumbled, feeling wretched. Not only was Jo Ann annoyed with her, Parker thought she was a fool. And there was little she could do to redeem herself in his eyes. The fact that it troubled her so much was something for the men with chaise longues in their offices to analyze. But trouble her it did.

If only Parker hadn't looked at her with those dark eyes of his—as if he was willing to reconsider his first assessment of her.

If only she hadn't looked back and felt that puzzling sensation come over her—the way a heroine does when she's met the man of her dreams.

The weekend passed, and although Bailey spent most of her time working on the rewrite of *Forever Yours,* she couldn't stop picturing the disgruntled look on Parker's face as he walked off the subway car. It hurt her pride that he assumed she was a liar. Granted, introducing herself as Janice Hampton had been a lie, but after that, she'd told only the truth. She was sure he didn't believe a single word she'd said. Still, he intrigued her so much she spent a couple of precious hours on Saturday afternoon on the Internet, learning everything she could about him, which unfortunately wasn't much.

When Monday's lunch hour arrived, she headed directly for Parker's building. Showing up at his door should merit her an award for courage—or one for sheer stupidity.

"May I help you?" the receptionist asked when Bailey walked into the architectural firm's outer office. It was the same woman who'd helped her the week before. The nameplate on her desk read Roseanne Snyder. Bailey hadn't noticed it during her first visit.

"Would it be possible to see Mr. Davidson for just a few minutes?" she asked in her most businesslike voice, hoping the woman didn't recognize her.

Roseanne glanced down at the appointment calendar. "You're the gal who was in to see Mr. Davidson the first part of last week, aren't you?"

So much for keeping her identity a secret. "Yes." It was embarrassing to admit that. Bailey prayed Parker hadn't divulged the details of their encounter to the firm's receptionist.

"When I mentioned your name to Mr. Davidson, he didn't seem to remember your family."

"Uh… I wasn't sure he would," Bailey answered vaguely.

"If you'll give me your name again, I'll tell him you're here."

"Bailey. Bailey York," she said with a silent sigh of relief. Parker didn't know her real name; surely he wouldn't refuse to see her.

"Bailey York," the friendly woman repeated. "But aren't you—?" She paused, staring at her for a moment before she pressed the intercom button. After a quick exchange, she nodded, smiling tentatively. "Mr. Davidson said to go right in. His office is the last one on the left," she said, pointing the way.

The door was open and Parker sat at his desk, apparently engrossed in studying a set of blueprints. His office was impressive, with a wide sweeping view of the Golden Gate Bridge and Alcatraz Island. As she stood in the doorway, Parker glanced up. His smile faded when he recognized her.

"What are you doing here?"

"Proving I'm not a liar." With that, she strode into his office and slapped a package on his desk.

"What's that?" he asked.

"Proof."

# *Four*

Parker stared at the manuscript box as though he feared it was a time bomb set to explode at any moment.

"Go ahead and open it," Bailey said. When he didn't, she lifted the lid for him. Awkwardly she flipped through the first fifteen pages until she'd gathered up the first chapter, which she shoved into his hands. "Read it."

"Now?"

"Start with the header," she instructed, and then pointed to the printed line on the top right-hand side of each page.

"York...Forever Yours...Page one," he read aloud, slowly and hesitantly.

Bailey nodded. "Now move down to the text." She used her index finger to indicate where she wanted him to read.

"Chapter one. Janice Hampton had dreaded the business meeting for weeks. She was—"

"That's enough," Bailey muttered, ripping the pages out of his hands. "If you want to look through the rest of the manuscript, you're welcome to."

"Why would I want to do that?"

"So you no longer have the slightest doubt that I wrote it," she answered in a severe tone. "So you'll believe that I *am* a writer—and not a liar or a maniac. The purpose of this visit, though, why I find it necessary to prove I'm telling you the truth, isn't clear to me yet. It just seemed…important."

As she spoke, she scooped up the loose pages and stuffed them back into the manuscript box, closing it with enough force to crush the lid.

"I believed you before," Parker said casually, leaning back in his chair as if he'd never questioned her integrity. Or her sanity. "No one could've made up that story about being a romance writer and kept a straight face."

"But you—"

"What I didn't appreciate was the fact that you called yourself by a false name."

"You caught me off guard! I gave you the name of my heroine because…well, because I saw you as the hero."

"I see." He raised one eyebrow—definitely a herolike mannerism, Bailey had to admit.

"I guess you didn't appreciate being followed around town, either," she said in a small voice.

"True enough," he agreed. "Take my advice, would you? The next time you want to research details about a man's life, hire a detective. You and your friend couldn't have been more obvious if you'd tried."

Bailey's ego had already taken one beating from this man, and she wasn't game for round two. "Don't worry, I've given up the chase. I've discovered there aren't any real heroes left in this world. I thought you might be one, but—" she shrugged elaborately "—alas, I was wrong."

"Ouch." Parker placed his hand over his heart as though her words had wounded him gravely. "I was just beginning to feel flattered. Then you had to go and ruin it."

"I know what I'm talking about when it comes to this hero business. They're extinct, except between the pages of women's fiction."

"Correct me if I'm wrong, but do I detect a note of bitterness?"

"I'm not bitter," Bailey denied vehemently. But she didn't mention the one slightly yellowed wedding dress hanging in her closet. She'd used her savings to pay for the elegant gown and been too mortified to return it unused. She tried to convince herself it was an investment, something that would gain value over the years, like gold. Or stocks. That was what she told herself, but deep down she knew better.

"I'm sorry to have intruded upon your busy day,"

she said, reaching for her manuscript. "I won't trouble you again."

"Do you object to my asking you a few questions before you go?" Parker asked, standing. He walked around to the front of his desk and leaned against it, crossing his ankles. "Writers have always fascinated me."

Bailey made a show of glancing at her watch. She had forty-five minutes left of her lunch hour; she supposed she could spare a few moments. "All right."

"How long did it take you to write *Forever and a Day?*"

"*Forever Yours,*" Bailey corrected. She suspected he was making fun of her. "Nearly six months, but I worked on it every night after work and on weekends. I felt like I'd completed a marathon when I finished." Bailey knew Janice and Michael were grateful, too. "Only I made a beginner's mistake."

"What's that?"

"I sent it off to a publisher."

"That's a mistake?"

Bailey nodded. "I should've had someone read it first, but I was too new to know that. It wasn't until later that I met Jo Ann and joined a writers' group."

Parker folded his arms across his broad chest. "I'm not sure I understand. Isn't having your work read by an editor the whole point? Why have someone else read it first?"

"Every manuscript needs a final polishing. It's important to put your best foot forward."

"I take it *Forever Yours* was rejected."

Bailey shook her head. "Not yet, but I'm fairly certain it will be. It's been about four months now, but meanwhile I've been working on revisions. And like Jo Ann says—no news is no news."

Parker arched his brows. "That's true."

"Well," she said, glancing at her watch again, but not because she was eager to leave. She felt foolish standing in the middle of Parker's plush office talking about her novel. Her guard was slipping and the desire to secure it firmly in place was growing stronger.

"I assume Jo Ann read the manuscript after you mailed it off?"

"Yes." Bailey punctuated her comment with a shrug. "She took it home and returned it the next morning with margin notes and a list of comments three pages long. When I read them over, I could see how right she was and, well, mainly the problem was with the hero."

"Michael?"

Bailey was surprised he remembered that. "Yes, with Michael. He's a terrific guy, but he needs a little help figuring out what women—in this case Janice Hampton—want."

"That's where I came in?"

"Right."

"How?"

Bailey made an effort to explain. "A hero, at least in romantic fiction, is determined, forceful and cool.

When I saw you the first time, you gave the impression of being all three."

"Was that before or after I hit you in the head?"

"After."

Parker grinned. "Did you ever consider that my umbrella might have caused a temporary lack of, shall we say, good judgment? My guess is that you don't normally follow men around town, taking notes about their behavior, do you?"

"No, you were my first," she informed him coldly. This conversation was becoming downright irritating.

"I'm pleased to hear that," he said with a cocky grin.

"Perhaps you're right. Perhaps I *was* hit harder than I realized." Just when she was beginning to feel reasonably comfortable around Parker, he'd do or say something to remind her that he was indeed a mere mortal. Any effort to base Michael's personality on his would only be a waste of time.

Bailey clutched her manuscript to her chest. "I really have to go now. I apologize for the intrusion."

"It's fine. I found our discussion…interesting."

No doubt he had. But it didn't help Bailey's dignity to know she was a source of amusement to one of the city's most distinguished architects.

"What else did he say?" Jo Ann asked early the following morning as they sat side by side on the crowded subway car.

Even before Bailey could answer, Jo Ann asked another question. "Did you get a chance to tell him that little joke about your story having a beginning, a *muddle* and an end?"

Jo Ann's reaction had surprised her. When Bailey admitted confronting Parker with her completed manuscript, Jo Ann had been enthusiastic, even excited. Bailey had supposed that her friend wouldn't understand her need to see Parker and correct his opinion of her. Instead, Jo Ann had been approving— and full of questions.

"I didn't have time to tell Parker any jokes," Bailey answered. "Good grief, I was only in his office, I don't know, maybe ten minutes."

"Ten minutes! A lot can happen in ten minutes."

Bailey crossed her long legs and prayed silently for patience. "Believe me, nothing happened. I accomplished what I set out to prove. That's it."

"If you were in there a full ten minutes, surely the two of you talked."

"He had a few questions about the business of writing."

"I see." Jo Ann nodded slowly. "So what did you tell him?"

Bailey didn't want to think about her visit with Parker. Not again. She'd returned from work that afternoon and, as was her habit, went directly to her computer. Usually she couldn't wait to get home to write. But that afternoon, she'd sat there, her hands poised on the keys, and instead of composing witty sparkling dialogue for Michael and Janice, she'd reviewed every word of her conversation with Parker.

He'd been friendly, cordial. And he'd actually sounded interested—when he wasn't busy being amused. Bailey hadn't expected that. What she'd expected was outright rejection. She'd come prepared to talk to a stone wall.

Michael, the first time around, had been like that. Gruff and unyielding. Poor Janice had been in the dark about his feelings from page one. It was as though her hero feared that revealing emotion was a sign of weakness.

In the second version Michael was so…amiable, so pleasant, that any conflict in the story had been watered down almost to nonexistence.

"As you might have guessed," Jo Ann said, breaking into her thoughts, "I like Parker Davidson. You were right when you claimed he's hero material. You'll have to forgive me for doubting you. It's just that I've never followed a man around before."

"You like Parker?" Bailey's musing about Michael and his shifting personality came to a sudden halt. 'You're married," Bailey felt obliged to remind her.

"I'm not interested in him for *me,* silly," Jo Ann said, playfully nudging Bailey with her elbow. "He's all yours."

"Mine!" Bailey couldn't believe what she was hearing. "You're nuts."

"No, I'm not. He's tall, dark and handsome, and we both know how perfect that makes him for a classic romance. And the way you zeroed in on Parker the instant you saw him proves he's got the compelling presence a hero needs."

"The only *presence* I noticed was his umbrella's! He nearly decapitated me with the thing."

"You know what I think?" Jo Ann murmured, nibbling on her bottom lip. "I think that something inside you, some innate sonar device, was in action. You're hungering to find Michael. Deep within your subconscious you're seeking love and romance."

"Wrong!" Bailey declared adamantly. "You couldn't be more off course. Writing and selling a romance are my top priorities right now. I'm not interested in love, not for myself."

"What about Janice?"

The question was unfair and Bailey knew it. So much of her own personality was invested in her heroine.

The train finally reached their station, and Bailey and Jo Ann stood up and made their way toward the exit.

"Well?" Jo Ann pressed, clearly unwilling to drop the subject.

"I'm not answering that and you know why," Bailey said, stepping onto the platform. "Now kindly get off this subject. I doubt I'll ever see Parker Davidson again, and if I do I'll ignore him just the way he'll ignore me."

"You're sure of that?"

"Absolutely positive."

"Then why do you suppose he's waiting for you? That *is* Parker Davidson, isn't it?"

Bailey closed her eyes and struggled to gather her wits. Part of her was hoping against hope that Parker would saunter past without giving either of them a second's notice. But another part of her, a deep womanly part, hoped he was doing exactly what Jo Ann suggested.

"Good morning, ladies," Parker said to them as he approached.

"Hello," Bailey returned, suspecting she sounded in need of a voice-box transplant.

"Good morning!" Jo Ann said with enough enthusiasm to make up for Bailey's sorry lack.

Parker bestowed a dazzling smile on them. Bailey felt the impact of it as profoundly as if he'd bent down and brushed his mouth over hers. She quickly shook her head to dispel the image.

"I considered our conversation," he said, directing his remark to Bailey. "Since you're having so many problems with your hero, I decided I might be able to help you, after all."

"Is that right?" Bailey knew she was coming across as defensive, but she couldn't seem to help it.

Parker nodded. "I assume you decided to follow me that day to learn pertinent details about my habits, personality and so on. How about if the two of us sit down over lunch and you just ask me what you want to know?"

Bailey recognized a gift horse when she saw one. Excitement welled up inside her; nevertheless she hesitated. This man was beginning to consume her thoughts already, and she'd be asking for trouble if she allowed it to continue.

"Would you have time this afternoon?"

"She's got time," Jo Ann said without missing a beat. "Bailey works as a paralegal and she can see you during her lunch hour. This afternoon would be perfect."

Bailey glared at her friend, resisting the urge to suggest *she* have lunch with Parker since she was so keen on the idea.

"Bailey?" Parker asked, turning his attention to her.

"I…suppose." She didn't sound very gracious, and the look Jo Ann flashed her told her as much. "This is, um, very generous of you, Mr. Davidson."

"Mr. Davidson?" Parker said. "I thought we were long past being formal with each other." He dazzled her with another smile. It had the same effect on Bailey as before, weakening her knees—and her resolve.

"Shall we say noon, then?" Parker asked. "I'll meet you on Fisherman's Wharf at the Sandpiper."

The Sandpiper was known for its wonderful seafood, along with its exorbitant prices. Parker might be able to afford to eat there, but it was far beyond Bailey's meager budget.

"The Sandpiper?" she repeated. "I…I was thinking we could pick up something quick and eat on the wharf. There are several park benches along Pier 39…"

Parker frowned. "I'd prefer the Sandpiper. I'm doing some work for them, and it's good business practice to return the favor."

"Don't worry, she'll meet you there," Jo Ann assured Parker.

Bailey couldn't allow her friend to continue speaking for her. "Jo Ann, if you don't mind, I'll answer for myself."

"Oh, sure. Sorry."

Parker returned his attention to Bailey, who inhaled sharply and nodded. "I can meet you there." Of course it would mean packing lunches for the next two weeks and cutting back on Max's expensive tastes in gourmet cat food, but she supposed that was a small sacrifice.

Parker was waiting for Bailey when she arrived at the Sandpiper at a few minutes after noon. He stood when the maitre d' ushered her to his table. The room's lighting, its thick dark red carpet and rich wood created a sense of intimacy and warmth that appealed to Bailey despite her nervousness.

She'd been inside the Sandpiper only once before, with her parents when they were visiting from Oregon. Her father had wanted to treat her to the best restaurant in town, and Bailey had chosen the Sand-piper, renowned for its elegance and its fresh seafood.

"We meet again," Parker said, raising one eye-brow—that hero quirk again—as he held out her chair.

"Yes. It's very nice of you to do this."

"No problem." The waiter appeared with menus. Bailey didn't need to look; she already knew what she wanted. The seafood Caesar salad, piled high with shrimp, crab and scallops. She'd had it on her last visit and thoroughly enjoyed every bite. Parker ordered sautéed scallops and a salad. He suggested a bottle of wine, but Bailey declined. She needed to remain completely alert for this interview, so she requested coffee instead. Parker asked for the same.

After they'd placed their order, Bailey took a pen and pad from her purse, along with her reading glasses. She had a list of questions prepared. "Do you mind if we get started?"

"Sure," Parker said, leaning forward. He propped his elbows on the table and stared at her intently. "How old are you, Bailey? Twenty-one, twenty-two?"

"Twenty-seven."

He nodded, but was obviously surprised. "According to Jo Ann you work as a paralegal."

"Yes." She paused. "You'll have to excuse Jo Ann. She's a romantic."

"That's what she said about *you*—that you're a ro-mantic."

"Yes, well, I certainly hope it works to her advantage *and* to mine."

"Oh?" His eyebrows lifted.

"We're both striving to becoming published novelists. It takes a lot more than talent, you know."

Hot crisp sourdough rolls were delivered to the table and Bailey immediately reached for one.

"The writer has to have a feel for the genre," she continued. "For Jo Ann and me, that means writing from the heart. I've only been at this for a few months, but there are several women in our writers' group who've been submitting their work for five or six years without getting published. Most of them are pragmatic about it. There are plenty of small successes we learn to count along the way."

"Such as?"

Bailey swallowed before answering. "Finishing a manuscript. There's a real feeling of accomplishment in completing a story."

"I see."

"Some people come into the group thinking they're going to make a fast buck. They think anyone should be able to throw together a romance. Generally they attend a couple of meetings, then decide writing is too hard, too much effort."

"What about you?"

"I'm in this for the long haul. Eventually I will sell because I won't stop submitting stories until I do. My dad claims I'm like a pit bull when I want something.

I clamp on and refuse to let go. That's how I feel about writing. I'm going to succeed at this if it's the last thing I ever do."

"Have you always wanted to be a writer?" Parker helped himself to a roll.

"No. I wasn't even on my high-school newspaper, although now I wish I had been. I might not have so much trouble with sentence structure and punctuation if I'd paid more attention back then."

"Then what made you decide to write romances?"

"Because I read them. In fact, I've been reading romances from the time I was in college, but it's only been in the past year or so that I started creating my own. Meeting Jo Ann was a big boost for me. I might have gone on making the same mistakes for years if it wasn't for her. She encouraged me, introduced me to other writers and took me under her wing."

The waiter arrived with their meals and Bailey sheepishly realized that she'd been doing all the talking. She had yet to ask Parker a single question.

The seafood Caesar salad was as good as Bailey remembered. After one bite she decided to treat herself like this more often. An expensive lunch every month or so wouldn't sabotage her budget.

"You were telling me it only took you six months to write *Forever Yours*," Parker commented between forkfuls of his salad. "Doesn't it usually take much longer for a first book?"

"I'm sure it does, but I devoted every spare minute to the project."

"I see. What about your social life?"

It was all Bailey could do not to snicker. What social life? She'd lived in San Francisco for more than a year, and this lunch with Parker was as close as she'd gotten to a real date. Which was exactly how she wanted it, she reminded herself.

"Bailey?"

"Oh, I get out occasionally," but she didn't mention that it was always with women friends. Since her second broken engagement, Bailey had given up on the opposite sex. Twice she'd been painfully forced to accept that men were not to be trusted. After fifteen months, Tom's deception still hurt.

Getting over Tom might not have been so difficult if it hadn't been for Paul. She'd been in love with him, too, in her junior year at college. But like Tom, he'd found someone else he loved more than he did her. The pattern just kept repeating itself, so Bailey, in her own sensible way, had put an end to it. She no longer dated.

There were times she regretted her decision. This afternoon was an excellent example. She could easily find herself becoming romantically interested in Parker. She wouldn't, of course, but the temptation was there.

Parker with his coffee-dark eyes and his devastating smile. Fortunately Bailey was wise to the fickle hearts of men. Of one thing she was sure: Parker Davidson hadn't reached his mid-thirties, still single, without breaking a few hearts along the way.

There were other times she regretted her decision to give up on dating. No men equaled no marriage. And no children. It was the children part that troubled her most, especially when she was around babies. Her decision hit her hard then. Without a husband she wasn't likely to have a child of her own, since she wasn't interested in being a single mother. But so far, all she had to do was avoid places where she'd run into mothers and infants. Out of sight, out of mind....

"Bailey?"

"I'm sorry," she mumbled, suddenly aware that she'd allowed her thoughts to run unchecked for several minutes. "Did I miss something?"

"No. You had a...pained look and I was wondering if your salad was all right?"

"Yes. It's wonderful. As fantastic as I remember." She briefly relayed the story of her parents treating her to dinner at the Sandpiper. What she didn't explain was that their trip south had been made for the express purpose of checking up on Bailey. Her parents were worried about her. They insisted she worked too hard, didn't get out enough, didn't socialize.

Bailey had listened politely to their concerns and then hugged them both, thanked them for their love and sent them back to Oregon.

Spotting her pad and pen lying beside her plate, Bailey sighed. She hadn't questioned Parker once, which was the whole point of their meeting. Glancing at her watch, she groaned inwardly. She only had another fifteen minutes. It wasn't worth the effort of getting started. Not when she'd just have to stop.

"I need to get back to the office," she announced regretfully. She looked around for the waiter so she could ask for her check.

"It's been taken care of."

It took Bailey a moment to realize that Parker was talking about her meal. "I can't let you do that," she insisted, reaching for her purse.

"Please."

If he'd argued with her, shoveled out some chauvinistic challenge, Bailey would never have allowed him to pay. But that one word, that one softly spoken word, was her undoing.

"All right," she agreed, her own voice just as soft.

"You didn't get a chance to ask your questions."

"I know." She found that frustrating, but had no one to blame but herself. "I got caught up talking about romance fiction and writing and—"

"Shall we try again? Another time?"

"It looks like we'll have to." She needed to be careful that lunch with Parker didn't develop into a habit.

"I'm free tomorrow evening."

"Evening?" Somehow that seemed far more threatening than meeting for lunch. "Uh…I generally reserve the hours after work for writing."

"I see."

Her heart reacted to the hint of disappointment in his voice. "I might be able to make an exception." Bailey was horrified as soon as the words were out. She couldn't believe she'd said that. For the entire hour, she'd been lecturing herself about the dangers of getting close to Parker. "No," she said firmly. "It's crucial that I maintain my writing schedule."

"You're sure?"

"Positive."

Parker took a business card from his coat pocket. He scribbled on the back and handed it to her. "This is my home number in case you change your mind."

Bailey accepted the card and thrust it into her purse, together with her notepad and pen. "I really have to write… I mean, my writing schedule is important to me. I can't be running out to dinner just because someone asks me." She stood, scraping back her chair in her eagerness to escape.

"Consider it research."

Bailey responded by shaking her head. "Thank you for lunch."

"You're most welcome. But I hope you'll reconsider having dinner with me."

She backed away from the table, her purse held tightly in both hands. "Dinner?" she echoed, still undecided.

"For the purposes of research," he added.

"It wouldn't be a *date*." It was important to make that point clear. The only man she had time for was Michael. But Parker was supposed to help her with Michael, so maybe… "Not a date, just research," she repeated in a more determined voice. "Agreed?"

He grinned, his eyes lighting mischievously. "What do you think?"

# Five

Max was waiting at the door when Bailey got home from work that evening. His striped yellow tail pointed straight toward the ceiling as he twisted and turned between her legs. His not-so-subtle message was designed to remind her it was mealtime.

"Just a minute, Maxie," she muttered. She leafed through the mail as she walked into the kitchen, pausing when she found a yellow slip.

"Meow."

"Max, look," she said, waving the note at him. "Mrs. Morgan's holding a package for us." The apartment manager was always kind enough to accept deliveries, saving Bailey more than one trip to the post office.

Leaving a disgruntled Max behind, Bailey hurried down the stairs to Mrs. Morgan's first-floor apartment, where she was greeted with a warm smile. Mrs.

Morgan was an older woman, a matronly widow who seemed especially protective of her younger tenants.

"Here you go, dear," she said, handing Bailey a large manila envelope.

Bailey knew the instant she saw the package that this wasn't an unexpected surprise from her parents. It was her manuscript—rejected.

"Thank you," she said, struggling to disguise her disappointment. From the moment Bailey had read Jo Ann's critique she'd realized *Forever Yours* would probably be rejected. What she hadn't foreseen was this stomach-churning sensation, this feeling of total discouragement. Koppen Publishing had kept the manuscript for nearly four months. Jo Ann had insisted no news was no news, and so Bailey had begun to believe that the editor had held on to her book for so long because she'd seriously considered buying it.

Bailey had fully expected that she'd have to revise her manuscript; nonetheless, she'd *hoped* to be doing it with a contract in her pocket, riding high on success.

Once again Max was waiting by the door, more impatient this time. Without thinking, Bailey walked into the kitchen, opened the refrigerator and dumped food into his bowl. It wasn't until she straightened that she realized she'd given her greedy cat the dinner she was planning to cook for herself.

No fool, Max dug into the ground turkey, edging his way between her legs in his eagerness. Bailey shrugged. The way she was feeling, she didn't have much of an appetite, anyway.

It took her another five minutes to find the courage to open the package. She carefully pried apart the seam. Why she was being so careful, she couldn't even guess. She had no intention of reusing the envelope. Once the padding was separated, she removed the manuscript box. Inside was a short letter that she quickly read, swallowing down the emotion that clogged her throat. The fact that the letter was personal, and not simply a standard rejection letter, did little to relieve the crushing disappointment.

Reaching for the phone, Bailey punched out Jo Ann's number. Her friend had experienced this more than once and was sure to have some words of wisdom to help Bailey through this moment. Jo Ann would understand how badly her confidence had been shaken.

After four rings, Bailey was connected to her friend's answering machine. She listened to the message, but didn't want to leave Jo Ann such a disheartening message, so she mumbled, "It's Bailey," and hung up.

Pacing the apartment in an effort to sort out her emotions didn't seem to help. She eyed her computer, which was set up in a corner of her compact living room, but the desire to sit down and start writing was nil. Vanished. Destroyed.

Jo Ann had warned her. So had others in their

writers' group. Rejections hurt. She just hadn't expected it to hurt so much.

Searching in her purse for a mint, she felt her fingers close around a business card. *Parker's* business
card. She slowly drew it out. He'd written down his
phone number….

Should she call him? No, she decided, thrusting the
card into her pocket. Why even entertain the notion?
Talking to Parker now would be foolish. And risky.
She was a big girl. She could take rejection. Anyone
who became a writer had to learn how to handle rejection.

Rejections were rungs on the ladder of success.
Someone had said that at a meeting once, and Bailey
had written it down and kept it posted on the bottom edge of her computer screen. Now was the time
to act on that belief. Since this was only the first
rung, she had a long way to climb, but the darn ladder was much steeper than she'd anticipated.

With a fumbling resolve, she returned to the
kitchen and reread the letter from Paula Albright, the
editor, who wrote that she was returning the manuscript "with regret."

"Not as much regret as I feel," Bailey informed
Max, who was busy enjoying *her* dinner.

"She says I show promise." But Bailey noted that
she didn't say promise of what.

The major difficulty, according to the editor, was
Michael. This wasn't exactly a surprise to Bailey. Ms.

Albright had kindly mentioned several scenes that needed to be reworked with this problem in mind. She ended her letter by telling Bailey that if she revised the manuscript, the editorial department would be pleased to reevaluate it.

Funny, Bailey hadn't even noticed that the first time she'd read the letter. If she reworked Michael, there was still a chance.

With sudden enthusiasm, Bailey grabbed the phone. She'd changed her mind—calling Parker now seemed like a good idea. A great idea. He might well be her one and only chance to straighten out poor misguided Michael.

Parker answered on the second ring, sounding distracted and mildly irritated at being interrupted.

"Parker," Bailey said, desperately hoping she wasn't making a first-class fool of herself, "this is Bailey York."

"Hello." His tone was a little less disgruntled.

Her mouth had gone completely dry, but she rushed ahead with the reason for her call. "I want you to know I've…I've been thinking about your dinner invitation. Could you possibly meet me tonight instead of tomorrow?" She wanted to start rehabilitating Michael as soon as possible.

"This is Bailey York?" He sounded as though he didn't remember who she was.

"The writer from the subway," she said pointedly, feeling like more of an idiot with every passing second. She should never have phoned him, but the impulse had been so powerful. She longed to put this rejection behind her and write a stronger romance, but she was going to need his help. Perhaps she should call him later. "Listen, if now is inconvenient, I could call another time." She was about to hang up when Parker spoke.

"Now is fine. I'm sorry if I seem rattled, but I was working and I tend to get absorbed in a project."

"I do that myself," she said, reassured by his explanation. Drawing a deep breath, she explained the reason for her unexpected call. "*Forever Yours* was rejected today."

"I'm sorry to hear that." His regret seemed genuine, and the soft fluttering sensation returned to her stomach at the sympathy he extended.

"I was sorry, too, but it didn't come as a big shock. I guess I let my hopes build when the manuscript wasn't immediately returned, which is something Jo Ann warned me about." She shifted the receiver to her other ear, surprised by how much better she felt having someone to talk to.

"What happens when a publisher turns down a manuscript? Do they critique the book?"

"Heavens, no. Generally manuscripts are returned with a standard rejection letter. The fact that the editor took the time to personally write me about revising is sort of a compliment. Actually, it's an excellent sign. Especially since she's willing to look at *Forever*

*Yours* again." Bailey paused and inhaled shakily. "I was wondering if I could take you up on that offer for dinner. I realize this is rather sudden and I probably shouldn't have phoned, but tonight would be best for me since…since I inadvertently gave Max my ground turkey and there's really nothing else in the fridge, but if you can't I understand…." The words had tumbled out in a nervous rush; once she'd started, she couldn't seem to make herself stop.

"Do you want me to pick you up, or would you rather meet somewhere?"

"Ah…" Despite herself, Bailey was astounded. She hadn't really expected Parker to agree. "The restaurant where you had lunch a couple of weeks ago looked good. Only, please, I insist on paying for my own meal this time."

"In Chinatown?"

"Yes. Would you meet me there?"

"Sure. Does an hour give you enough time?"

"Oh, yes. An hour's plenty." Once again Bailey found herself nearly tongue-tied with surprise—and pleasure.

Their conversation was over so fast that she was left staring at the phone, half wondering if it had really happened at all. She took a couple of deep breaths, then dashed into her bedroom to change, renew her makeup and brush her hair.

Bailey loved Chinese food, especially the spicy Szechuan dishes, but she wasn't thinking about dinner as the taxi pulled up in front of the restaurant. She'd decided to indulge herself by taking a cab to Chinatown. It did mean she'd have to take the subway home, though.

Parker, who was standing outside the restaurant waiting for her, hurried forward to open the cab door. Bailey was terribly aware of his hand supporting her elbow as he helped her out.

"It's good of you to meet me like this on such short notice," she said, smiling up at Parker.

"No problem. Who's Max?"

"My cat."

Parker grinned and, clasping her elbow more firmly, led her into the restaurant. The first thing that caught Bailey's attention was a gigantic, intricately carved chandelier made of dark polished wood. She'd barely had a chance to examine it, however, when they were escorted down a long hallway to a narrow room filled with wooden booths, high-backed and private, each almost a little room of its own.

"Oh, my, this is nice," she breathed, sliding into their booth. She slipped the bag from her shoulder and withdrew the same pen and notepad she'd brought with her when they'd met for lunch.

The waiter appeared with a lovely ceramic teapot and a pair of tiny matching cups. The menus were tucked under his arm.

Bailey didn't have nearly as easy a time making her

choice as she had at the Sandpiper. Parker suggested they each order whatever they wished and then share. There were so many dishes offered, most of them sounding delectable and exciting, that it took Bailey a good ten minutes to make her selection—spicy shrimp noodles. Parker chose the less adventurous almond chicken stir-fry.

"All right," Bailey said, pouring them each some tea. "Now let's get down to business."

"Sure." Parker relaxed against the back of the booth, crossing his arms and stretching out his legs. "Ask away," he said, motioning with his hand when she hesitated.

"Maybe I'd better start by giving you a brief outline of the story."

"However you'd like to do this."

"I want you to understand Michael,' she explained. "He's a businessman, born on the wrong side of the tracks. He's a little bitter, but he's learned to forgive those who've hurt him through the years. Michael's in his mid-thirties, and he's never been married."

"Why not?"

"Well, for one thing he's been too busy building his career."

"As what?"

"He's in the exporting business."

"I see."

"You're frowning." Bailey hadn't asked a single one of her prepared questions yet, and already Parker was looking annoyed.

"It's just that a man doesn't generally reach the ripe old age of thirty-five without a relationship or two. If he's never had any, then there's a problem."

"You're thirty-something and you're not married," she felt obliged to point out. "What's your excuse?"

Parker shrugged. "My college schedule was very heavy, which didn't leave a lot of time for dating. Later I traveled extensively, which again didn't offer much opportunity. Oh, there were relationships along the way, but nothing ever worked out. I guess you could say I haven't found the right woman. But that doesn't mean I'm not interested in marrying and settling down some day."

"Exactly. That's how Michael feels, except he thinks getting married would only complicate his life. He's ready to fall in love with Janice, but he doesn't realize it."

"I see," Parker said with a nod, "go on. I shouldn't have interrupted you."

"Well, basically, Michael's life is going smoothly until he meets Janice Hampton. Her father has retired and she's taking over the operation of his manufacturing firm. A job she's well qualified for, I might add."

"What does she manufacture?"

"I was rather vague about that, but I let the reader assume it has something to do with computer parts. I tossed in a word here and there to give that suggestion."

Parker nodded. "Continue. I'll try not to butt in again."

"That's okay," she said briskly. "Anyway, Janice's father is a longtime admirer of Michael's, and the old coot would like to get his daughter and Michael together. Neither one of them's aware of it, of course. At least not right away."

Parker reached for the teapot and refilled their cups. "That sounds good."

Bailey smiled shyly. "Thanks. One of the first things that happens is Janice's father maneuvers Michael and Janice under the mistletoe at a Christmas party. Everyone's expecting them to kiss, but Michael is furious and he—"

"Just a minute." Parker held up one hand, stopping her. "Let me see if I've got this straight. This guy is standing under the mistletoe with a beautiful woman and he's furious. What's wrong with him?"

"What do you mean?"

"No man in his right mind is going to object to kissing a beautiful woman."

Bailey picked up her teacup and leaned against the hard back of the wooden booth, considering. Parker was right. And Janice hadn't been too happy about the situation herself. Was that any more believable? Imagine standing under the mistletoe with a man like Parker Davidson. Guiltily she shook off the thought and returned her attention to his words.

"Unless…" he was saying pensively.

"Yes?"

"Unless he recognizes that he was manipulated into kissing her and resents it. He may even think she's in cahoots with her father."

Brightening, Bailey nodded, making a note on her pad. "Yeah, that would work." Parker was as good at tossing ideas around as Jo Ann, which was a pleasant surprise.

"Still…" He hesitated, sighing. "A pretty woman is a pretty woman and he isn't going to object too strongly, regardless of the circumstances. What happens when he does kiss her?"

"Not too much. He does it grudgingly, but I've decided I'm going to change that part. You're right. He shouldn't make too much of a fuss. However, this happens early on in the book and neither of them's aware of her father's scheme. I don't want to tip the reader off so soon as to what's happening."

Bailey's mind was spinning as she reworked the scene. She could picture Michael and Janice standing under the mistletoe, both somewhat uneasy with the situation, but as Parker suggested, not objecting too strongly. Janice figures they'll kiss, and that'll be the end of it…until they actually do the kissing.

That was the part Bailey intended to build on. When Michael's and Janice's lips met it would be like…like throwing a match on dry tinder, so intense would be the reaction.

The idea began to gather momentum in her mind.

Then, not only would Janice and Michael be fighting her father's outrageous plot, they'd be battling their feelings for each other.

"This is great," Bailey whispered, "really great." She started to tell Parker her plan when they were interrupted by the waiter who brought their dinner, setting the steaming dishes before them.

By then, Bailey's appetite had fully recovered and she reached eagerly for the chopsticks. Parker picked up his own. They both reached for the shrimp noodles. Bailey withdrew her chopsticks.

"You first."

"No, you." He waved his hand, encouraging her.

She smiled and scooped up a portion of the noodles. The situation felt somehow intimate, comfortable, and yet they were still basically strangers.

They ate in silence for several minutes and Bailey watched Parker deftly manipulate the chopsticks. It was the first time she'd dated a man who was as skilled at handling them as she was herself.

*Dated a man.*

The words leapt out at her. Bright red warning signs seemed to be flashing in her mind. Her head shot up and she stared wide-eyed at the man across the table from her.

"Bailey? Are you all right?"

She nodded and hurriedly looked away.

"Did you bite into a hot pepper?"

"No," she assured him, quickly shaking her head.

"I'm fine. Really, I'm all right." Only she wasn't, and she suspected he knew it.

The remainder of their meal passed with few comments.

Naturally Parker had no way of knowing about her experiences with Paul and Tom. Nor would he be aware that there was an unused wedding dress hanging in her closet, taunting her every morning when she got ready for work. The wedding gown was an ever-present reminder of why she couldn't put any faith in the male of the species.

The danger came when she allowed her guard to slip. Before she knew it, she'd be trusting a man once again, and that was a definite mistake. Parker made her feel somehow secure; she felt instinctively that he was a man of integrity, of candor—and therein lay the real risk. Maybe he *was* a real live breathing hero, but Bailey had been fooled twice before. She wasn't going to put her heart on the line again.

They split the tab. Parker clearly wasn't pleased about that, but Bailey insisted. They were about to leave the restaurant when Parker said, "You started to say something about rewriting that scene under the mistletoe."

"Yes," she answered, regaining some of her former enthusiasm. "I'm going to have that kiss make a dynamite impact on them both. Your suggestions were very helpful. I can't tell you how much I appreciate your willingness to meet with me like this."

It was as though Parker hadn't heard her. His forehead creased as he held open the door for her and they stepped onto the busy sidewalk.

"You're frowning again," Bailey noted aloud.

"Have you ever experienced that kind of intense sensation when a man kissed you?"

Bailey didn't have to think about it. "Not really."

"That's what I thought."

"But I like the idea of that happening between Janice and Michael," she argued. "It adds a whole new dimension to the plot. I can use that. Besides, there's a certain element of fantasy in a traditional romance novel, a larger-than-life perspective."

"Oh, I'm not saying a strong reaction between them shouldn't happen. I'm just wondering how you plan to write such a powerfully emotional scene without any real experience of it yourself."

"That's the mark of a good writer," Bailey explained, ignoring his less-than-flattering remark. She'd been kissed before! Plenty of times. "Being able to create an atmosphere of romance just takes imagination. You don't expect me to go around kissing strange men, do you?"

"Why not? You had no qualms about *following* a strange man. Kissing me wouldn't be any different. It's all research."

"Kissing you?"

"It'll add credibility to your writing. A confidence you might not otherwise have."

"If I were writing a murder mystery would you suggest I go out and kill someone?" Bailey had to argue with him before she found herself *agreeing* to this craziness!

"Don't be ridiculous! Murder would be out of the question, but a kiss…a kiss is very much within your grasp. It would lend authenticity to your story. I suggest we go ahead with it, Bailey."

They were strolling side by side. Bailey was deep in thought when Parker casually turned into a narrow alley. She guessed it was the same one he'd hauled her into the day she'd followed him.

"Well," he said, resting his hands on her shoulders and staring down at her. "Are you game?"

Was she? Bailey didn't know anymore. He was right; the scene would have far more impact if she were to experience the same sensations as Janice. Kissing Parker would be like Janice kissing Michael. The sale of her book could hinge on how well she developed the attraction between hero and heroine in that all-important first chapter.

"Okay," she said, barely recognizing her own voice.

No sooner had she spoken than Parker gently cupped her chin and directed her mouth toward his. "This is going to be good," she heard him whisper just before his lips settled over hers.

Bailey's eyes drifted shut. This *was* good. In fact, it was wonderful. So wonderful, she felt weak and dizzy—and yearned to feel even weaker and dizzier.

Despite herself, she clung to Parker, literally hanging in his arms. Without his support, she feared she would have slumped to the street.

He tasted so warm and familiar, as if she'd spent a lifetime in his arms, as if she were *meant* to spend a lifetime there.

The fluttering sensation in her stomach changed to a warm heaviness. She felt strange and hot. Bailey was afraid that if this didn't end soon, she'd completely lose control.

"No more," she pleaded, breaking off the kiss. She buried her face in his shoulder and dragged in several deep breaths in an effort to stop her trembling.

It wasn't fair that Parker could make her feel this way. For Janice and Michael's sake, it was the best thing that could have happened, but for her own sake, it was the worst. She didn't *want* to feel any of this. The protective numbness around her heart was crumbling just when it was so important to keep it securely in place.

The hot touch of his lips against her temple caused her to jump away from him. "Well," she said, rubbing her palms briskly together once she found her voice. "That was certainly a step in the right direction."

"I beg your pardon?" Parker was staring at her as though he wasn't sure he'd heard her accurately.

"The kiss. It had pizzazz and a certain amount of charm, but I was looking for a little more...something. The kiss between Michael and Janice has got to have spark."

"Our kiss had spark." Parker's voice was deep, brooding.

"Charm," she corrected, then added brightly, "I will say one thing, though. You're good at this. Lots of practice, right?" Playfully she poked his ribs with her elbow. "Well, I've got to be going. Thanks again for meeting me on such short notice. I'll be seeing you around." Amazingly the smile on her lips didn't crack. Even more amazing was the fact that she managed to walk away from him on legs that felt like overcooked pasta.

She was about five blocks from the BART station, walking as fast as she could, mumbling to herself all the way. She behaved like an idiot every time she even came near Parker Davidson!

She continued mumbling, chastising herself, when he pulled up at the curb beside her in a white sports car. She didn't know much about cars, but she knew expensive when she saw it. The same way she knew his suit hadn't come from a department store.

"Get in," he said gruffly, slowing to a stop and leaning over to open the passenger door.

"Get in?" she repeated. "I was going to take BART."

"Not at this time of night you're not."

"Why shouldn't I?" she demanded.

"Don't press your luck, Bailey. Just get in."

She debated whether she should or not, but from the stubborn set of his jaw, she could see it would do no good to argue. She'd never seen a more obstinate-looking jaw in her life. As she recalled, it was one of the first things she'd noticed about Parker.

"What's your address?" he asked after she'd slipped inside.

Bailey gave it to him as she fiddled with the seat belt, then sat silently while he sped down the street, weaving his way in and out of traffic. He braked sharply at a red light and she glanced in his direction.

"Why are you so angry?" she demanded. "You look as if you're ready to bite my head off."

"I don't like it when a woman lies to me."

"When did I lie?" she asked indignantly.

"You lied a few minutes ago when you said our kiss was…lacking." He laughed humorlessly and shook his head. "We generated more electricity with that one kiss than the Hoover Dam does in a month. You want to kid yourself, then fine, but I'm not playing your game."

"I'm not playing any game," she informed him primly. "Nor do I appreciate having you come at me like King Kong because my assessment of a personal exchange between us doesn't meet yours."

"A personal exchange?" he scoffed. "It was a kiss, sweetheart."

"I only agreed to it for research purposes."

"If that's what you want to believe, fine, but we both know better."

"Whatever," she muttered. Parker could think

what he wanted. She'd let him drive her home because he seemed to be insisting on it. But as far as having anything further to do with him—out of the question. He was obviously placing far more significance on their kiss than she'd ever intended.

Okay, so she *had* felt something. But to hear him tell it, that kiss rivaled the great screen kisses of all time.

Parker drove up in front of her apartment building and turned off the engine. "All right," he said coolly. "Let's go over this one last time. Do you still claim our kiss was merely a 'personal exchange'? Just research?"

"Yes," she stated emphatically, unwilling to budge an inch.

"Then prove it."

Bailey sighed. "How exactly am I supposed to do that?"

"Kiss me again."

Bailey could feel the color drain out of her face. "I'm not about to sit outside my apartment kissing you with half the building looking on."

"Fine, then invite me in."

"Uh…it's late."

"Since when is nine o'clock late?" he taunted.

Bailey was running out of excuses. "There's nothing that says a woman is obligated to invite a man into her home, is there?" she asked in formal tones. Her spine was Sunday-school straight and her eyes were focused on the street ahead of her.

Parker's laugh took her by surprise. She twisted around to stare at him and found him smiling roguishly. "You little coward," he murmured, pulling her toward him for a quick peck on the cheek. "Go on. Run home before I change my mind."

## Six

"I like it," Jo Ann said. "The way you changed that first kissing scene under the mistletoe is a stroke of genius." She smiled happily. "This is exactly the kind of rewriting you'll need to turn that rejection into a sale. You've taken Michael and made him proud and passionate, but very real and spontaneous. He's caught off guard by his attraction to Janice and is reacting purely by instinct." Jo Ann tapped her fingers on the top page of the revised first chapter. "This is your most powerful writing yet."

Bailey was so pleased she could barely restrain herself from leaping up and dancing a jig down the center of the congested subway-car aisle. Through sheer determination, she managed to confine her response to a smile.

"It's interesting how coming at this scene from a slightly different angle puts everything in a new light, isn't it?"

"It sure is," Jo Ann concurred. "If the rest of the book reads as well as this chapter, I honestly think you might have a chance."

It was too much to hope for. Bailey had spent the entire weekend in front of her computer. She must have rewritten the mistletoe scene no less than ten times, strengthening emotions, exploring the heady response Michael and Janice had toward each other. She'd worked hard to capture the incredulity they'd experienced, the shock of their unexpected fascination. Naturally, neither one could allow the other to know what they were feeling yet—otherwise Bailey wouldn't have any plot.

Michael had been dark and brooding afterward. Janice had done emotional cartwheels in an effort to diminish the incident. But neither of them could forget it.

If the unable-to-forget part seemed particularly realistic, there was a reason. Bailey's reaction to Parker had been scandalously similar to Janice's feelings about Michael's kiss. The incredulity was there. The wonder. The shock. And it never should have happened.

Unfortunately Bailey had suspected that even before she'd agreed to the "research." Who did she think she was fooling? Certainly not herself. She'd wanted Parker to kiss her long before he'd offered her the excuse.

Halfway through their dinner, Bailey had experienced all the symptoms. She knew them well. The palpitating heart, the sweating palms, the sudden loss of appetite. She'd tried to ignore them, but as the meal had progressed she'd thought of little else.

Parker had gone suspiciously quiet, too. Then, later, he'd kissed her and everything became much, much worse. She'd felt warm and dizzy. A tingling sensation had slowly spread through her body. It seemed as though every cell in her body was aware of him. The sensations had been so overwhelming, she'd had to pretend nothing had happened. The truth was simply too risky.

"What made you decide to rework the scene that way?" Jo Ann asked, breaking into her thoughts.

Bailey stared at her friend and blinked rapidly.

"Bailey?" Jo Ann asked. "You look as if your mind's soaring through outer space."

"Uh…I was just thinking."

"A dangerous habit for a writer. We can't seem to get our characters out of our minds, can we? They insist on following us everywhere."

Characters, nothing! It was Parker Davidson she couldn't stop thinking about. As for the *following* part… Had her thoughts conjured him up? There he was, large as life, casually strolling toward them as though he'd sought her out. He hadn't, she told herself sternly. Nonetheless she searched for him every morning. She couldn't seem to help it. She'd never been so frighteningly aware of a man before, so eager—yet so reluctant to see him. Often she found herself scanning the faces around her, hoping to catch a glimpse of him.

Now here he was. Bailey quickly looked out the window into the tunnel's darkness, staring at the reflections in the glass.

"Good morning, ladies," Parker said jovially, standing directly in front of them, his feet braced slightly apart. The morning paper was tucked under his arm, and he looked very much as he had the first time she'd noticed him. Forceful. Appealing. Handsome.

"Morning," Bailey mumbled. She immediately turned back to the window.

"Hello again," Jo Ann replied warmly, smiling up at him.

For one wild second Bailey experienced a flash of resentment. Parker was *her* hero, not Jo Ann's! Her friend was greeting him like a long-lost brother or something. But what bothered Bailey even more was how delighted *she* felt. These were the very reactions she'd been combating all weekend.

"So," Parker said smoothly, directing his words to Bailey, "have you followed any strange men around town lately?"

She glared at him, annoyed at the way his words drew the attention of those sitting nearby. "Of course not," she snapped.

"I'm glad to hear it."

She'd just bet! She happened to glance at the man

standing next to Parker. He was a distinguished-look-ing older gentleman who was peeking at her curiously over the morning paper.

"Did you rewrite the kissing scene?" Parker asked next.

The businessman gave up any pretense of reading, folded his paper and studied Bailey openly.

"She did a fabulous job of it," Jo Ann said with a mentor's pride.

"I was sure she would," Parker remarked. A hint of a smile raised the corners of his mouth and made his eyes sparkle. Bailey wanted to demand that he cease and desist that very instant. "I suspect it had a ring of sincerity to it," Parker added, his eyes meet-ing Bailey's. "A depth, perhaps, that was missing in the first account."

"It did," Jo Ann confirmed, looking mildly sur-prised. "The whole scene is beautifully written. Every emotion, every sensation, is right there, so vividly de-scribed it's difficult to believe the same writer is re-sponsible for both versions."

Parker's expression reminded Bailey of Max when he'd discovered ground turkey in his dish instead of soggy cat food. His full sensuous mouth curved with satisfaction.

"I only hope Bailey can do as well with the danc-ing scene," Jo Ann said.

"The dancing scene?" Parker asked intently.

"That's several chapters later," Bailey explained,

jerking the manuscript out of Jo Ann's lap. She shoved it inside a folder and slipped it into her spacious shoulder bag.

"It's romantic the way it's written, but there's something lacking," said Jo Ann. "Unfortunately I haven't been able to put my finger on what's wrong."

"The problem is and always has been Michael," Bailey inserted, not wanting the conversation to continue in this vein. She hoped her hero would forgive her for blaming her shortcomings as a writer on him.

"You can't fault Michael for the dancing scene," Jo Ann disagreed. "Correct me if I'm wrong, but as I recall, Michael and Janice were manipulated—by Janice's father—into attending a Pops concert. The only reason they went was that they couldn't think of a plausible excuse."

"Yes," she admitted grudgingly. "A sixties rock group was performing."

"Right. Then, as the evening went on, several couples from the audience started to dance. The young man sitting next to Janice asked her—"

"The problem is with Michael," Bailey insisted again. She glanced hopefully at the older gentleman, but he just shrugged, eyes twinkling.

"What did Michael do that was so wrong?" Jo Ann asked with a puzzled frown.

"He…he should never have let Janice dance with another man," Bailey said in a desperate voice.

"Michael couldn't have done anything else," Jo

Ann argued, "otherwise he would've looked like a jealous fool." She turned to Parker for confirmation.

"I may be new to this hero business, but I can't help agreeing."

Bailey was irritated with both of them. This was *her* story and she'd write it as she saw fit. However, she refrained from saying so—just in case they were right. She needed time to mull over their opinions.

The train screeched to a halt and people surged toward the door. Bailey noted, gratefully, that this was Parker's stop.

"I'll give you a call later," he said, looking directly into Bailey's eyes. He didn't wait for a response.

He knew she didn't want to hear from him. She was frightened. Defensive. Guarded. With good reason. Only he didn't fully understand what that reason was. But a man like Parker wouldn't let her attitude go unchallenged.

"He's going to call you." Jo Ann sighed enviously. "Isn't that thrilling? Doesn't that excite you?"

Bailey shook her head, contradicting everything she was feeling inside. "Excite me? Not really."

Jo Ann frowned at her suspiciously. "What's the matter?"

"Nothing," Bailey answered with calm determination. She'd strolled down the path of romantic delusion twice before, but this time her eyes were wide open. Romance was wonderful, exciting, inspiring— and it was best limited to the pages of a well-crafted novel. Men, at least the men in her experience, inevitably proved to be terrible disappointments. Painful disappointments.

"Don't you like Parker?" Jo Ann demanded. "I mean, who wouldn't? He's hero material. You recognized it immediately, even before I did. Remember?"

Bailey wasn't likely to forget. "Yes, but that was in the name of research."

"Research?" Jo Ann cocked her eyebrows in flagrant disbelief. "Be honest, Bailey. You saw a whole lot more than Michael in Parker Davidson. You're not the type of woman who dashes off subways to follow a man. Some deep inner part of your being was reaching out to him."

Bailey forced a short laugh. "I hate to say it, Jo Ann, but I think you've been reading too many romances lately."

Jo Ann shrugged in a lie-to-yourself-if-you-insist manner. "Maybe, but I doubt it."

Nevertheless, her friend had given Bailey something to ponder.

The writing didn't go well that evening. Bailey, dressed in warm gray sweats, sans makeup and shoes, sat in front of her computer, staring blankly at the screen. "Inspiration is on vacation," she muttered, and that bit of doggerel seemed the best she could manage at the moment. Her usual warmth and humor escaped her. Every word she wrote sounded flat. She was tempted to erase the entire chapter.

Max, who had appointed himself the guardian of her printer, was curled up fast asleep on top of it. Bailey had long ago given up trying to keep him off. She'd quickly surrendered and taken to folding a towel over the printer to protect its internal workings from cat hair. Whenever she needed to print out a chapter, she nudged him awake; Max was always put out by the inconvenience and let her know it.

"Something's wrong," she announced to her feline companion. "The words just aren't flowing."

Max didn't reveal the slightest concern. He stretched out one yellow striped leg and examined it carefully, then settled down for another lengthy nap. He was fed and content and that was all that mattered.

Crossing her ankles, Bailey leaned back and clasped her hands behind her head. Chapter two of *Forever Yours* was just as vibrant and fast-paced as chapter one. But chapter three… She groaned and reread Paula Albright's letter for the umpteenth time, wanting desperately to capture the feelings and emotions the editor had suggested.

The phone rang in the kitchen, startling her. Bailey sighed irritably, then got up and rushed into the other room.

"Hello," she said curtly, realizing two important things at the same time. The first was how unfriendly and unwelcoming she sounded, and the second…the second was that she'd been unconsciously anticipating this call the entire evening.

"Hello," Parker returned in an affable tone. He didn't seem at all perturbed by her disagreeable mood. "I take it you're working, but from the sound of your voice I'd guess the rewrite isn't going well."

"It's coming along nicely." Bailey didn't know why she felt the need to lie. She was immediately consumed by guilt, then tried to disguise that by being even less friendly. "In fact, you interrupted a critical scene. I have so little time to write as it is, and my evenings are important to me."

There was an awkward silence. "Then I won't keep you," Parker said with cool politeness.

"It's just that it would be better if you didn't phone me." Her explaining didn't seem to improve the situation.

"I see," he said slowly.

And Bailey could tell that he *did* understand. She'd half expected him to argue, or at least attempt to cajole her into a more responsive mood. He didn't.

"Why don't you call me when you have a free moment," was all he said.

"I will," she answered, terribly disappointed and not sure why. It *was* better this way, with no further contact between them, she reminded herself firmly. "Goodbye, Parker."

"Goodbye," he said after another uncertain silence.

Bailey was still gripping the receiver when she

heard a soft click followed by the drone of the disconnected line. She'd been needlessly abrupt and standoffish—as if she was trying to prove something. Trying to convince herself that she wanted nothing more to do with Parker.

*Play it safe, Bailey. Don't involve your heart. You've learned your lesson.* Her mind was constructing excuses for her tactless behavior, but her heart would accept none of it.

Bailey felt wretched. She went back to her chair and stared at the computer screen for a full five minutes, unable to concentrate.

*He's only trying to help,* her heart told her.

*Men aren't to be trusted,* her mind said. *Haven't you learned that yet? How many times does it take to teach you something?*

*Parker isn't like the others,* her heart insisted.

Her mind, however, refused to listen. *All men are alike.*

But if she'd done the right thing, why did she feel so rotten? Yet she knew that if she gave in to him now, she'd regret it. She was treading on thin ice with this relationship; she remembered how she'd felt when he kissed her. Was she willing to risk the pain, the heartache, all over again?

Bailey closed her eyes and shook her head. Her thoughts were hopelessly tangled. She'd done what she knew was necessary, but she didn't feel good about it. In fact, she was miserable. Parker had gone out of his way to help her with this project, offering her his time and his advice. He'd given her valuable insights into the male point of view. And when he kissed her, he'd reminded her how it felt to be a desirable woman....

Bailey barely slept that night. On Tuesday morning she decided to look for Parker, even if it meant moving from one subway car to the next, something she rarely did. When she did run into him, she intended to apologize, crediting her ill mood to creative temperament.

"Morning," Jo Ann said, meeting her on the station platform the way she did every morning.

"Hello," Bailey murmured absently, scanning the windows of the train as it slowed to a stop, hoping to spot Parker. If Jo Ann noticed anything odd, she didn't comment.

"I heard back from the agent I wrote to a couple of months back," Jo Ann said, grinning broadly. Her eyes fairly sparkled.

"Irene Ingram?" Bailey momentarily forgot about Parker as she stared at her friend. Her sagging spirits lifted with the news. For weeks Jo Ann had been poring over the agent list, trying to decide whom to approach first. After much deliberation and thought, Jo Ann had decided to aim high. Many of the major publishers were no longer accepting non-agented material, and finding one willing to represent a beginner had been a serious concern. Irene was listed as one of the top romance-fiction agents in the industry. She represented a number of prominent names.

"And?" Bailey prompted, although she was fairly sure the news was positive.

"She's read my book and—" Jo Ann tossed her hands in the air "—she's crazy about it!"

"Does that mean she's going to represent you?" They were both aware how unusual it was for an established New York agent to represent an unpublished author. It wasn't unheard of, but it didn't happen all that often.

"You know, we never got around to discussing that—I assume she is. I mean, she talked to me about doing some minor revisions, which shouldn't take more than a week. Then we discussed possible markets. There's an editor she knows who's interested in historicals set in this time period. Irene wants to send it to her first, just as soon as I've finished with the revisions."

"Jo Ann," Bailey said, clasping her friend's hands tightly, "this is fabulous news!"

"I'm still having trouble believing it. Apparently Irene phoned while I was still at work and my eight-year-old answered. When I got home there was this scribbled message that didn't make any sense. All it said was that a lady with a weird name had phoned."

"Leave it to Bobby."

"He wasn't even home for me to question."

"He didn't write down the phone number?" Bailey asked.

"No, but he told Irene I was at work and she phoned me at five-thirty, our time."

"Weren't you the one who told me that being a writer means always knowing what time it is in New York?"

"The very one," Jo Ann teased. "Anyway, we spoke for almost an hour. It was crazy. Thank goodness Dan was home. I was standing in the kitchen with this stunned look on my face, frantically taking down notes. I didn't have to explain anything. Dan started dinner and then raced over to the park to pick up Bobby from Little League practice. Sarah set the table, and by the time I was off the phone, dinner was ready."

"I'm impressed." Several of the women in their writers' group had complained about their husbands' attitudes toward their creative efforts. But Jo Ann was fortunate in that department. Dan believed in her talent as strongly as Jo Ann did herself.

Jo Ann's dream was so close to being realized that Bailey could feel her own excitement rise. After three years of continuous effort, Jo Ann deserved a sale more than anyone she knew. She squeezed her writing in between dental appointments and Little League practices, between a full-time job and the demands of being a wife and mother. In addition, she was the driving force behind their writers' group. Jo Ann

Webster had paid her dues, and Bailey sincerely hoped that landing Irene Ingram as her agent would be the catalyst to her first sale.

"I refuse to get excited," Jo Ann said matter-of-factly.

Bailey stared at her incredulously. "You're kidding, aren't you?"

"I suppose I am. It's impossible not to be thrilled, but there's a saying in the industry we both need to remember. Agents don't sell books, good writing does. Plotting and characterization are what interest an editor. Agents negotiate contracts, but they don't sell books."

"You should've phoned and told me she called," Bailey chastised.

"I meant to. Honest, I did, but when I'd finished the dinner dishes, put the kids to bed and reviewed my revision notes, it was too late. By the way, before I forget, did Parker call you?"

He was the last person Bailey wanted to discuss. If she admitted he had indeed phoned her, Jo Ann was bound to ask all kinds of questions Bailey preferred not to answer. Nor did she want to lie about it.

So she compromised. "He did, but I was writing at the time and he suggested I call him back later."

"Did you?" Jo Ann asked expectantly.

"No," Bailey said in a small miserable voice. "I should have, but...I didn't."

"He's marvelous, you know."

"Would it be okay if we didn't discuss Parker?" Bailey asked. She'd intended to seek him out, but she decided against it, at least for now. "I've got so much on my mind and I...I need to clear away a few cobwebs."

"Of course." Jo Ann's look was sympathetic. "Take your time, but don't take too long. Men like Parker Davidson don't come along often. Maybe once in a lifetime, if you're lucky."

This wasn't what Bailey wanted to hear.

Max was curled up on Bailey's printer later that same evening. She'd worked for an hour on the rewrite and wasn't entirely pleased with the results. Her lack of satisfaction could be linked, however, to the number of times she'd inadvertently typed Parker's name instead of Michael's.

That mistake was simple enough to understand. She was tired. Parker had been in her thoughts most of the day. Good grief, when *wasn't* he in her thoughts?

Then, when she decided to take a break and scan the evening paper, Parker's name seemed to leap right off the page. For a couple of seconds, Bailey was convinced the typesetter had made a mistake, just as she herself had a few minutes earlier. Peering at the local-affairs page, she realized that yes, indeed, Parker was in the news.

She sat down on the kitchen stool and carefully read the brief article. Construction crews were breaking ground for a high-rise bank in the financial district. Parker Davidson was the project's architect.

Bailey read the item twice and experienced a swelling sense of pride and accomplishment.

She had to phone Parker. She owed him an explanation, an apology; she owed him her gratitude. She'd known it the moment she'd abruptly ended their conversation the night before. She'd known it that morning when she spoke with Jo Ann. She'd known it the first time she'd substituted Parker's name for Michael's. Even the afternoon paper was telling her what she already knew.

Something so necessary shouldn't be so difficult, Bailey told herself, standing in front of her telephone. Her hand still on the receiver, she hesitated. What could she possibly say to him? Other than to apologize for her behavior and congratulate him on the project she'd read about, which amounted to about thirty seconds of conversation.

Max sauntered into the kitchen, no doubt expecting to be fed again.

"You know better," she muttered, glaring down at him.

Pacing the kitchen didn't lend her courage. Nor did examining the contents of her refrigerator. The only thing that did was excite Max, who seemed to think she'd changed her mind, after all.

"Oh, for heaven's sake," she muttered, furious with herself. She picked up the phone, punched out

Parker's home number—and waited. The phone rang once, twice, three times.

Parker was apparently out for the evening. Probably with some tall blond bombshell, celebrating his success. Every woman's basic nightmare. Four rings. Well, what did she expect? He was handsome, appealing, generous, kind—

"Hello?"

He caught her completely off guard. "Parker?"

"Bailey?"

"Yes, it's me," she said brightly. "Hello." The things she'd intended to say had unexpectedly disintegrated.

"Hello." His voice softened a little.

"Am I calling at a bad time?" she asked, wrapping the telephone cord around her index finger, then her wrist and finally her elbow. "I could call back later if that's more convenient."

"Now is fine."

"I saw your name in the paper and wanted to congratulate you. This project sounds impressive."

He shrugged it off, as she knew he would. Silence fell between them, the kind of silence that needed to be filled or explained or quickly extinguished.

"I also wanted to apologize for the way I acted last night, when you phoned," Bailey said, the cord so tightly drawn around her hand that her fingers had gone numb. She loosened it now, her movements almost frantic. "I was rude and tactless and you didn't deserve it."

"So you ran into a snag with your writing?"

"I beg your pardon?"

"You're having a problem with your novel."

Bailey wondered how he knew that. "Uh…"

"I suggest it's time to check out the male point of view again. Get my insights. Am I right or wrong?"

"Right or wrong? Neither. I called to apologize."

"How's the rewrite coming?"

"Not too well." She sighed.

"Which tells me everything I need to know."

Bailey was mystified. "If you're implying that the only reason I'm calling is to ask for help with *Forever Yours* you couldn't be more mistaken."

"Then why *did* you call?"

"If you must know, it was to explain."

"Go on, I'm listening."

Now that she had his full attention, Bailey was beginning to feel foolish. "My mother always told me there's no excuse for rudeness, so I wanted to tell you something—something that might help you understand." Suddenly she couldn't utter another word.

"I'm listening," Parker repeated softly.

Bailey took a deep breath and closed her eyes. "Uh, maybe you *won't* understand, but you should know there's…there's a slightly used wedding dress hanging in my closet."

# *Seven*

Of all the explanations Bailey could have given, all the excuses she could have made to Parker, she had no idea why she'd mentioned the wedding dress. Sheer embarrassment dictated her next action.

She hung up the phone.

Immediately afterward it started ringing and she stared at it in stupefied horror. Placing her hands over her ears, she walked into the living room, sank into the overstuffed chair and tucked her knees under her chin.

Seventeen rings.

Parker let the phone ring so many times Bailey was convinced he was never going to give up. The silence that followed the last peal seemed to reverberate loudly through the small apartment.

She was just beginning to gather her thoughts when there was an impatient pounding on her door.

Max imperiously raised his head from his position on her printer as though to demand she do something. Obviously all the disruptions this evening were annoying him.

"Bailey, open this door," Parker ordered in a tone even she couldn't ignore.

Reluctantly she got up and pulled open the door, knowing intuitively that he would've gotten in one way or another. If she'd resisted, Parker would probably have had Mrs. Morgan outside her door with a key.

He stormed into her living room as though there was a raging fire inside that had to be extinguished. He stood in the center of the room and glanced around, running his hand through his hair. "What was that you said about a wedding dress?"

Bailey, who still clutched the doorknob, looked up at him and casually shrugged. "You forgot the slightly used part."

"Slightly used?"

"That's what I tried to explain earlier," she returned, fighting the tendency to be flippant.

"Are you married?" he asked harshly.

The question surprised her, although she supposed it shouldn't have. After all, they were talking about wedding dresses. "Heavens, no!"

"Then what the hell did you mean when you said it was slightly used?"

"I tried it on several times, paid for it, walked

around in it. I even had my picture taken in it, but that dress has never, to the best of my knowledge, been inside a church." She closed the door and briefly leaned against it.

"Do you want to tell me what happened?"

"Not particularly," she said, joining him in the middle of the room. "I really don't understand why I even brought it up. But now that you're here, do you want a cup of coffee?" She didn't wait for his response, but went into her kitchen and automatically took down a blue ceramic mug.

"What was his name?"

"Which time? The first time around it was Paul. Tom followed a few years later," Bailey said with matter-of-fact sarcasm as she filled the mug and handed it to him. She poured a cup for herself.

"I take it you've had to cancel two weddings, then?"

"Yes," she said leading the way back into her living area. She curled up on the couch, her feet tucked beneath her, leaving the large overstuffed chair for Parker. "This isn't something I choose to broadcast, but I seem to have problems holding on to a man. To be accurate, I should explain I bought the dress for Tom's and my wedding. He was the second fiancé. Paul and I hadn't gotten around to the particulars before he...left." The last word was barely audible.

"Why'd you keep the dress?" Parker asked, his dark eyes puzzled.

Bailey looked away. She didn't want his pity any more than she needed his tenderness, she told herself. But if that was the case, why did she feel so cold and alone?

"Bailey?"

"It's such a beautiful dress." Chantilly lace over luxurious white silk. Pearls along the full length of the sleeves. A gently tapered bodice; a gracefully draped skirt. It was the kind of dress every woman dreamed she'd wear once in a lifetime. The kind of dress that signified love and romance…

Instead of leaving the wedding gown with her parents, Bailey had packed it up and transported it to San Francisco. Now Parker was asking her why. Bailey supposed there was some psychological reason behind her actions. Some hidden motive buried in her subconscious. A reminder, perhaps, that men were not to be trusted?

"You loved them?" Parker asked carefully.

"I thought I did," she whispered, staring into her coffee. "To be honest, I…I don't know anymore."

"Tell me about Paul."

"Paul," she repeated in a daze. "We met our junior year of college." That seemed like a lifetime ago now.

"And you fell in love," he finished for her.

"Fairly quickly. He intended to go into law. He was bright and fun and opinionated. I could listen to him for hours. Paul seemed to know exactly what he wanted and how to get it."

"He wanted you," Parker inserted.

"At first." Bailey hesitated, struggling against the pain before it could tighten around her heart the way it once had. "Then he met Valerie. I don't think he intended to fall in love with her." Bailey had to believe that. She knew Paul had tried to hold on to his love for her, but in the end it was Valerie he chose. "I dropped out of college afterward," she added, her voice low and trembling. "I couldn't bear to be there, on campus, seeing the two of them together." It sounded cowardly now. Her parents had been disappointed, but she'd continued her studies at a business college, graduating as a paralegal a year later.

"I should've known Paul wasn't a hero," she said, glancing up at Parker and risking a smile.

"How's that?"

"He drank blush wine."

Parker stared at her a moment without blinking. "I beg your pardon?"

"You prefer straight Scotch, right?"

"Yes." Parker was staring at her. "How'd you know?"

"You also get your hair cut by a real barber and not a hairdresser."

He nodded.

"You wear well-made conservative clothes and prefer socks with your shoes."

"That's all true," Parker agreed, as though he'd missed the punch line in a joke. "But how'd you know?" he asked again.

"You like your coffee in a mug instead of a cup."

"Yes." His voice was even more incredulous.

"You're a hero, remember?" She sent him another smile, pleased with how accurately she'd assessed his habits. "At least I've learned one thing in all of this, and that's how to recognize a real man."

"Paul and Tom weren't real men?"

"No, they were costly imitations. Costly to my pride, that is." She altered her position and pulled her knees beneath her chin, wrapping her arms around her legs. She'd consciously assumed a defensive position—just in case he felt the need to comfort her. "Before you leap to conclusions, I think you should know that the only reason I need a hero is for the sake of *Forever Yours.* You're perfect as a model for Michael."

"But you don't want to become personally involved with me."

"Exactly." Now that everything was out in the open, Bailey felt an immediate sense of relief. Now that Parker understood, the pressure would be gone. There would be no unrealistic expectations. "I write romances and you're a hero type. Our relationship is strictly business. Though of course I'm grateful for your...friendship," she added politely.

Parker seemed to mull over her words for several seconds before shaking his head. "I could accept that—except there's one complication."

"Oh?" Bailey's gaze sought Parker's.

"The kiss."

Abruptly she dropped her gaze as a chill raced up her spine. "Foul!" she wanted to yell. "Unfair!" Instead, she muttered, "Uh, I don't think we should discuss that."

"Why not?"

"It was research," she said forcefully. "That's all." She was working hard to convince herself. Harder still at smiling blandly in his direction, hoping all the while he'd leave her comment untouched.

He didn't.

"Well, then it wouldn't hurt to experiment a second time, would it?" he argued. Unfortunately she had to acknowledge the logic of that—but she wouldn't admit it.

"No, please, there isn't any need," she told him, neatly destroying her own argument with her impassioned plea.

"I disagree," Parker said, standing up and striding toward her.

"Ah…" She clasped her bent legs even more tightly.

"There's nothing to worry about," Parker assured her.

"Isn't there? I mean…of course, there isn't. It's just that kissing makes me uncomfortable."

"Why's that?"

Couldn't the man accept a simple explanation? Just once?

Bailey sighed. "All right, you can kiss me if you insist," she said ungraciously, dropping her feet to the floor. She straightened her sweatshirt, dutifully squeezed her eyes shut, puckered her lips and waited.

And waited.

Finally she grew impatient and opened her eyes to discover Parker sitting next to her, staring. His face was inches from her own. A smile nipped at the corners of his mouth, making his lips quiver slightly.

"I amuse you?" she asked, offended. He was the one who'd requested this demonstration in the first place. He was the one who'd demanded proof.

"Not exactly *amuse*," Parker said, but from the gleam in his eyes she suspected he was fighting the urge to laugh out loud.

"I think we should forget the whole thing." She spoke with as much dignity as possible then got up to carry her cup into the kitchen. Turning to collect Parker's mug from the living room, she walked head-long into his arms.

His hands rested on her shoulders. "Both of those men were fools," he whispered, his gaze warm, his words soft.

Trapped between his body and the kitchen counter, Bailey felt the flutterings of panic. Her heart soared to her throat, beating wildly. He'd had his chance to kiss her, to prove his point. He should've done it then. Not now. Not when she wasn't steeled and ready. Not when his words made her feel so helpless and vulnerable.

Gently his mouth claimed hers. The kiss was straightforward, uncomplicated by need or desire. A tender kiss. A kiss to erase the pain of rejection and the grief of loss.

Bailey didn't respond. Not at first. Then her lips trembled to life in a slow awakening.

Like the first time Parker had kissed her, Bailey felt besieged by confusion and a sense of shock. She wasn't ready for this! She jerked herself free of his arms and twisted around. "There!" she said, her voice quavering. "Are you happy?"

"No," he answered starkly. "You can try to fool yourself if you want, but we both know the truth. You've been burned."

"Since I can't stand the heat," she said in a reasonable tone, "I got out of the kitchen." The fact that she'd just been kissed by him *in* the kitchen only made her situation more farcical. She brushed the hair back from her forehead, managed a false smile and turned around to face him. "I should never have said anything about the wedding dress. I don't know why I did. I'm not even sure what prompted that display of hysteria."

"I'm glad you did. And, Bailey, don't feel you have to apologize to me."

"Thank you," she mumbled, leading the way to her door.

Parker stopped to pat Max, who didn't so much as open his eyes to investigate. "Does he always sleep on your printer?"

"No, he sometimes insists on taking up a large portion of my pillow, generally when I'm using it myself."

Parker grinned. Bailey swore she'd never met a man with a more engaging smile. It was like watching the sun break through the clouds after a heavy downpour. It warmed her spirit, and only with the full strength of her will was she able to look away.

"I'll be seeing you," he said, pausing at the door.

"Yes," she whispered, yearning to see him again, yet in the same heartbeat hoping it wouldn't be soon.

"Bailey," Parker said, pressing his hand to her cheek, "just remember you haven't been the only one betrayed by love. It happens to all of us."

Perhaps, Bailey thought, but Parker was a living, breathing hero. The type of man women bought millions of books a year to read about, to dream about. She doubted he knew what it was like to have love humiliate him and break his heart.

"You look like you don't believe me."

Bailey stared at him, surprised he'd read her reaction so clearly.

"You're wrong," he said quietly. "I lost someone I loved, too." With that he dropped his hand and walked out, closing the door behind him.

By the time Bailey had recovered her wits enough to race after him, question him, the hallway was empty. Parker had lost at love, too? No woman in her right mind would walk away from Parker Davidson.

He was a hero.

★ ★ ★

"I'm afraid I did it again," Bailey announced to Jo Ann as they walked briskly toward their respective office buildings. The noise on the subway that morning had made private conversation impossible.

"Did what?"

"Put my foot in my mouth with Parker Davidson. He—"

"Did you see his name in the paper last night?" Jo Ann asked excitedly, cutting her off. "It was a small piece in the local section. I would've phoned you, but I knew I'd see you this morning and I didn't want to interrupt your writing time."

"I saw it."

"Dan was impressed that we even knew Parker. Apparently he's made quite a name for himself in the past few years. I never pay attention to that sort of thing. If it doesn't have to do with medical insurance or novel-writing, it's lost on me. But Dan's heard of him. He would, being in construction and all. Did you know Parker won a major national award for an innovative house he designed last year?"

"N-no."

"I'm sorry, I interrupted you, didn't I?" Jo Ann said, stopping midstride. "What were you about to say?"

Bailey wasn't sure how much she should tell her. "He stopped by my apartment—"

"Parker came to your place?" Jo Ann sounded

awestruck, as though Bailey had experienced a heavenly visitation.

Bailey didn't know what was wrong with Jo Ann. She wasn't letting her get a word in edgewise. "I made the mistake of telling him about the wedding dress in my closet. And at first I think he assumed I was married."

Jo Ann came to an abrupt halt. Her eyes narrowed. "There's a wedding dress in your closet?"

Bailey had forgotten she'd never told Jo Ann about Paul and Tom. She felt neither the inclination nor the desire to explain now, especially on a cold February day in the middle of a busy San Francisco sidewalk.

"My, my, will you look at the time?" Bailey muttered, staring down at her watch. It was half-past frustration and thirty minutes to despair. The only way she could easily extricate herself from this mess was to leave—now.

"Oh, no, you don't, Bailey York," Jo Ann cried, grasping her forearm. "You're not walking away from me yet. Not without filling me in first."

"It's nothing. I was engaged."

"When? Recently?"

"Yes and no," Bailey responded cryptically with a longing glance at her office building two blocks south.

"What does that mean?" Jo Ann demanded.

"I was engaged to be married twice, and both times the man walked out on me. All right? Are you satisfied now?"

Her explanation didn't seem to appease Jo Ann. "Twice? But what's any of this got to do with Parker? It wasn't his fault those other guys dumped you, was it?"

"Of course not," Bailey snapped, completely exasperated. She'd lost her patience. It had been a mistake to ever mention the man's name. Jo Ann had become Parker's greatest advocate. Never mind that she was also *her* good friend and if she was going to champion anyone, it should be Bailey. However, in Jo Ann's starry-eyed view, Parker apparently could do no wrong.

"He assumed you were married?"

"Don't worry, I explained everything," she said calmly. "Listen, we're going to be late for work. I'll talk to you later."

"You bet you will. You've got a lot more explaining to do." She took a couple of steps, walking backward, staring at Bailey. "You were engaged? To different men each time?" she repeated. "Two different men?"

Bailey nodded and held up two fingers as they continued to back away from each other. "Two times, two different men."

Unexpectedly Jo Ann's face broke into a wide smile. "You know what they say, don't you? Third time's the charm, and if Parker Davidson is anything, it's charming. Talk to you this evening." With a quick wave, her friend turned and hurried down the street.

★ ★ ★

By lunchtime, Bailey decided the day was going to be a disaster. She'd misfiled an important folder, accidentally disconnected a client on the phone and worst of all spent two hours typing up a brief, then pressed the wrong key and lost the entire document. Following the fiasco with the computer, she took an early lunch and decided to walk off her frustration.

Either by accident or unconscious design—she couldn't decide which—Bailey found herself outside Parker's office building. She gazed at it for several minutes, wavering with indecision. She wanted to ask him what he'd meant about losing someone he loved. It was either that or spend the second half of the day infuriating her boss and annoying important clients. She was disappointed in Parker, she decided. He shouldn't have walked away without explaining. It wasn't fair. He'd been willing enough to listen to the humiliating details of *her* love life, but hadn't shared his own pain.

Roseanne Snyder, the firm's receptionist, brightened when Bailey walked into the office. "Oh, Ms. York, it's good to see you again."

"Thank you," Bailey answered, responding naturally to the warm welcome.

"Is Mr. Davidson expecting you?" The receptionist was flipping through the pages of the engagement calendar. "I'm terribly sorry if I—"

"No, no," Bailey said, stepping close to the older

woman's desk. "I wasn't even sure Parker would be in."

"He is, and I know he'd be pleased to see you. Just go on back and I'll tell him you're coming. You know the way, don't you?" She turned in her chair and pointed down the hallway. "Mr. Davidson's office is the last door on your left."

Bailey hesitated, more doubtful than ever that showing up like this was the right thing to do. She would have left, crept quietly away, if Roseanne hadn't spoken into the intercom just then and gleefully announced her presence.

Before Bailey could react, Parker's office door opened. He waited there, hands in his pockets, leaning indolently against the frame.

Fortifying her resolve, she hurried toward him. He moved aside and closed the door when she entered. Once again she was struck by the dramatically beautiful view of the bay, but she couldn't allow that to deter her from her purpose.

"This is an unexpected surprise," Parker said.

Her nerves were on edge, and her words were more forceful than she intended. "That was a rotten thing you did."

"What? Kissing you? Honestly, Bailey are we going to go through all that again? You've got to stop lying to yourself."

"My day's a complete waste," she said, clenching her hands, "and this has nothing to do with our kiss."

"It doesn't?"

She sank down in a chair. "I dragged my pride through the mud of despair for you," she said dramatically.

He blinked as though she'd completely lost him.

"All right," she admitted with a flip of her hand, "that may be a little on the purple side."

"Purple?"

"Purple prose." Oh, it was so irritating having to explain everything to him. "Do you think I enjoy sharing my disgrace? It isn't every woman who'd willingly dig up the most painful episodes in her past and confess them to you. It wasn't easy, you know."

Parker walked around to his side of the desk, sat down and rubbed the side of his jaw. "Does this conversation have anything to do with the slightly used wedding dress?"

"Yes," she returned indignantly. "Oh, it was perfectly acceptable for me to describe how two—not one, mind you, but two—different men dumped me practically at the altar steps."

The amusement faded from Parker's eyes. "I realize that."

"No, you don't," she said, "otherwise you'd never have left on that parting shot."

"Parting shot?"

She shut her eyes for a moment and prayed for patience. "As you were leaving, you oh-so-casually mentioned something about losing someone you loved. Why was it fine for me to share my humiliation but not for you? I'm disappointed and—" Her throat closed before she could finish.

Parker was strangely quiet. His eyes held hers, his look somber. "You're right. That was rude of me, and I don't have any excuse."

"Oh, but you do," she said dryly. She should have known. He was a hero, wasn't he? She shook her head, angry with herself as much as with him.

"I do?" Parker countered.

"Yes, I should've figured it out sooner. Heroes often have a difficult time exposing their vulnerabilities. Obviously this…woman you loved wounded your pride. She unmasked your vulnerability. Believe me, I know about that from experience. You don't have to explain it to me." She stood up to go, guiltily aware that she'd judged Parker too harshly.

"But you're right," he argued. "You shared a deep part of yourself and I should have been willing to do the same. It was unfair of me to leave the way I did."

"Perhaps, but it was true to character." She would have said a quick goodbye and walked out the door if not for the pain that suddenly entered his eyes.

"I'll tell you. It's only fair that you know. Sit down."

Bailey did as he requested, watching him carefully.

Parker smiled, but this wasn't the winsome smile she was accustomed to seeing. This was a strained smile, almost a grimace.

"Her name was Maria. I met her while I was traveling in Spain about fifteen years ago. We were both so young and in love. I wanted to marry her, bring her back with me to the States, but her family…well, suffice it to say her family didn't want their daughter marrying a foreigner. Several hundred years of tradition and pride stood between us, and when Maria was forced to choose between her family and me, she chose to remain in Madrid." He paused, shrugging one shoulder. "She did the right thing, I realize that now, much as it hurt at the time. I also realize how difficult her decision must have been. I learned a few months later that she'd married someone far more acceptable to her family than an American student."

"I'm sorry."

He shook his head as though to dispel the memories. "There's no reason you should be. Although I loved her a great deal, the relationship would never have lasted. Maria would've been miserable in this country. I understand now how perceptive she was."

"She loved you."

"Yes," he said. "She loved me as much as she dared, but in the end duty and family were more important to her than love."

Bailey didn't know what to say. Her heart ached for the young man who had lost his love, and yet she couldn't help admiring the brave woman who had sacrificed her heart for her family and her deepest beliefs.

"I think what hurt the most was that she married someone else so soon afterward," Parker added.

"Paul and Tom got married, too…I think." Bailey understood his pain well.

The office was quiet for a moment, until Parker broke the silence. "Are we going to sit around and mope all afternoon? Or are you going to let me take you to lunch?"

Bailey smiled. "I think you might be able to talk me into it." Her morning had been miserable, but the afternoon looked much brighter now. She got to her feet, still smiling at Parker. "One thing I've learned over the years is that you can't allow misery to interfere with mealtimes."

Parker laughed and the robust sound of it was contagious. "I have a small surprise for you," he told her, reaching inside his suit pocket. "I was going to save it for later, but now seems more fitting." He handed her two tickets.

Bailey stared at them, speechless.

"The Pops concert," Parker said. "They're having a rock group from the sixties perform. It seems only fitting that Janice and Michael attend."

# Eight

It wasn't until they'd finished lunch that Bailey noticed what a good time she was having with Parker. They'd sat across the table from each other and chatted like old friends. Bailey had never felt more at ease with him, nor had she ever allowed herself to be more open. Her emotions had undergone a gradual but profound change.

Fear and caution had been replaced by genuine contentment. And by hope.

After lunch they strolled through Union Square tossing breadcrumbs to the greedy pigeons. The early-morning fog had burned away and the sun was out in a rare display of brilliance. The square was filled with tourists, groups of old men and office workers taking an outdoor lunch. Bailey loved Union Square. Being there now, with Parker, seemed especially…fitting. And not just because Janice and Michael did the same thing in chapter six!

He was more relaxed with her, as well. He talked freely about himself, something he'd never done before. He was the oldest of three boys and the only one still unmarried.

"I'm the baby of the family," Bailey explained. "Pampered and spoiled. Overprotected, I'm afraid. My parents tried hard to dissuade me from moving to California." She paused.

"What made you leave Oregon?"

Bailey waited for the tightness that always gripped her heart when she thought of Tom, but it didn't come. It simply wasn't there anymore.

"Tom," she admitted, glancing down at the squawking birds, fighting over crumbs.

"He was fiancé number two?" Parker's hands were locked behind his back as they strolled along the paved pathway.

Bailey couldn't resist wondering if he'd hidden his hands to keep from touching her. "I met Tom a couple of years after…Paul. He was, is, a junior partner in the law firm where I worked as a paralegal. We'd been dating off and on for several months, nothing serious for either of us. Then we got involved in a case together and ended up spending a lot of time in each other's company. Within three months we were engaged."

Parker placed his hand lightly on her shoulder as though to lend her support. She smiled up at him in appreciation. "Actually it doesn't hurt as much to talk about it now." Time did heal all wounds, or as she preferred to think, time wounds all heels.

"I'm not sure when he met Sandra," she continued. "For all I know, they might have been childhood sweethearts. What I do remember is that we were only a few weeks away from the wedding. The invitations were all finished and waiting to be picked up at the printer's when Tom told me there was someone else."

"Were you surprised?"

"Shocked. In retrospect, I suppose I should have recognized the signs, but I'd been completely wrapped up in preparing for the wedding—shopping with my bridesmaids for their dresses, arranging for the flowers, things like that. In fact, I was so busy picking out china patterns I didn't even notice that my fiancé had fallen out of love with me."

"You make it sound as though it was your fault."

Bailey shrugged. "In some ways I think it was. I'm willing to admit that now, to see my own faults. But that doesn't make up for the fact that he was engaged to me and seeing another woman on the sly."

"No, it doesn't," Parker agreed. "What did you say when he told you?" By now, his hand was clasping her shoulder and she was leaning into him. The weight of her humiliation no longer seemed as crushing, but it was still there, and talking about it produced a flood of emotions she hadn't wanted to face. It was ironic that she could do so now, after all this time, and with another man.

"Have you forgiven him?"

Bailey paused and nudged a fallen leaf with the toe of her shoe. "Yes. Hating him, even disliking him, takes too much energy. He was truly sorry. By the time he talked to me, I think poor Tom was completely and utterly miserable. He tried so hard to avoid doing or saying anything to hurt me. I swear it took him fifteen minutes to get around to telling me he wanted to call off the wedding and another thirty to confess that there was someone else. I remember the sick feeling in my stomach. It was like coming down with a bad case of the flu, having all the symptoms hit me at once." Her mind returned to that dreadful day and how she'd sat and stared at Tom in shocked disbelief. He'd been so uncomfortable, gazing at his hands, guilt and confusion muffling his voice.

"I didn't cry," Bailey recalled. "I wasn't even angry, at least not at first. I don't think I felt any emotion." She gave Parker a chagrined smile. "In retrospect I realize my pride wouldn't allow it. What I do remember is that I said the most nonsensical things."

"Like what?"

Bailey's gaze wandered down the pathway. "I told him I expected him to pay for the invitations. We'd had them embossed with gold, which had been considerably more expensive. Besides, I was already out the money for the wedding dress."

"Ah, the infamous slightly used wedding dress."

"It was expensive!"

"I know," Parker said, his eyes tender. "Actually you were just being practical."

"I don't know what I was being. It's crazy the way the mind works in situations like that. I remember thinking that Paul and Tom must have been acquainted with each other. I was convinced the two of them had plotted together, which was utterly ridiculous."

"I take it you decided to move to San Francisco after Tom broke the engagement."

She nodded. "Within a matter of hours I'd given my notice at the law firm and was making plans to move."

"Why San Francisco?"

"You know," she said, laughing lightly, "I'm not really sure. I'd visited the area several times over the years and the weather was always rotten. Mark Twain wrote somewhere that the worst winter he ever spent was a summer in San Francisco. I guess the city, with its overcast skies and foggy mornings, suited my mood. I couldn't have tolerated bright sunny days and moonlit nights in the weeks after I left Oregon."

"What happened to Tom?"

"What do you mean?" Bailey cocked her head to look up at him, taken aback by the question.

"Did he marry Sandra?"

"Heavens, I don't know."

"Weren't you curious?"

Frankly she hadn't been. He obviously hadn't

wanted *her,* and that was the only thing that mattered to Bailey. She'd felt betrayed, humiliated and abandoned. If Tom ever regretted his decision or if things hadn't worked out between him and Sandra, she didn't know. She hadn't stuck around to find out. Furthermore, she wouldn't have cared, not then, anyway.

She'd wanted out. Out of her job, Out of Oregon. Out of her dull life. If she was going to fall in love, why did it have to be with weak men? Men who couldn't make up their minds. Men who fell in and out of love, men who were never sure of what they wanted.

Perhaps it was some flaw in her own character that caused her to choose such men. That was the very reason she'd given up on relationships and dating and the opposite sex in general. And she knew it was also why she enjoyed reading romances, why she enjoyed writing them. Romance fiction offered her the happy ending that had been so absent in her own life.

The novels she read and wrote were about men who were *real* men—strong, traditional, confident men—and everyday women not unlike herself.

She'd been looking for a hero when she stumbled on Parker Davidson. Yes, she could truly say her heart was warming toward him. Warming, nothing! It was *on fire* and had been for weeks, although she'd refused to acknowledge that until now.

Parker's dark eyes caressed hers. "I'm glad you moved to the Bay area."

"So am I."

"You won't change your mind, will you?" he asked as they began to walk back. He must have read the confusion in her eyes because he added, "The concert tonight? It's in honor of Valentine's Day."

"No, I'm looking forward to going." She hadn't even realized what day this was. Bailey suddenly felt a thrill of excitement at the thought of spending the most romantic evening of the year with Parker Davidson. Although of course it would mean no time to work on *Forever Yours*...

"Think of the concert as research," Parker said, grinning down at her.

"I will." A woman could be blinded by eyes as radiant as Parker's. They were alight with the sensitivity and strength of his nature.

"Goodbye," she said reluctantly, lifting her hand in a small wave.

"Until tonight," Parker said, sounding equally reluctant to part.

"Tonight," she repeated softly. She'd seen her pain reflected in his eyes when she told him about Tom. He understood what it was to lose someone you loved, regardless of the circumstances. She sensed that in many ways the two of them were alike. During that short walk around Union Square, Bailey had felt a closeness to Parker, a comfortable and open honesty she'd rarely felt with anyone before.

"I'll pick you up at seven," he said.

"Perfect." Bailey was convinced he would have kissed her if they hadn't been standing in such a public place. And she would have let him.

The afternoon flew by. Whereas the morning had been excruciatingly slow, filled with one blunder after another, the hours after her lunch with Parker were trouble free. No sooner had she returned to the office than it seemed time to pack up her things and head for the subway.

True to form, Max was there to greet her when she walked in the door. She set her mail, two bills and an ad for the local supermarket, on the kitchen counter, and quickly fed him. Max seemed mildly surprised at her promptness and stared at his food for several minutes, as though he was hesitant about eating it.

Grumbling that it was impossible to please the dratted cat, Bailey stalked into her bedroom, throwing open the closet door.

For some time she did nothing but stare at the contents. She finally made her decision, a printed dress she'd worn when she was in college. The paisley print was bright and cheerful, the skirt widely pleated. The style was slightly dated, but it was the best she could do. If Parker had given her even a day's notice she would have gone out and bought something new. Something red in honor of Valentine's Day.

* * *

The seats Parker had purchased for the concert at Civic Center were among the best in the house. They were situated in the middle about fifteen rows from the front.

The music was fabulous. Delightful. Romantic. There were classical pieces she recognized, interspersed with soft rock, and a number of popular tunes and "golden oldies."

The orchestra was spectacular, and being this close to the stage afforded Bailey an opportunity so special she felt tears of appreciation gather in her eyes more than once. Nothing could ever duplicate a live performance.

The warm generous man in her company made everything perfect. At some point, early in the program, Parker reached for her hand. When Bailey's heartbeat finally settled down to a normal rate, she felt an emotion she hadn't experienced in more than a year, not since the day Tom had called off their wedding.

*Contentment.* Complete and utter contentment.

She closed her eyes to savor the music and when she opened them again, she saw Parker studying her. She smiled shyly and he smiled back. And at that moment, cymbals clanged. Bailey jumped in her seat as though caught doing something illegal. Parker chuckled and raised her hand to his lips, gently brushing her knuckles with a kiss.

The second group, Hairspray, performed after the intermission. Bailey found their music unfamiliar with the exception of two or three classic rock numbers. But the audience responded enthusiastically to the group's energy and sense of fun. Several people got to their feet, swaying to the music. After a while some couples edged into the aisles and started dancing. Bailey would have liked to join them, but Parker seemed to prefer staying where they were. She couldn't very well leave him sitting there while she sought out a partner. Especially when the only partner she wanted was right beside her.

Eventually nearly everyone around them rose and moved into the aisle, which meant a lot of awkward shifting for Parker and Bailey. She was convinced they were the only couple in the section not on their feet.

She glanced at Parker, but he seemed oblivious to what was happening around them. At one point she thought she heard him grumble about not being able to see the band because of all those people standing.

"Miss?" An older balding man moved into their nearly empty row and tapped Bailey on the shoulder in an effort to get her attention. He wore his shirt open to the navel and had no less than five pounds of gold draped around his neck. Clearly he'd never left the early seventies. "Would you care to dance?"

"Uh…" Bailey certainly hadn't been expecting an invitation. She wasn't entirely confident of the protocol. She'd come with Parker and he might object.

"Go ahead," Parker said, reassuring her. He actually seemed relieved someone else had asked her. Perhaps he was feeling guilty about not having done so himself, Bailey mused.

She shrugged and stood, glancing his way once more to be sure he didn't mind. He urged her forward with a wave of his hand.

Bailey was disappointed. She wished with all her heart that it was Parker taking her in his arms. Parker, not some stranger.

"Matt Cooper," the man with the gold chains said, holding out his hand.

"Bailey York."

He grinned as he slipped his arm around her waist. "There must be something wrong with your date to leave you sitting there."

"I don't think Parker dances."

It had been a long while since Bailey had danced, and she wasn't positive she'd even remember how. She needn't have worried. The space was so limited that she couldn't move more than a few inches in any direction.

The next song Hairspray performed was an old rock song from the sixties. Matt surprised her by placing two fingers in his mouth and whistling loudly. The piercing sound cut through music, crowd noises and applause. Despite herself, Bailey laughed.

The song was fast-paced and Bailey began swaying her hips and moving to the beat. Before she was sure how it had happened, she was quite a distance from her friend. She found herself standing next to a tall good-looking man about Parker's age, who was obviously enjoying the group's performance.

He smiled at Bailey and she smiled shyly back. The next song was another oldie, one written with young lovers in mind and perfect for slow dancing.

Bailey tried to make it down the aisle to Parker's seat, but the row was empty. Although she glanced all around she couldn't locate him.

"We might as well," the good-looking man said, holding out his hands to her. "My partner has taken off for parts unknown."

"Mine seems to have disappeared, too." Scanning the crowd, she still couldn't find Parker but then, the area was so congested it was impossible to see anyone clearly. A little worried, she wondered how they'd ever find each other when the concert was over.

She and her new partner danced two or three dances without ever exchanging names. He twirled her about with an expertise that masterfully disguised her own less-inspired movements. They finished a particularly fast dance, and Bailey fanned her face, flushed from the exertion, with one hand.

When Hairspray introduced another love ballad, it seemed only natural for Bailey to slip into her temporary partner's arms. He said something and laughed. Bailey hadn't been able to make out his words, but she grinned back at him. She was about to say something herself when she saw Parker edging toward them, scowling.

"My date's here," she said, breaking away from the man who held her. She gave him an apologetic look and he released her with a decided lack of enthusiasm.

"I thought I'd lost you," she said when Parker made it to her side.

"I think it's time we left," he announced in clipped tones.

Bailey blinked, surprised by his irritation. "But the concert isn't over yet." Cutting a path through the horde of dancers would be difficult, perhaps impossible. "Shouldn't we at least stay until Hairspray is finished?"

"No."

"What's wrong?"

Parker shoved his hands in his pockets. "I didn't mind you dancing with that Barry Gibb look-alike, but the next thing I know, you've taken off with someone else."

"I didn't *take off* with anyone," she said, disliking his tone as much as his implication. "We were separated by the crowds."

"Then you should've come back to me."

"You didn't honestly expect me to fight my way through this mass of humanity, did you? Can't you see how crowded the aisles are?"

"I made it to you."

Bailey sighed, fighting the urge to be sarcastic. And lost. "Do you want a Boy Scout award? I didn't know they issued them for pushing and shoving."

Parker's eyes flashed with resentment. "I didn't push anyone. I think it would be best if we sat down," he said, gripping her by the elbow and leading her back into a row, "before you make an even greater spectacle of yourself."

"A spectacle of myself," Bailey muttered furiously. "If anyone was a spectacle, it was you! You were the only person in ten rows who wasn't dancing."

"I certainly didn't expect my date to take off with another man." He sank down in a seat and crossed his arms as though he had no intention of continuing this discussion.

"Your date," she repeated, struggling to hold on to her temper by clenching her fists. "May I remind you this entire evening was for the purposes of research and nothing more?"

Parker gave a disbelieving snort. "That's not how I remember it. At the time, you seemed eager enough." He laughed, a cynical, unpleasant sound. "I'm not the one who chased after you."

Standing there arguing with him was attracting more attention than Bailey wanted. Reluctantly she sat down, primly folding her hands in her lap, and stared directly ahead. "I didn't chase after you," she informed him through gritted teeth. "I have *never* chased after any man."

"Oh, forgive me, then. I could have sworn it was you who followed me off the subway. Were you aware that someone who closely resembles you stalked me all the way into Chinatown?"

"Oh-h-h," Bailey moaned, throwing up her hands, "you're impossible."

"What I am is correct."

Bailey didn't deign to reply. She crossed her legs and swung her ankle ferociously until the concert finally ended.

Parker didn't say a word as he escorted her to his car, which was fine with Bailey. She'd never met a more unreasonable person in her life. Less than an hour earlier, they'd practically been drowning in each other's eyes. She'd allowed herself to get caught up in the magic of the moment, that was all. Some Valentine's Day!

They parted with little more than a polite goodnight. Bailey informed him there was no need to see her to her door. Naturally he claimed otherwise, just to be obstinate. She wanted to argue, but knew it would be a waste of breath.

Max was at the door to greet her, his tail waving in the air. He stayed close to her, rubbing against her legs, and Bailey nearly tripped over him as she hurriedly undressed. She started to tell him about her evening, changed her mind and got into bed. She pulled the covers up to her chin, forcing the cantankerous Parker Davidson from her mind.

★ ★ ★

Jo Ann was waiting for her outside the BART station the following morning. "Well?" she said, racing to Bailey's side. "How was your date?"

"What date? You couldn't possibly call that outing with Parker a date."

"I couldn't?" Jo Ann was clearly puzzled.

"We attended the Pops Concert—"

"For research," Jo Ann finished for her. "I gather the evening didn't go well?" They filed through the turnstile and rode the escalator down to the platform where they'd board the train.

"The whole night was a disaster."

"Tell Mama everything," Jo Ann urged.

Bailey wasn't in the mood to talk, but she made the effort to explain what had happened and how unreasonable Parker had been. She hadn't slept well, convinced she'd made the same mistake with Parker as she had with the other men in her life. All along she'd assumed he was different. Not so. Parker was pompous, irrational and arrogant. She told Jo Ann that. "I was wrong about him being a hero," she said bleakly,

Jo Ann frowned. "Let me see if I've got this straight. People started dancing. One man asked you to dance, then you got separated and danced with another guy and Parker acted like a jealous fool."

"Exactly." It infuriated Bailey every time she thought about it, which she'd been doing all morning.

"Of course he did," Jo Ann said enthusiastically, as

though she'd just made an important discovery. "Don't you see? He was being true to character. Didn't more or less the same thing happen between Janice and Michael when they went to the concert?"

Bailey had completely forgotten. "Now that you mention it, yes," she admitted slowly.

The train arrived. When the screeching came to a halt, Jo Ann said, "I told Parker all about that scene myself, remember?"

Bailey did, vaguely.

"When you sit down to rewrite it, you'll know from experience exactly what Janice was feeling and thinking because those were the very thoughts you experienced yourself. How can you be angry with him?"

Bailey wasn't finding it difficult.

"You should be grateful."

"I should?"

"Oh, yes," Jo Ann insisted. "Parker Davidson is more of a hero than either of us realized."

# Nine

"Don't you understand what Parker did?" Jo Ann asked when they met for lunch later that same day. The topic was one she refused to drop.

"You bet I understand. He's a…Neanderthal, only he tried to be polite about it. As if that makes any difference."

"Wrong," Jo Ann argued, looking downright mysterious. "He's given you some genuine insight into your character's thoughts and actions."

"What he did," Bailey said, waving her spoon above her cream-of-broccoli soup, "was pretty well ruin what started out as a perfect evening."

"You said he acted like a jealous fool, but you've got to remember that's exactly how Michael reacted when Janice danced with another man."

"Then he went above and beyond the call of duty, and I'm not about to reward that conduct in a man, hero or not." She crumbled her soda crackers into her soup, then brushed her palms free of crumbs.

Until Bailey accepted the invitation to dance, her evening with Parker had been wonderfully romantic. They'd sat together holding hands, while the music swirled and floated around them. Then the dancing began and her knight in shining armor turned into a fire-breathing dragon.

"You haven't forgotten the critique group is meeting tonight, have you?" Jo Ann asked, abruptly changing the subject.

Bailey's head was so full of Parker that she had, indeed, forgotten. She'd been absentminded lately. "Tonight?"

"Seven, at Darlene's house. You'll be there, won't you?"

"Of course." Bailey didn't need to think twice. Every other week, women from their writing group took turns hosting a session in which they evaluated one another's work.

"Oh, good. For a moment I wondered whether you'd be able to come."

"Why wouldn't I?" Bailey demanded. She was as dedicated as the other writers. She hadn't missed a single meeting since the group was formed two months ago.

"Oh, I thought you might be spending the evening with Parker. You two need to work out your differences. You're going to be miserable until this is resolved."

Bailey slowly lowered her spoon. "Miserable?" she repeated, giving a brief, slightly hysterical laugh. "Do I look like I'm the least bit heartbroken? Honestly, Jo Ann, you're making a mountain out of a molehill. The two of us had a falling out. I don't want to see him, and I'm sure he feels the same way. I won't have any problem making the group tonight."

Jo Ann calmly drank her coffee, then just as calmly stated, "You're miserable, only you're too proud to admit it."

"I am *not* miserable," Bailey asserted, doing her utmost to smile serenely.

"How much sleep did you get last night?"

"Why? Have I got circles under my eyes?"

"No. Just answer the question."

Bailey swallowed uncomfortably. "Enough. What's with you? Have you taken up writing mystery novels? Parker Davidson and I had a parting of the ways. It would have happened eventually. Besides, it's better to learn these sorts of things in the beginning of a…relationship." She shrugged comically. "A bit ironic to have it end on Valentine's Day."

"So you won't be seeing him again?" Jo Ann made that sound like the most desolate of prospects.

"We probably won't be able to avoid a certain amount of contact, especially while he's taking the subway, but for the record, no. I don't intend to ever go out with him again. He can save his caveman tactics for someone else."

"Someone else?" Jo Ann filled the two words with tearful sadness. Until Parker, Bailey had seen only the tip of the iceberg when it came to her friend's romantic nature.

Bailey finished her soup and, glancing at her watch, realized she had less than five minutes to get back to the office.

"About tonight—I'll give you a ride," Jo Ann promised. "I'll be by to pick you up as close to six-thirty as I can. It depends on how fast I can get home and get everyone fed."

"Thanks," Bailey said. "I'll see you then."

They parted and Bailey hurried back to her office. The large vase of red roses on the reception desk was the first thing she noticed when she walked in.

"Is it your birthday, Martha?" she asked as she removed her coat and hung it on the rack.

"I thought it must be yours," the secretary replied absently.

"Mine?"

"The card has your name on it."

Bailey's heart went completely still. Had Parker sent her flowers? It seemed too much to hope for, yet... "My name's on the card?"

"A tall good-looking man in a suit delivered them not more than ten minutes ago. He seemed disappointed when I said you'd taken an early lunch. Who is that guy, anyway? He looks vaguely familiar."

Bailey didn't answer. Instead she removed the envelope and slipped out the card. It read, "Forgive me, Parker."

She felt the tightness around her heart suddenly ease.

"Oh, I nearly forgot," Martha said, reaching for a folded slip of paper next to the crystal vase. "Since you weren't here, he left a message for you."

Carrying the vase with its brilliant red roses in one hand and her message in the other, Bailey walked slowly to her desk. With eager fingers, she unfolded the note.

"Bailey," it said. "I'm sorry I missed you. We need to talk. Can you have dinner with me tonight? If so, I'll pick you up at seven. Since I'll be tied up most of the afternoon, leave a message with Roseanne."

He'd written down his office number. Bailey reached for the phone with barely a thought. The friendly—and obviously efficient—receptionist answered on the first ring.

"Hello, Roseanne, this is Bailey York."

"Oh, Bailey, yes. It's good to hear from you. Mr. Davidson said you'd be phoning."

"I missed him by only a few minutes."

"How frustrating for you both. I've been concerned about him this morning."

"You have?"

"Why, yes. Mr. Davidson came into the office and he couldn't seem to sit still. He got himself a cup of coffee, then two minutes later came out again and poured a second cup. When I pointed out that he already had coffee, he seemed surprised. That was when he started muttering under his breath. I've worked with Mr. Davidson for several years now and I've never known him to mutter."

"He was probably thinking about something important regarding his work." Bailey was willing to offer a face-saving excuse for Parker's unprecedented behavior.

"That's not it," the woman insisted. "He went into his office again and came right back out, asking me if I read romance novels. I have on occasion, and that seemed to satisfy him. He pulled up a chair and began asking me questions about a hero's personality. I answered him as best I could."

"I'm sure you did very well."

"I must have, because he cheered right up and asked me what kind of flowers a woman enjoys most. I told him roses, and a minute later, he's looking through my phone book for a florist. Unfortunately no florist could promise a delivery this morning, so he said he'd drop them off personally. He phoned a few minutes ago to tell me you'd be calling in sometime today and that I should take a message."

"I just got back from lunch."

So Parker's morning hadn't gone any better than her own, Bailey mused, feeling almost jubilant. She'd managed to put on a good front for Jo Ann, but Bailey had felt terrible. Worse than terrible. She hadn't wanted to discuss her misery, either. It was much easier to pretend that Parker meant nothing to her.

But Jo Ann had been right. She *was* miserable.

"Could you tell Mr. Davidson I'll be ready at seven?" She'd call Jo Ann later and tell her she wouldn't be able to make the critique group, after all.

"Oh, my, that *is* good news," Roseanne said, sounding absolutely delighted. "I'll pass the message along as soon as he checks in. I'm so pleased. Mr. Davidson is such a dear man, but he works too hard. I've been thinking he needed to meet a nice girl like you. Isn't it incredible that the two of you have known each other for so long?"

"We have?"

"Oh, yes, don't you remember? You came into the office that morning and explained how Mr. Davidson is a friend of your family's. You must have forgotten you'd told me that."

"Oh. Oh, yes," Bailey mumbled, embarrassed by the silly lie. "Well, if you'd give him the message, I'd be most grateful."

"I'll let Mr. Davidson know," Roseanne said. She hesitated, as though she wanted to add something else and wasn't sure she should. Then, decision apparently made, the words rushed out. "As I said before, I've been with Mr. Davidson for several years and I think you should know that to the best of my knowledge, this is the first time he's ever sent a woman roses."

\* \* \*

For the rest of the afternoon, Bailey was walking on air. At five o'clock, she raced into the department store closest to her office, carrying one long-stemmed rose. Within minutes she found a lovely purple-and-gold silk dress. Expensive, but it looked wonderful. Then she hurried to the shoe department and bought a pair of pumps. In accessories, she chose earrings and a matching gold necklace.

From the department store she raced to the subway, clutching her purchases and the single red rose. She'd spent a fortune but didn't bother to calculate how many "easy monthly installments" it would take to pay everything off. Looking nice for Parker was worth the cost. No man had ever sent her roses, and every time she thought about it, her heart positively melted. It was such a *romantic* thing to do. And to think he'd conferred with Roseanne Snyder.

By six-thirty she was almost ready. She needed to brush her hair and freshen her makeup, but that wouldn't take long. She stood in front of the mirror in a model's pose, one hand on her hip, one shoulder thrust forward, studying the overall effect, when there was a knock at the door.

Oh, no! Parker was early. Much too early. It was either shout at him from this side of the door to come back later, or make the best of it. Running her fingers through her hair, she shook her head for the breezy effect and opted to make the best of it.

"Are you ready?" Jo Ann asked, walking inside, her book bag in one hand and her purse in the other. She gaped openly at Bailey's appearance. "Nice," she said, nodding, "but you might be a touch overdressed for the critique group."

"Oh, no, I forgot to call you." How could she have let it slip her mind?

"Call me?"

Bailey felt guilty—an emotion she was becoming increasingly familiar with—for not remembering tonight's arrangement. It was because of Parker. He'd occupied her thoughts from the moment he'd first kissed her.

There had been no kiss last night. The desire—no more than desire, the *need*—for his kiss, his touch had flared into urgent life. Since the breakup with Tom she'd felt frozen, her emotions lying dormant. But under the warmth of Parker's humor and generosity, she thawed a little more each time she saw him.

"Someone sent you a red rose," Jo Ann said matter-of-factly. She walked farther into the room, lifting the flower to her nose and sniffing appreciatively. "Parker?"

Bailey nodded. "There were a dozen waiting for me when I got back to the office."

Jo Ann's smile was annoyingly smug.

"He stopped by while I was at lunch—we'd missed each other…" Bailey mumbled in explanation.

Jo Ann circled her, openly admiring the dress.

"He's taking you to dinner?" Her gaze fell to the purple suede pumps that perfectly matched the dress.

"Dinner? What gives you that idea?"

"The dress is new."

"This old thing?" Bailey gave a nervous giggle.

Jo Ann tugged at the price tag dangling from Bailey's sleeve and pulled it free.

"Very funny!" Bailey groaned. She glanced at her watch, hoping Jo Ann would take the hint.

Jo Ann was obviously pleased about Parker's reappearance. "So, you're willing to let bygones be bygones?" she asked in a bracing tone.

"Jo Ann, he's due here any minute."

Her friend disregarded her pleas. "You're really falling for this guy, aren't you?"

If it was any more obvious, Bailey thought, she'd be wearing a sandwich board and parading in front of his office building. "Yes."

"Big time?"

"Big time," Bailey admitted.

"How do you feel about that?"

Bailey was sorely tempted to throw up her arms in abject frustration. "How do you think it makes me feel? I've been jilted twice. I'm scared to death. Now, isn't it time you left?" She coaxed Jo Ann toward the door, but when her friend ignored that broad hint, Bailey gripped her elbow. "Sorry you had to leave so soon, but I'll give your regards to Parker."

"All right, all right," Jo Ann said, sighing, "I can take a hint when I hear one."

Bailey doubted it. "Tell the others that...something came up, but I'll be there next time for sure." Her hands were at the small of Jo Ann's back, urging her forward. "Goodbye, Jo Ann."

"I'm going, I'm going," her friend said from the other side of the threshold. Suddenly earnest, she turned to face Bailey. "Promise me you'll have a good time."

"I'm sure we will." *If* she could finish getting ready before Parker arrived. *If* she could subdue her nerves. *If*...

Once Jo Ann was gone, Bailey slammed the door and rushed back to her bathroom. She was dabbing cologne on her wrists when there was a second knock. Inhaling a calming breath, Bailey opened the door, half expecting to find Jo Ann on the other side, ready with more advice.

"Parker," she whispered unsteadily, as though he was the last person she expected to see.

He frowned. "I did get the message correctly, didn't I? You were expecting me?"

"Oh, yes, of course. Come inside, please."

"Good." His face relaxed.

He stepped into the room, but his eyes never left hers. "I hope I'm not too early."

"Oh, no." She twisted her hands, staring down at her shoes like a shy schoolgirl.

"You got the roses?"

"Oh, yes," she said breathlessly, glancing at the one she'd brought home from her office. "They're beautiful. I left the others on my desk at work. It was so sweet of you."

"It was the only way I could think to apologize. I didn't know if a hero did that sort of thing or not."

"He...does."

"So once again, I stayed in character."

"Yes. Very much so."

"Good." His mouth slanted charmingly with the slight smile he gave her. "I realize this dinner is short notice."

"I didn't mind changing my plans," she told him. The critique group was important, but everyone missed occasionally.

"I suppose I should explain we'll be eating at my parents' home. Do you mind?"

His parents? Bailey's stomach tightened instantly. "I'd enjoy meeting your family," she answered, doing her best to reassure him. She managed a fleeting smile.

"Mom and Dad are anxious to meet you."

"They are?" Bailey would have preferred not to know that. The fact that Parker had even mentioned her to his family came as a surprise.

"So, how was your day?" he asked, walking casually over to the window.

Bailey lowered her gaze. "The morning was difficult, but the afternoon...the afternoon was wonderful."

"I behaved like a jealous fool last night, didn't I?" He didn't wait for her to respond. "The minute I saw you in that other man's arms, I wanted to get you away from him. I'm not proud of how I acted." He shoved his fingers through his hair, revealing more than a little agitation. "As I'm sure you've already guessed, I'm not much of a dancer. When that throwback from the seventies asked you to dance with him, I had no objections. If you want the truth, I was relieved. I guess men are supposed to be able to acquit themselves on the dance floor, but I've got two left feet. No doubt I've blown this whole hero business, but quite honestly that's the least of my worries. I know it matters to you, but I can't change who I am."

"I wouldn't expect you to."

He nodded. "The worst part of the whole evening was the way I cheated myself out of what I was looking forward to the most."

"Which was?"

"Kissing you again."

"Oh, Parker…"

He was going to kiss her. She realized that at about the same time she knew she'd cry with disappointment if he didn't. Bailey wasn't sure who reached out first. What she instantly recognized was the perfect harmony between them, how comfortable she felt in his arms—as though they belonged together.

His mouth found hers with unerring ease. A moan of welcome and release spilled from her throat as she began to tremble. An awakening, slow and sure, unfolded within her like the petals of a hothouse rose.

That sensation was followed by confusion. She pulled away from Parker and buried her face in his strong neck. The trembling became stronger, more pronounced.

"I frighten you?"

If only he knew. "Not in the way you think," she said slowly. "It's been so long since a man's held me like this. I tried to convince myself I didn't want to feel this way ever again. I didn't entirely succeed."

"Are you saying you *wanted* me to kiss you?"

"Yes." His finger under her chin raised her eyes to his. Bailey thought they would have gone on gazing at each other forever if Max hadn't chosen that moment to walk across the back of the sofa, protesting loudly. This was his territory and he didn't take kindly to invasions.

"We'd better leave," Parker said reluctantly.

"Oh, sure…" Bailey said. She was nervous about meeting Parker's family. More nervous than she cared to admit. The last set of parents she'd been introduced to had been Tom's. She'd met them a few days before they'd announced their engagement. As she recalled, the circumstances were somewhat similar. Tom had unexpectedly declared that it was time to meet his family. That was when Bailey had realized how serious their relationship had grown. Tom's family was very nice, but Bailey had felt all too aware of being judged and, she'd always suspected, found wanting.

Bailey doubted she said more than two words as Parker drove out to Daley City. His family's home was an elegant two-story white stone house with a huge front garden.

"Here we are," Parker said needlessly, placing his hand on her shoulder when he'd helped her out of the car.

"Did you design it?"

"No, but I love this house. It gave birth to a good many of my ideas."

The front door opened and an older couple stepped outside to greet them. Parker's mother was tall and regal, her white hair beautifully waved. His father's full head of hair was a distinguished shade of gray. He stood only an inch or so taller than his wife.

"Mom, Dad, this is Bailey York." Parker introduced her, his arm around her waist. "Bailey, Yvonne and Bradley Davidson, my parents."

"Welcome, Bailey," Bradley Davidson said with a warm smile.

"It's a pleasure to meet you," Yvonne said, walking forward. Her eyes briefly connected with Parker's before she added, "at last."

"Come inside," Parker's father urged, leading the way. He stood at the door and waited for them all to walk into the large formal entry. The floor was made of black-and-white squares of polished marble, and there was a long circular stairway on the left.

"How about something to drink?" Bradley suggested. "Scotch? A mixed drink? Wine?" Bailey and Parker's mother both chose white wine, Parker and his father, Scotch.

"I'll help you, Dad," Parker offered, leaving the two women alone.

Yvonne took Bailey into the living room, which was strikingly decorated in white leather and brilliant red.

Bailey sat on the leather couch. "Your home is lovely."

"Thank you," Yvonne murmured. A smile trembled at the edges of her mouth, and Bailey wondered what she found so amusing. Perhaps there was a huge run in her panty hose she knew nothing about, or another price tag dangling from her dress.

"Forgive me," the older woman said. "Roseanne Snyder and I are dear friends, and she mentioned your name to me several weeks back."

Bailey experienced a moment of panic as she recalled telling Parker's receptionist that she was an old family friend. "I…guess you're wondering why I claimed to know Parker."

"No, although it did give me a moment's pause. I couldn't recall knowing any Yorks."

"You probably don't." Bailey folded her hands in her lap, uncertain what to say next.

"Roseanne's right. You really are a charming young lady."

"Thank you."

"I was beginning to wonder if Parker was ever going to fall in love again. He was so terribly hurt by Maria, and he was so young at the time. He took it very hard…." She hesitated, then spoke briskly. "But I suppose that's neither here nor there."

Bailey decided to ignore the implication that Parker had fallen in love with her. Right now there were other concerns to face. "Did Parker tell you how we met?" She said a silent prayer that he'd casually mentioned something about the two of them bumping into each other on the subway.

"Of course I did," Parker answered for his mother, as he walked into the room. He sat on the arm of the sofa and draped his arm around Bailey's shoulders. His laughing eyes held hers. "I did mention Bailey's a budding romance writer, didn't I, Mom?"

"Yes, you did," his mother answered. "I hope you told her I'm an avid reader."

"No, I hadn't gotten around to that."

Bailey shifted uncomfortably in her chair. No wonder Yvonne Davidson had trouble disguising her amusement if Parker had blabbed about the way she'd followed him off the subway.

Parker's father entered the room carrying a tray of drinks, which he promptly dispensed.

Then he joined his wife, and for some time, the foursome chatted amicably.

"I'll just go and check on the roast," Yvonne said eventually.

"Can I help, dear?"

"Go ahead, Dad," Parker said, smiling. "I'll entertain Bailey with old family photos."

"Parker," Bailey said once his parents were out of earshot. "How *could* you?"

"How could I what?"

"Tell your mother how we met? She must think I'm crazy!"

Instead of revealing any concern, Parker grinned widely. "Honesty is the best policy."

"In principle I agree, but our meeting was a bit…unconventional."

"True, but I have to admit that being described as classic hero material was flattering to my ego."

"I take everything back," she muttered, crossing her legs.

Parker chuckled and was about to say something else when his father came into the room carrying a bottle of champagne.

"Champagne, Dad?" Parker asked when his father held out the bottle for Parker to examine. "This is good stuff."

"You're darn right," Bradley Davidson said. "It isn't every day our son announces he's found the woman he wants to marry."

# *Ten*

Bailey's gaze flew to Parker's in shocked disbelief. She found herself standing, but couldn't remember rising from the chair. The air in the room seemed too thin and she had difficulty catching her breath.

"Did I say something I shouldn't have?" Bradley Davidson asked his son, distress evident on his face.

"It might be best if you gave the two of us a few minutes alone," Parker said, frowning at his father.

"I'm sorry, son, I didn't mean to speak out of turn."

"It's fine, Dad."

His father left the room.

Bailey walked over to the massive stone fireplace and stared into the grate at the stacked logs and kindling.

"Bailey?" Parker spoke softly from behind her.

She whirled around to face him, completely speechless, able only to shake her head in bemused fury.

"I know this must come as…something of a surprise."

"Something of a surprise?" she shrieked.

"All right, a shock."

"We…we met barely a month ago."

"True, but we know each other better than some couples who've been dating for months."

The fact that he wasn't arguing with her didn't comfort Bailey at all. "I… Isn't it a bit presumptuous of you…to be thinking in terms of an engagement?" She'd made it plain from the moment they met that she had no intention of getting involved with a man. Who could blame her after the experiences she'd had with the opposite sex? Another engagement, even with someone as wonderful as Parker, was out of the question.

"Yes, it was presumptuous."

"Then how could you suggest such a thing? Engagements are disastrous for me! I won't go through that again. I won't!"

He scowled. "I agree I made a mistake."

"Obviously." Bailey stalked to the opposite side of the room to stand behind a leather-upholstered chair, one hand clutching its back. "Twice, Parker, twice." She held up two fingers. "And both times, *both* times, they fell out of love with me. I couldn't go through that again. I just couldn't."

"Let me explain," Parker said, walking slowly toward her. "For a long time now, my parents have wanted me to marry."

"So in other words, you used me. I was a decoy. You made up this story? How courageous of you."

She could tell from the hard set of his jaw that Parker was having difficulty maintaining his composure. "You're wrong, Bailey."

"Suddenly everything is clear to me." She made a sweeping gesture with her hand.

"It's obvious that nothing is clear to you," he countered angrily.

"I suppose I'm just so naive it was easy for me to fall in with your…your fiendish plans."

"*Fiendish* plans? Don't you think you're being a bit melodramatic?"

"Me? You're talking to a woman who's been jilted. Twice. Almost every man I've ever known has turned into a fiend."

"Bailey, I'm not using you." He crossed the room, stood directly in front of her and rested his hands on her shoulders. "Think what you want of me, but you should know the truth. Yes, my parents are eager for me to marry, and although I love my family, I would never use you or anyone else to satisfy their desires."

Bailey frowned uncertainly. His eyes were so sincere, so compelling…. "Then what possible reason could you have for telling them you'd found the woman you want to marry?"

"Because I have." His beautiful dark eyes brightened. "I'm falling in love with you. I have been almost from the moment we met."

Bailey blinked back hot tears. "You may believe you're in love with me now," she whispered, "but it won't last. It never does. Before you know it, you'll meet someone else, and you'll fall in love with her and not want me anymore."

"Bailey, that's not going to happen. You're going to wear that slightly used wedding dress and you're going to wear it for me."

Bailey continued to stare up at him, doubtful she could trust what she was hearing.

"The mistake I made was in telling my mother about you. Actually Roseanne Snyder couldn't wait to mention you to Mom. Next thing I knew, my mother was after me to bring you over to the house so she and Dad could meet you. To complicate matters, my father got involved and over a couple of glasses of good Scotch I admitted that my intentions toward you were serious. Naturally both my parents were delighted."

"Naturally." The sinking feeling in her stomach refused to go away.

"I didn't want to rush you, but since Dad's brought everything out into the open, maybe it's best to clear the air now. My intentions are honorable."

"Maybe they are now," she argued, "but it'll never last."

Parker squared his shoulders and took a deep breath. "It will last. I realize you haven't had nearly enough time to figure out your feelings for me. I'd hoped—" he hesitated, his brow furrowed "—that we could have this discussion several months down the road when our feelings for each other had matured."

"I'll say it one more time—engagements don't work, at least not with me."

"It'll be different this time."

"If I was ever going to fall in love with anyone, it would be you. But Parker, it just isn't going to work. I'm sorry, really I am, but I can't go through with this." Her hands were trembling and she bit her lower lip. She was in love with Parker, but she was too frightened to acknowledge it outside the privacy of her own heart.

"Bailey, would you listen to me?"

"No," she said. "I'm sorry, but everything's been blown out of proportion here. I'm writing a romance novel and you…you're the man I'm using for the model." She gave a resigned shrug. "That's all."

Parker frowned. "In other words, everything between us is a farce. The only person guilty of using anyone is you."

Bailey clasped her hands tightly in front of her, so tightly that her nails cut deep indentations in her palms. A cold sweat broke out on her forehead. "I never claimed anything else."

"I see." The muscles in his jaw tightened again. "Then all I can do is beg your forgiveness for being so presumptuous."

"There's no need to apologize." Bailey felt terrible, but she had to let him believe their relationship *was* a farce, otherwise everything became too risky. Too painful.

A noise, the muffled steps of Parker's mother entering the room, distracted them. "My dears," she said, "dinner's ready. I'm afraid if we wait much longer, it'll be ruined."

"We'll be right in," Parker said.

Bailey couldn't remember a more uncomfortable dinner in her life. The tension was so thick, she thought wryly, it could have been sliced and buttered.

Parker barely spoke during the entire meal. His mother, ever gracious, carried the burden of conversation. Bailey did her part to keep matters civilized, but the atmosphere was so strained it was a virtually impossible chore.

The minute they were finished with the meal, Parker announced it was time to leave. Bailey nodded and thanked his parents profusely for the meal. It was an honor to have met them, she went on, and this had been an exceptionally pleasant evening.

"Don't you think you overdid that a little?" Parker muttered once they were in the car.

"I had to say something," she snapped. "Especially since you were so rude."

"I wasn't rude."

"All right, you weren't rude, you were completely tactless. Couldn't you see how uncomfortable your father was? He felt bad enough about mentioning your plans. You certainly didn't need to complicate everything with such a rotten attitude."

"He deserved it."

"That's a terrible thing to say."

Parker didn't answer. For someone who, only hours before, had declared tender feelings for her, he seemed in an almighty hurry to get her home, careering around corners as though he were in training for the Indianapolis 500.

To Bailey's surprise he insisted on walking her to the door. The night before, he'd also escorted her to the door, and after a stilted good-night, he'd left. This evening, however, he wasn't content to leave it at that.

"Invite me in," he said when she'd unlatched the lock.

"Invite you in," Bailey echoed, listening to Max meowing plaintively on the other side.

"I'm coming in whether you invite me or not." His face was devoid of expression, and Bailey realized he would do exactly as he said. Her stomach tightened with apprehension.

"All right," she said, opening the door. She flipped on the light and removed her coat. Max, obviously sensing her state of mind, immediately headed for the bedroom. "I'd make some coffee, but I don't imagine you'll be staying that long."

"Make the coffee."

Bailey was grateful to have something to do. She concentrated on preparing the coffee and setting out mugs.

"Whatever you have to say isn't going to change my mind," Bailey told him. She didn't sound as calm and controlled as she'd hoped.

Parker ignored her. He couldn't seem to stand still, but rapidly paced her kitchen floor, pausing only when Bailey handed him a steaming mug of coffee. She'd seen Parker when he was angry and frustrated, even when he was jealous and unreasonable, but she'd never seen him quite like this.

"Say what you want to say," she prompted, resting her hip against the kitchen counter. She held her cup carefully in both hands.

"All right." Parker's eyes searched hers. "I resent having to deal with your irrational emotions."

"My irrational emotions!"

"Admit it, you're behaving illogically because some other man broke off his engagement to you."

"Other *men,*" Bailey corrected sarcastically. "Notice the plural, meaning more than one. Before you judge me too harshly, *Mr.* Davidson, let me remind you that every person is the sum of his or her experiences. If you stick your hand in the fire and get burned, you're not as likely to play around the campfire again, are you? It's as simple as that. I was fool enough to risk the fire twice, but I'm not willing to do it a third time."

"Has it ever occurred to you that you weren't in love with either Paul or Tom?"

Bailey blinked at the unexpectedness of the question. "That's ridiculous. I agreed to marry them. No woman does that without being in love."

"They both fell for someone else."

"How kind of you to remind me."

"Yet when they told you, you did nothing but wallow in your pain. If you'd been in love, deeply in love, you would've done everything within your power to keep them. Instead you did nothing. Absolutely nothing. What else am I to think?"

"Frankly I don't care what you think. I know what was in my heart and I was in love with both of them. Is it any wonder I refuse to fall in love again? An engagement is out of the question!"

"Then marry me now."

Bailey's heart leapt in her chest, then sank like a dead weight. "I—I'm not sure I heard you correctly."

"You heard. Engagements terrify you. I'm willing to accept that you've got a valid reason, but you shouldn't let it dictate how you live the rest of your life."

"In other words, bypassing the engagement and rushing to the altar is going to calm my fears?"

"You keep repeating that you refuse to go through another engagement. I can understand your hesitancy," he stated calmly. "Reno is only a couple of hours away." He glanced at his watch. "We could be married by this time tomorrow."

"Ah…" Words twisted and turned in her mind, but no coherent thought emerged.

"Well?" Parker regarded her expectantly.

"I…we…elope? I don't think so, Parker. It's rather…heroic of you to suggest it, actually, but it's an impossible idea."

"Why? It sounds like the logical solution to me."

"Have you stopped to consider that there are other factors involved in this? Did it occur to you that I might not be in love with you?"

"You're so much in love with me you can't think straight," he said with ego-crushing certainty.

"How do you know that?"

"Easy. It's the way you react, trying too hard to convince yourself you don't care. And the way you kiss me. At first there's resistance, then gradually you warm to it, letting your guard slip just a little, enough for me to realize you're enjoying the kissing as much as I am. It's when you start to moan that I know everything I need to know."

A ferocious blush exploded in Bailey's cheeks. "I do not moan," she protested heatedly.

"Do you want me to prove it to you?"

"No," Bailey cried, backing away.

A smug smile moved over his mouth, settling in his eyes.

Bailey's heart felt heavy. "I'm sorry to disappoint you, Parker, but I'd be doing us both a terrible disservice if I agreed to this."

Parker looked grim. She stared at him and knew, even as she rejected his marriage proposal, that if ever there was a man who could restore peace to her heart, that man was Parker. But she wasn't ready yet; she still had healing and growing to do on her own. But soon… Taking her courage in both hands, she whispered, "Couldn't we take some time to decide about this?"

Parker had asked her to be his wife. Parker Davidson, who was twice the man Paul was and three times the man Tom could ever hope to be. And she was so frightened all she could do was stutter and tremble and plead for time.

"Time," he repeated. Parker set his mug down on the kitchen counter, then stepped forward and framed her face in his large hands. His thumbs gently stroked her cheeks. Bailey gazed up at him, barely breathing. Warm anticipation filled her as he lowered his mouth.

She gasped sharply as his lips touched hers, moving over them slowly, masterfully. A moan rose deep in her throat, one so soft it was barely audible. A small cry of longing and need.

Parker heard it and responded, easing her closer and wrapping her in his arms. He kissed her a second time, then abruptly released her and turned away.

Bailey clutched the counter behind her to keep from falling. "What was that for?"

A slow easy grin spread across his face. "To help you decide."

★ ★ ★

"The worst part of this whole thing is that I haven't written a word in an entire week," Bailey complained as she sat on her living-room carpet, her legs pulled up under her chin. Pages of Jo Ann's manuscript littered the floor. Max, who revealed little or no interest in their writing efforts, was asleep as usual atop her printer.

"In an entire week?" Jo Ann sounded horrified. Even at Christmas neither of them had taken more than a three-day break from writing.

"I've tried. Each and every night I turn on my computer and then I sit there and stare at the screen. This is the worst case of writer's block I've ever experienced. I can't seem to make myself work."

"Hmm," Jo Ann said, leaning against the side of the couch. "Isn't it also an entire week since you saw Parker? Seems to me the two must be connected."

She nodded miserably. Jo Ann wasn't telling her anything she didn't already know. She'd relived that night in her memory at least a dozen times a day.

"You've never told me what happened," Jo Ann said, studying Bailey closely.

Bailey swallowed. "Parker is just a friend."

"And pigs have wings."

"My only interest in Parker is as a role model for Michael," she tried again, but she didn't know who she was trying to convince, Jo Ann or herself.

She hadn't heard from him all week. He'd left,

promising to give her the time she'd requested. He'd told her the kiss was meant to help her decide if she wanted him. Wanted him? Bailey didn't know if she'd ever *stop* wanting him, but she was desperately afraid that his love for her wouldn't last. It hadn't with Paul or Tom, and it wouldn't with Parker. And with Parker, the pain of rejection would be far worse.

Presumably Parker had thought he was reassuring her by suggesting they skip the engagement part and rush into a Nevada marriage. What he didn't seem to understand, what she couldn't seem to explain, was that it wouldn't make any difference. A wedding ring wasn't a guarantee. Someday, somehow, Parker would have a change of heart; he'd fall out of love with her.

"Are you all right?" Jo Ann asked.

"Of course I am." Bailey managed to keep her voice steady and pretend a calm she wasn't close to feeling. "I'm just upset about this writer's block. But it isn't the end of the world. I imagine everything will return to normal soon and I'll be back to writing three or four pages a night."

"You're sure about that?"

Bailey wasn't sure about anything. "No," she admitted.

"Just remember I'm here any time you want to talk."

A trembling smile touched the edges of Bailey's mouth and she nodded.

* * *

Bailey saw Parker three days later. She was waiting at the BART station by herself—Jo Ann had a day off—when she happened to glance up and see him walking in her direction. At first she tried to ignore the quaking of her heart and focus her attention away from him. But it was impossible.

She knew he saw her, too, although he gave no outward indication of it. His eyes met hers as though challenging her to ignore him. When she took a hesitant step toward him, his mouth quirked in a mocking smile.

"Hello, Parker."

"Bailey."

"How have you been?"

He hesitated a split second before he answered, which made Bailey hold her breath in anticipation.

"I've been terrific. How about you?"

"Wonderful," she lied, astonished that they could stand so close and pretend so well. His gaze lingered on her lips and she felt the throb of tension in the air. Parker must have rushed to get to the subway—his hair was slightly mussed and he was breathing hard.

He said something but his words were drowned out by the clatter of the approaching train. It pulled up and dozens of people crowded out. Neither Parker nor Bailey spoke as they waited to board.

He followed her inside, but sat several spaces away. She looked at him, oddly shocked and disappointed that he'd refused to sit beside her.

There were so many things she longed to tell him. Until now she hadn't dared admit to herself how much she'd missed his company. How she hungered to talk to him. They'd known each other for such a short while and yet he seemed to fill every corner of her life.

That, apparently, wasn't the case with Parker. Not if he could so casually, so willingly, sit apart from her. She raised her chin and forced herself to stare at the advertising panels that ran the length of the car.

Bailey felt Parker's eyes on her. The sensation was so strong his hand might as well have touched her cheek, held her face the way he had when he'd last left her. When she could bear it no longer, she turned and glanced at him. Their eyes met and the hungry desire in his tore at her heart.

With every ounce of strength she possessed, Bailey looked away. Eventually he would find someone else, someone he loved more than he would ever love her. Bailey was as certain of that as she was of her own name.

She kept her gaze on anything or anyone except Parker. But she felt the pull between them so strongly that she had to turn her head and look at him. He was staring at her, and the disturbing darkness of his eyes seemed to disrupt the very beat of her heart. A rush of longing jolted her body.

The train was slowing and Bailey was so grateful it was her station she jumped up and hurried to the exit.

"I'm still waiting," Parker whispered from directly behind her. She was conscious as she'd never been before of the long muscled legs so close to her own, of his strength and masculinity. "Have you decided yet?"

Bailey shut her eyes and prayed for the courage to do what was right for both of them. She shook her head silently; she couldn't talk to him now. She couldn't make a rational decision while the yearning in her heart was so great, while her body was so weak with need for him.

The crowd rushed forward and Bailey rushed with them, leaving him behind.

The writers' group met the following evening, for which Bailey was thankful. At least she wouldn't have to stare at a blank computer screen for several hours while she tried to convince herself she was a writer. Jo Ann had been making headway on her rewrite, whereas Bailey's had come to a complete standstill.

The speaker, an established historical-romance writer who lived in the San Francisco area, had agreed to address their group. Her talk was filled with good advice and Bailey tried to take notes. Instead, she drew meaningless doodles. Precise three-dimensional boxes and neat round circles in geometric patterns.

It wasn't until she was closing her spiral notebook at the end of the speech that Bailey realized all the circles on her page resembled interlocking wedding bands. About fifteen pairs of them. Was her subconscious sending her a message? Bailey had given up guessing.

"Are you going over to the diner for coffee?" Jo Ann asked as the group dispersed. Her eyes didn't meet Bailey's.

"Sure." She studied her friend and knew instinctively that something was wrong. Jo Ann had been avoiding her most of the evening. At first she'd thought it was her imagination, but there was a definite strain between them.

"All right," Bailey said, once they were outside. "What is it? What's wrong?"

Jo Ann sighed deeply. "I saw Parker this afternoon. I know it's probably nothing and I'm a fool for saying anything but, Bailey, he was with a woman and they were definitely more than friends."

"Oh?" Bailey's legs were shaky as she moved down the steps to the street. Her heart felt like a stone in the center of her chest.

"I'm sure it doesn't mean anything. For all I know, the woman could be his sister. I…I hadn't intended on saying a word, but then I thought you'd want to know."

"Of course I do," Bailey said, swallowing past the tightness in her throat. Her voice was firm and steady, revealing none of the chaos in her thoughts.

"I think Parker saw me. In fact, I'm sure he did. It was almost as if he *wanted* me to see him. He certainly didn't go out of his way to disguise who he was with—which leads me to believe it was all very innocent."

"I'm sure it was," Bailey lied. Her mouth twisted in a wry smile. She made a pretense of looking at her watch. "My goodness, I didn't realize it was so late. I think I'll skip coffee tonight and head on home."

Jo Ann grabbed her arm. "Are you all right?"

"Of course." But she was careful not to look directly at her friend. "It really doesn't matter, you know—about Parker."

"Doesn't matter?" Jo Ann echoed.

"I'm not the jealous type."

Her stomach was churning, her head spinning, her hands trembling. Fifteen minutes later, Bailey let herself into her apartment. She didn't stop to remove her coat, but walked directly into the kitchen and picked up the phone.

Parker answered on the third ring. His greeting sounded distracted. "Bailey," he said, "it's good to hear from you. I've been trying to call you most of the evening."

"I was at a writers' meeting. You wanted to tell me something?"

"As a matter of fact, yes. You obviously aren't going to change your mind about the two of us."

"I…"

"Let's forget the whole marriage thing. There's no need to rush into this. What do you think?"

# *Eleven*

"Oh, I agree one hundred percent," Bailey answered. It didn't surprise her that Parker had experienced a change of heart. She'd been expecting it to happen sooner or later. It was a blessing that he'd recognized his feelings so early on.

"No hard feelings then?"

"None," she assured him, raising her voice to a bright confident level. "I've gotten used to it. Honestly, you don't have a thing to worry about."

"You seem…cheerful."

"I am," Bailey answered, doing her best to sound as though she'd just won the lottery and was only waiting until she'd finished with this phone call to celebrate.

"How's the writing going?"

"Couldn't be better." Couldn't be worse actually, but she wasn't about to admit that. Not to Parker, at any rate.

"I'll be seeing you around then," he said.

"I'm sure you will." Maintaining this false enthusiasm was killing her. "One question."

"Sure."

"Where'd you meet her?"

"Her?" Parker hesitated. "You must mean Lisa. We've known each other for ages."

"I see." Bailey had to get off the phone before her facade cracked. But her voice broke as she continued, "I wish you well, Parker."

He paused as though he were debating whether or not to say something else. "You, too, Bailey."

Bailey replaced the receiver, her legs shaking so badly she stumbled toward the chair and literally fell into it. She covered her face with her hands, dragging deep gulps of air into her lungs. The burning ache in her stomach seemed to ripple out in hot waves, spreading to the tips of her fingers, to the bottoms of her feet.

By sheer force of will, Bailey lifted her head, squared her shoulders and stood up. She'd been through this before. Twice. Once more wouldn't be any more difficult than the first two times. Or so she insisted to herself.

After all, this time there was no ring to return, no wedding arrangements to cancel, no embossed announcements to burn.

No one, with the exception of Jo Ann, even knew about Parker, so the embarrassment would be kept to a minimum.

Getting over Parker should be quick and easy.

It wasn't.

A hellishly slow week passed and Bailey felt as if she were living on another planet. Outwardly nothing had changed, and yet the world seemed to be spinning off its axis. She went to work every morning, discussed character and plot with Jo Ann, worked an eight-hour day, took the subway home and plunked herself down in front of her computer, working on her rewrite with demonic persistence.

She appeared to have everything under control. Yet her life was unfolding in slow motion around her, as though she was a bystander and not a participant.

It must have shown in her writing because Jo Ann phoned two days after Bailey had given her the complete rewrite.

"You finished reading it?" Bailey couldn't hide her excitement. If Jo Ann liked it, then Bailey could mail it right off to Paula Albright, the editor who'd asked to see the revised manuscript.

"I'd like to come over and discuss a few points. Have you got time?"

Time was the one thing Bailey had in abundance. She hadn't realized how large a role Parker had come to play in her life or how quickly he'd chased away the emptiness. The gap he'd left behind seemed impossible to fill. Most nights she wrote until she was exhausted. But because she couldn't sleep anyway, she usually just sat in the living room holding Max.

Her cat didn't really care for the extra attention she was lavishing on him. He grudgingly endured her stroking his fur and scratching his ears. An extra serving of canned cat food and a fluffed-up pillow were appreciated, but being picked up and carted across the room to sit in her lap wasn't. To his credit, Max had submitted to two or three sessions in which she talked out her troubles, but his patience with such behavior had exhausted itself.

"Put on a pot of coffee and I'll be over in a few minutes," Jo Ann said, disturbing Bailey's musings.

"Fine. I'll see you when I see you," Bailey responded, then frowned. My goodness, *that* was an original statement. If she was reduced to such a glaring lack of originality one week after saying farewell to Parker, she hated to consider how banal her conversation would be a month from now.

Jo Ann arrived fifteen minutes later, Bailey's manuscript tucked under her arm.

"You didn't like it," Bailey said in a flat voice. Her friend's expression couldn't have made it any plainer.

"It wasn't that, exactly," Jo Ann told her, setting the manuscript on the coffee table and curling up in the overstuffed chair.

"What seems to be the problem this time?"

"Janice."

"Janice?" Bailey cried, restraining the urge to argue. She'd worked so hard to make the rewrite of

*Forever Yours* work. "I thought *Michael* was the source of all the trouble."

"He was in the original version. You've rewritten him just beautifully, but Janice seemed so—I hate to say this—weak."

"Weak?" Bailey shouted. "Janice isn't weak! She's strong and independent and—"

"Foolish and weak-willed," Jo Ann finished. "The reader loses sympathy for her halfway through the book. She acts like a robot with Michael."

Bailey was having a difficult time not protesting. She knew Jo Ann's was only one opinion, but she'd always trusted her views. Jo Ann's evaluation of the manuscript's earlier versions had certainly been accurate.

"Give me an example," Bailey said, making an effort to keep her voice as even and unemotional as possible.

"Everything changed after the scene at the Pops concert."

"Parker was a real jerk," Bailey argued. "He deserved everything she said and did."

"Parker?" Jo Ann's brows arched at her slip of the tongue.

"Michael," Bailey corrected. "You know who I meant!"

"Indeed I did."

During the past week, Jo Ann had made several awkward attempts to drop Parker's name into conversation, but Bailey refused to discuss him.

"Michael did act a bit high-handed," Jo Ann continued, "but the reader's willing to forgive him, knowing he's discovering his true feelings for Janice. The fact that he felt jealous when she danced with another man hit him like an expected blow. True, he did behave like a jerk, but I understood his motivation and was willing to forgive him."

"In other words, the reader will accept such actions from the hero but not the heroine?" Bailey asked aggressively.

"That's not it at all," Jo Ann responded, sounding surprised. "In the original version Janice comes off as witty and warm and independent. The reader can't help liking her and sympathize with her situation."

"Then what changed?" Bailey demanded, raising her voice. Her inclination was to defend Janice as she would her own child.

Jo Ann shrugged. "I wish I knew what happened to Janice. All I can tell you is that it started after the scene at the Pops concert. From that point on I had problems identifying with her. I couldn't understand why she was so willing to accept everything Michael said and did. It was as if she'd lost her spirit. By the end of the book, I actively disliked her. I wanted to take her by the shoulders and shake her."

Bailey felt like weeping. "So I guess it's back to the drawing board," she said, putting on a cheerful front. "I suppose I should be getting used to that."

"My best advice is to put the manuscript aside for

a few weeks," Jo Ann said in a gentle tone. "Didn't you tell me you had another plot idea you wanted to develop?"

Bailey nodded. But that was before. Before almost all her energy was spent just surviving from day to day. Before she'd begun pretending her life was perfectly normal although the pain left her barely able to function. Before she'd lost hope...

"What will putting it aside accomplish?" she asked.

"It will give you perspective," Jo Ann advised. "Look at Janice. Really look at her. Does she deserve a man as terrific as Michael? You've done such a superb job writing him."

It went without saying that Parker had been the source of her inspiration.

"In other words Janice is unsympathetic?"

Jo Ann's nod was regretful. "I'm afraid so. But remember that this is strictly my opinion. Someone else may read *Forever Yours* and feel Janice is a fabulous heroine. You might want to have some of the other writers in the group read it. I don't mean to be discouraging, Bailey, really I don't."

"I know that."

"It's only because you're my friend that I can be so honest."

"That's what I wanted," Bailey admitted slowly. Who was she kidding? She was as likely to become a published writer as she was a wife. The odds were so bad it would be a sucker's bet.

"I don't want to discourage you," Jo Ann repeated in a worried voice.

"If I'd been looking for someone to tell me how talented I am, I would've given the manuscript to my mother."

Jo Ann laughed, then glanced at her watch. "I've got to scoot. I'm supposed to pick up Dan at the muffler shop. The station wagon's beginning to sound like an army tank. If you have any questions give me a call later."

"I will." Bailey led the way to the door and held it open as Jo Ann gathered up her purse and coat. Her friend paused, looking concerned. "You're not too depressed about this, are you?"

"A little," Bailey said. "All right, a lot. But it's all part of the learning process, and if I have to rewrite this manuscript a hundred times, then I'll do it. Writing isn't for the faint of heart."

"You've got that right."

Jo Ann had advised her to set the story aside but the instant she was gone, Bailey tore into the manuscript, leafing carefully through the pages.

Jo Ann's notes in the margins were valuable—and painful. Bailey paid particular attention to the comments following Michael and Janice's fateful evening at the concert. It didn't take her long to connect this scene in her novel with its real-life equivalent, her evening with Parker.

*She acts like a robot with Michael,* Jo Ann had said.

As Bailey read through the subsequent chapters, she couldn't help but agree. It was as though her feisty, spirited heroine had lost the will to exert her own personality. For all intents and purposes, she'd lain down and died.

*Isn't that what you've done?* her heart asked.

But Bailey ignored it. She'd given up listening to the deep inner part of herself. She'd learned how painful that could be.

"By the end of the book I actively disliked her." Jo Ann's words resounded like a clap of thunder in her mind. Janice's and Bailey's personalities were so intimately entwined that she no longer knew where one stopped and the other began.

"Janice seemed so…so weak."

Bailey resisted the urge to cover her ears to block out Jo Ann's words. It was all she could do not to shout, "You'd be spineless too if you had a slightly used wedding dress hanging in your closet!"

When Bailey couldn't tolerate the voices any longer, she reached for her jacket and purse and escaped. Anything was better than listening to the accusations echoing in her mind. The apartment felt unfriendly and confining. Even Max's narrowed green eyes seemed to reflect her heart's questions.

The sky was overcast—a perfect accompaniment to Bailey's mood. She walked without any real destination until she found herself at the BART station and her heart suddenly started to hammer. She chided herself for the small surge of hope she felt. What were the chances of running into Parker on a Saturday afternoon? Virtually none. She hadn't seen him in over a week. More than likely he'd been driving to work to avoid her.

Parker.

The pain she'd managed to hold at bay for several days bobbed to the surface. Tears spilled from her eyes. She kept on walking, her pace brisk as though she was in a hurry to get somewhere. Bailey's destination was peace and she had yet to find it. Sometimes she wondered if she ever would.

Men fell in love with her easily enough, but they seemed to fall out of love just as effortlessly. Worst of all, most demeaning of all, was the knowledge that there was always another woman involved. A woman they loved more than Bailey. Paul, Tom and now Parker.

Bailey walked for what felt like miles. Somehow, she wasn't altogether shocked when she found herself on Parker's street. He'd mentioned it in passing the evening they'd gone to the concert. The condominiums were a newer addition to the neighborhood, ultramodern, ultra-expensive, ultra-appealing to the eye. It wouldn't surprise her to learn that Parker had been responsible for their design. Although the dinner conversation with his parents had been stilted and uncomfortable, Parker's mother had taken delight in highlighting her son's many accomplishments. Parker obviously wasn't enthusiastic about his mother's bragging, but Bailey had felt a sense of pride in the man she loved.

*The man she loved.*

Abruptly Bailey stopped walking. She closed her eyes and clenched her hands into tight fists. She did *not* love Parker. If she did happen to fall in love again, it wouldn't be with a man as fickle or as untrustworthy as Parker Davidson, who apparently fell in and out of love at the drop of a—

*You love him, you fool. Now what are you going to do about it?*

Bailey just wanted these questions, these revelations, to stop, to leave her alone. Alone in her misery. Alone in her pain and denial.

An anger grew in Bailey. One born of so much strong emotion she could barely contain it. Without sparing a thought for the consequences, she stormed into the central lobby of the condominium complex. The doorman stepped forward.

"Good afternoon," he said politely.

Bailey managed to smile at him. "Hello." Then, when she noticed that he was waiting for her to continue, she added, "Mr. Parker Davidson's home, please," her voice remarkably calm and impassive. They were going to settle this once and for all, and no one, not a doorman, not even a security guard, was going to stand in her way.

"May I ask who's calling?"

"Bailey York," she answered confidently.

"If you'll kindly wait here," He was gone only a moment. "Mr. Parker says to send you right up. He's in unit 204."

"Thank you." Bailey's determination hadn't dwindled by the time her elevator reached the second floor.

It took Parker a couple of minutes to answer his door. When he did, Bailey didn't wait for an invitation. She marched into his apartment, ignoring the spectacular view and the lush traditional furnishings of polished wood and rich fabric.

"Bailey." He seemed surprised to see her.

Standing in the middle of the room, hands on her hips, she glared at him with a week's worth of indignation flashing from her eyes. "Don't Bailey me," she raged. "I want to know who Lisa is and I want to know *now*."

Parker gaped at her as though she'd taken leave of her senses.

"Don't give me that look." She walked a complete circle around him; he swiveled slowly, still staring. "There's no need to stand there with your mouth hanging open. It's a simple question."

"What are you doing here?"

"What does it look like?"

"Frankly I'm not sure."

"I've come to find out exactly what kind of man you are." That sounded good, and she said it in a mocking challenging way bound to get a response.

"What kind of man I am? Does this mean I have to run through a line of warriors waiting to flog me?"

Bailey was in no mood for jesting. "It just might." She removed one hand from her hip and waved it under his nose. "I'll have you know Janice has been ruined and I blame you."

"Who?"

"My character Janice," she explained with exaggerated patience. "The one in my novel, *Forever Yours.* She's wishy-washy, submissive and docile. Reading about her is like…like vanilla pudding instead of chocolate."

"I happen to be partial to vanilla pudding."

Bailey sent him a furious look. "I'll do the talking here."

Parker raised both hands. "Sorry."

"You should be. So…exactly what kind of man *are* you?"

"I believe you've already asked that question." Bailey spun around to scowl at him. "Sorry," he muttered, his mouth twisting oddly. "I forgot you're doing the talking here."

"One minute you claim you're in love with me. So much in love you want me to marry you." Her voice faltered slightly. "And the next you're involved with some woman named Lisa and you want to put our relationship on hold. Well, I've got news for you, Mr. Unreliable. I refuse to allow you to play with my heart. You asked me to marry you…" Bailey paused at the smile that lifted the corners of his mouth. "Is this discussion amusing you?" she demanded.

"A little."

"Feel free to share the joke," she said, motioning with her hand.

"Lisa's my sister-in-law."

The words didn't immediately sink in. "Your what?"

"She's my brother's wife."

Bailey slumped into a chair. A confused moment passed while she tried to collect her scattered thoughts. "You're in love with your brother's wife?"

"No." He sounded shocked that she'd even suggest such a thing. "I'm in love with you."

"You're not making a lot of sense."

"I figured as much, otherwise—"

"Otherwise what?"

"Otherwise you'd either be in my arms or finding ways to inflict physical damage on my person."

"You'd better explain yourself," she said, frowning, hardly daring to hope.

"I love you, Bailey, but I didn't know how long it would take you to discover you love me, too. You were so caught up in the past—"

"With reason," she reminded him.

"With reason," he agreed. "Anyway I asked you to marry me."

"To be accurate, your father's the one who did the actual speaking," Bailey muttered.

"True, he spoke out of turn, but it was a question I was ready to ask…"

"But…" she supplied for him. There was always a "but" when it came to men and love.

"But I didn't know if your feelings for me were genuine."

"I beg your pardon?"

"Was it me you fell for or Michael?" he asked quietly.

"I don't think I understand."

"The way I figure it, if you truly loved me you'd do everything in your power to win me back."

"Win you back? I'm sorry, Parker, but I still don't get it."

"All right, let's backtrack a bit. When Paul announced he'd found another woman and wanted to break your engagement, what did you do?"

"I dropped out of university and signed up for paralegal classes at the business college."

"What about Tom?"

"I moved to San Francisco."

"My point exactly."

Bailey lost him somewhere between Paul and Tom. "*What* is your point exactly?"

Parker hesitated, then looked straight into her eyes. "I wanted you to love me enough to fight for me," he told her simply. "Don't worry. Lisa and I are not, repeat not, in love."

"You just wanted me to think so?"

"Yes," he said with obvious embarrassment. "She reads romances, too. Quite a few women do apparently. I was telling her about our relationship, and she came up with the idea of using the 'other woman' the way some romance novels do."

"That's the most underhand unscrupulous thing I've ever heard."

"Indulge me for a few more minutes, all right?"

"All right," she agreed.

"When Paul and Tom broke off their engagements to you, you didn't say or do anything to convince them of your love. You calmly accepted that they'd met someone else and conveniently got out of their lives."

"So?"

"So I needed you to want me so much, love me so much, that you wouldn't give me up. You'd put aside that damnable pride of yours and confront me."

"Were you planning to arrange a mud-wrestling match between Lisa and me?" she asked wryly.

"No!" He looked horrified at the mere thought. "I wanted to provoke you—just enough to come to me. What took you so long?" He shook his head. "I was beginning to lose heart."

"You're going to lose a whole lot more than your heart if you ever pull that stunt again, Parker Davidson."

His face lit up with a smile potent enough to dissolve her pain and her doubts. He opened his arms then, and Bailey walked into his embrace.

"I should be furious with you," she mumbled.

"Kiss me first, then be mad."

His mouth captured hers in hungry exultation. In a single kiss Parker managed to make up for the long cheerless days, the long lonely nights. She was breathless when he finally released her.

"You really love me?" she whispered, needing to hear him say it. Her lower lip trembled and her hands tightened convulsively.

"I really love you," he whispered back, smiling down at her. "Enough to last us two lifetimes."

"Only two?"

His hand cradled the back of her head. "At least four." His mouth claimed hers again, then he abruptly broke off the kiss. "Now, what was it you were saying about Janice? What's wrong with her?"

A slow thoughtful smile spread across Bailey's face. "Nothing that a wedding and a month-long honeymoon won't cure."

# *Epilogue*

Bailey paused to read the sign in the bookstore window, announcing the autographing session for two local authors that afternoon.

"How does it feel to see your name in lights?" Jo Ann asked.

"You may be used to this, but I feel...I feel—" Bailey hesitated and flattened her palms on the smooth roundness of her stomach "—I feel almost the same as I did when I found out I was pregnant."

"It does funny things to the nervous system, doesn't it?" Jo Ann teased. "And what's this comment about me being used to all this? I've only got two books published to your one."

The bookseller, Caroline Dryer, recognized them when they entered the store and hurried forward to greet them, her smile welcoming. "I'm so pleased you could both come. We've had lots of interest." She steered them toward the front where a table, draped in lace, and two chairs were waiting. Several women were already lined up patiently, looking forward to meeting Jo Ann and Bailey.

They did a brisk business for the next hour. Family, friends and other writers joined the romance readers who stopped by to wish them well.

Bailey was talking to an older woman, a retired schoolteacher, when Parker and Jo Ann's husband, Dan, casually strolled past the table. The four were going out for dinner following the autograph session. There was a lot to celebrate. Jo Ann had recently signed a two-book contract with her publisher and Bailey had just sold her second romance. After weeks of work, Parker had finished the plans for their new home. Construction was scheduled to begin the following month and with luck would be completed by the time the baby arrived.

"What I loved best about *Forever Yours* was Michael," the older woman was saying to Bailey. "The scene where he takes her in his arms right in the middle of the merry-go-round and tells her he's tired of playing childish games and that he loves her was enough to steal my heart."

"He stole mine, too," Bailey said, her eyes linking with her husband's.

"Do you think there are any men like that left in this world?" the woman asked. "I've been divorced for years, and now that I'm retired, well, I wouldn't mind meeting someone."

"You'd be surprised how many heroes there are all around us," Bailey said, her gaze still holding Parker's. "They take the subway and eat peanut-butter sandwiches and fall in love—like you and me."

"Well, there's hope for me, then," the teacher said jauntily. "And I plan to have a good time looking." She smiled. "That's why I enjoy romance novels so much. They give me encouragement, they're fun— and they tell me it's okay to believe in love," she confided. "Even for the second time."

"Or the third," Parker inserted quietly.

Bailey grinned. She couldn't argue with that!

# #1 *New York Times* Bestselling Author
# DEBBIE MACOMBER

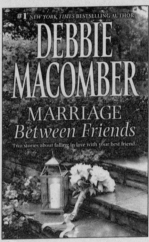

**First comes friendship…**

Back in high school,
Maggie Kingsbury and
Glenn Lambert were close friends.
But life took them in different
directions. Now they meet again—
as maid of honor and best man—at
a wedding in San Francisco full of
*White Lace and Promises*….

**And *then* comes marriage!**

Lily Morrissey decides it's time
to find a husband, preferably a
wealthy one. It's a strictly practical
decision, and she enlists the help
of her best friend, Jake Carson,
in the Great Husband Search.

That's when Lily's feelings for Jake start to change. Because they're
*Friends…And Then Some.*

## Available wherever books are sold.

**Be sure to connect with us at:**
Harlequin.com/Newsletters
Facebook.com/HarlequinBooks
Twitter.com/HarlequinBooks

MDM1580

#### #1 *New York Times* bestselling author

# DEBBIE MACOMBER

*brings you two classic stories of timeless romance in one heartwarming collection*

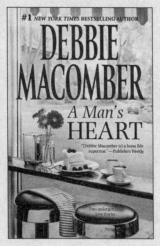

## The Way to a Man's Heart

Meghan O'Day and Grey Carlyle couldn't be more different. He's a sophisticated professor of literature; she's a waitress with a high-school education and a love of the classics. But he returns time and again to the diner where she works—and it's not just for the coffee and pie....

## A Hasty Wedding

On the day of her closest friend's Las Vegas wedding, Clare Gilroy fears that her own walk down the aisle will never happen...until she finds herself falling for best man— and town outcast—Reed Tonasket. Then, after a dizzying night in the glitter of Vegas, Clare wakes to find a ring on her finger and a husband by her side!

## Available wherever books are sold.

**Be sure to connect with us at:**

Harlequin.com/Newsletters

Facebook.com/HarlequinBooks

Twitter.com/HarlequinBooks

HARLEQUIN® MIRA®
www.Harlequin.com

MDM1587

SPECIAL EXCERPT FROM

Ⓗ HARLEQUIN®

SPECIAL EDITION

*When Mallory Dickinson is reunited with her first love, she has to decide whether to tell him her deepest secret—that her young son is his biological child!*

\*\*\*

Mallory took a deep breath, probably trying to gather her thoughts—or maybe to lie.

But it didn't take a brain surgeon to see the truth. She'd kept the baby she was supposed to have given up for adoption, and she'd let ten years go by without telling Rick.

Betrayal gnawed at his gut.

"Lucas called you a doctor," she said, arching a delicate brow.

"I'm a veterinarian. My clinic is just down the street."

As she mulled that over, Lucas sidled up to Rick wearing a bright-eyed grin. "Did you come to ask my mom about Buddy?"

No, the dog was the last thing he'd come to talk to Mallory about. And while he hadn't been sure just how the conversation was going to unfold when he arrived, it had just taken a sudden and unexpected turn.

"Why would he come to talk to me about his dog?" Mallory asked her son.

Or rather *their* son. Who else could the boy be?

Lucas, who wore a smile that indicated he was completely oblivious to the tension building between the adults, approached Mallory. "Because Buddy needs a home. Since we have a yard now, can I have him? *Please?* I promise to take care of him and walk him and everything."

She said, "We'll talk about it later."

"Okay. Thanks." He flashed Rick a smile, then turned and headed toward the stairs.

As Lucas was leaving, Rick's gaze traveled from the boy to Mallory and back again. Finally, when they were alone, Rick folded his arms across his chest, shifted his weight to one hip and smirked.

"Cute kid," he said.

Mallory flushed brighter still, and she wiped her palms along her hips.

*Nervous, huh?* Rick's internal B.S. detector slipped into overdrive.

Well, she ought to be.

When Rick had found out about her pregnancy, he'd been only seventeen, but he'd offered to quit school, get a job and marry her. However, her grandparents had decided that she was too young and convinced her that adoption was the only way to go. So they'd sent her to Boston to live with her aunt Carrie until the birth.

Yet in spite of what she'd promised him when she left, she hadn't come back to Brighton Valley. And within six months' time, he'd lost all contact with her—through no fault of his own.

Apparently, she'd had a change of heart about the adoption. And about the feelings she'd claimed she'd had for him, too.

\*\*\*

*Enjoy this sneak peek from* USA TODAY *bestselling author Judy Duarte's* THE DADDY SECRET, *the first book in* RETURN TO BRIGHTON VALLEY, *a brand-new miniseries coming in March 2014!*

Copyright © 2014 by Judy Duarte

# SPECIAL EDITION

**Life, Love and Family**

Coming next month from reader-favorite author
Teresa Southwick

## *FINDING A FAMILY...AND FOREVER?*

Kidnapped as a child, Emma Robbins heads to
Blackwater Lake to find her birth family.
In the process, she becomes the nanny to
Dr. Justin Flint's young son. The handsome
widower is unwillingly attracted to the lovely
newcomer, who loves the boy as her own, but
secrets and lies may undermine the family they
begin to build.

*Look for the latest in the
Bachelors of Blackwater Lake miniseries next
month from Harlequin® Special Edition®,
wherever books and ebooks are sold!*

HSE65802